SCANDAL OF VANDALS

FRANK F. WEBER

SCANDAL OF VANDALS

Front and back cover photo:
Trisha Spencer of Xsperience Photography

Cover Design: Jill Kurtz Libby
Cover Art Graphics: Jill Kurtz Libby

ISBN: 979-8-89443-346-2
EISBN: 979-8-89480-832-1

Published in partnership with BookBaby
7905 N. Crescent Blvd.
Pennsauken, NJ 08110
And
The Story Laboratory, www.writeeditdesignlab.com

Published by Moon Finder Press
500 Park Avenue
P.O. Box 496, Pierz, MN 56364

This book is dedicated to my mother, Rosetta Kapsner Weber: I hear music playing, think of Mom laughing, and the memories are tangible again. I had the present of Rosetta Kapsner Weber's guidance, and by her presence my honor was formed. She was unshakable in her faith. She believed that if you had the opportunity to laugh and enjoy the moment, you should.

Thank you, Allie Toenies, for your cover model work. You were perfect!

Trisha Spencer, Xperience Photography, once again, thank you for your amazing photography work on another cover.

Thank you, Kelly Sauer, for the first edit of this book. Your expertise is much appreciated!

Chris Marcotte, thank you for the peer review and well-thought-out feedback on my work.

Emily Piller, I am grateful for your final edit of *Scandal of Vandals.* Emily, you are truly amazing, and I hope to work with you again!

A special thanks to the Honorable Jeffery Thompson for his work in the justice system and his insightful contributions to this novel.

The Jon Frederick series,
by Frank F. Weber, includes:

Murder Book (2017)
The I-94 Murders (2018)
Last Call (2019)
Lying Close (2020)
Burning Bridges (2021)
Black and Blue (2022)
The Haunted House of Hillman (2023)
Scandal of Vandals (2024)
The Sun (2025)

It is important to note that this story is based on a true crime case. When you're reading portions that seem improbable, they are typically genuine, from the pizza-stealing seagull to children being returned to school while their mom was in critical condition, to the victim's children being ghosted by friends, to my learning about a tragedy in my family while testifying in court. Once touted as "the crime of the century," the investigation was hampered by odd but true circumstances: The crime took place in an affluent neighborhood at 9:00 a.m., and nobody witnessed the victim drag her bloodied body to four consecutive houses for help, and no one saw the perpetrator leave. *The names were changed to protect the innocent.*

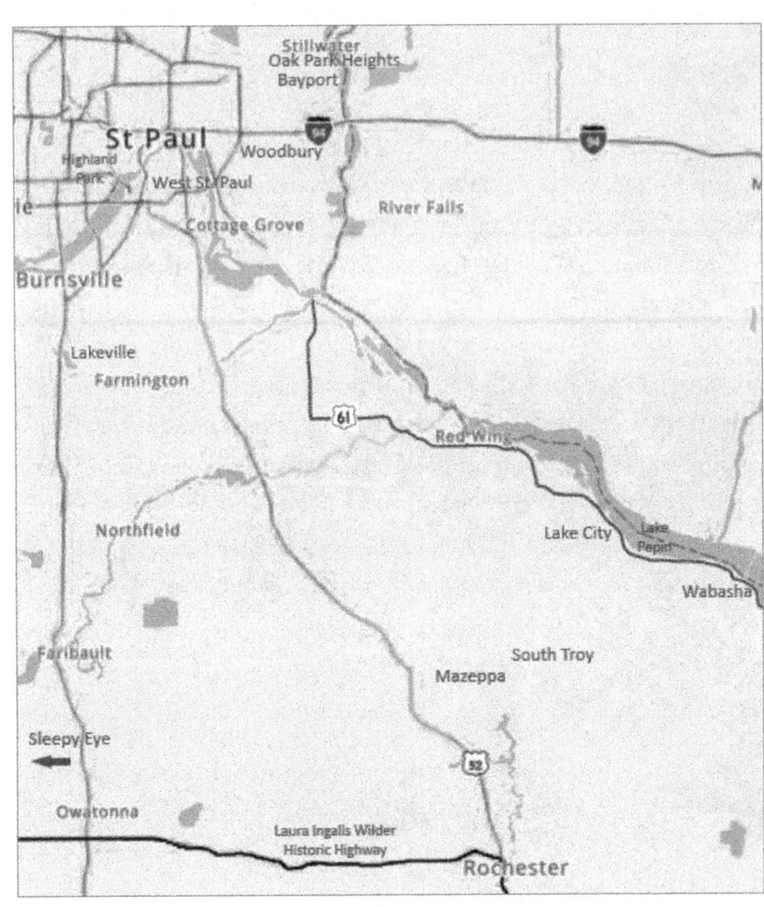
Stillwater
Oak Park Heights
Bayport
St Paul
Woodbury
Highland Park
West St Paul
River Falls
Cottage Grove
Burnsville
Lakeville
Farmington
61
Red Wing
Northfield
Lake City
Lake Pepin
Wabasha
Faribault
South Troy
Mazeppa
Sleepy Eye
52
Owatonna
Laura Ingalls Wilder
Historic Highway
Rochester

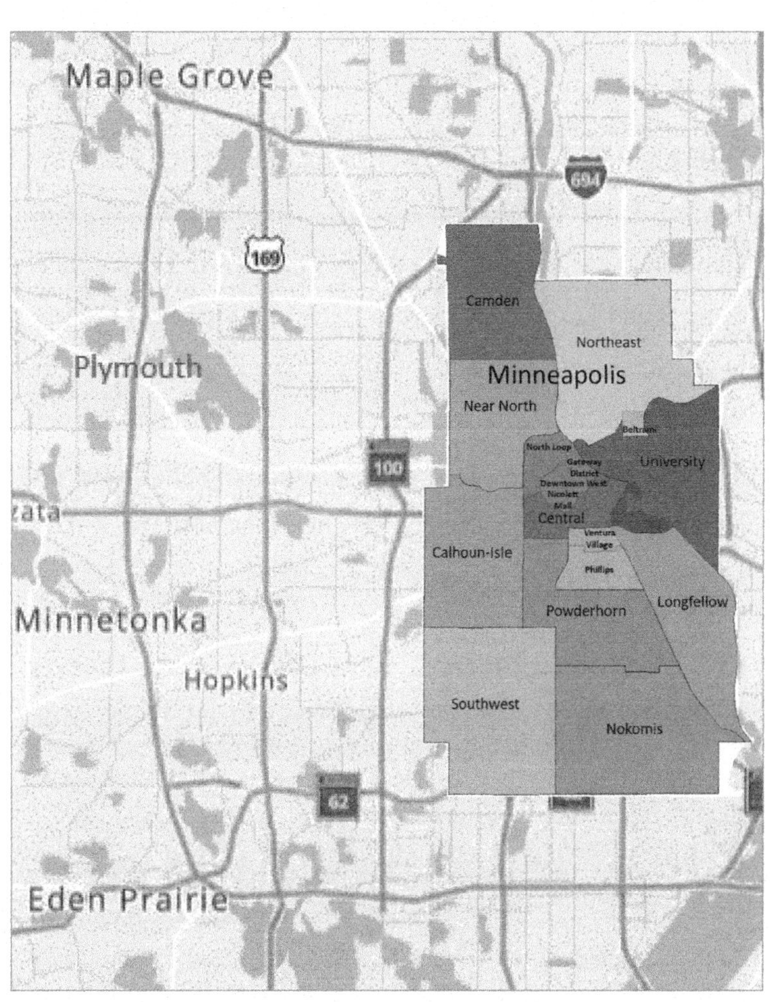

Maple Grove
694
169
Plymouth
100
zata
Minnetonka
Hopkins
62
Eden Prairie
Camden
Northeast
Minneapolis
Near North
Beltrami
North Loop
University
Gateway District
Downtown West
Nicolett Mall
Central
Calhoun-Isle
Ventura Village
Phillips
Longfellow
Powderhorn
Southwest
Nokomis

List of Characters

Richard "Ricky" Day .... Adolescent Farm Boy

Beth, Misty, Michael, and Blake .... *Richard's siblings*

Halle Day ..... Beth Day's daughter (Therapist as an adult)

Tony Shileto .... Sheriff's Deputy

Doris Shileto .... Tony's spouse

Vicki Ament .... Tony's Driver

Tug Grant .... Defense Attorney

Debra Grant .... Homemaker and Tug's Wife

Lincoln, Rebecca, Mary and Audrey Grant .... *Tug and Debra's Children*

Greta and Otto Scarpetta .... Debra Grant's Parents

Bridget Bare .... Hennepin County Prosecutor

Melanie Pearson .... Legal Secretary

Sophie .... Melanie's friend

Roan Caruso .... Minneapolis Combination Boss, Catania's spouse & Debra Grant's Ex

Catania Turrisi .... *Restaurateur & Roan's spouse*

Lorenzo Turrisi Caruso .... *Roan and Catania's Son*

Jon Frederick .... Bureau of Criminal Apprehension (BCA) Investigator

Serena Frederick .... Private Investigator & Homemaker

Nora and Jackson .... *Jon and Serena's children*

Taytum Hanson .... Legal Assistant and later Attorney

Lily Walker .... Legal Secretary

Xavier "Zave" Williams....... Minneapolis Police Investigator

Lauren Herald .... Sketch Artist

Keyshawn Harris .... Restaurateur

Paula Fineday .... BCA Investigator

Jada Anderson .... News Reporter

Wesley "Dreads" Washington .... Disciples Gang Member

Deondre Smith .... Disciples Gang Member,
Car Jacker, and Father

Latrice Johnson .... Deondre's lover

Montrel Johnson .... Disciples Gang Member

Jamarcus "Jam" Smith .... Disciples Gang Member

Ahmad Smith .... Disciples Gang Member

The Fox .... Disciples Governor (Leader)

Dick Doden .... Acquaintance of Roan Caruso

THE NAME AT THE TOP OF EACH CHAPTER
INDICATES FROM WHOSE PERSPECTIVE
THIS PART OF THE STORY IS TOLD.

1

JON FREDERICK

8:45 P.M., SATURDAY, DECEMBER 16, 2002
PIERZ

It was 46 degrees today, the warmest it would be all month. My cool cheeks felt like a mask on this starless night. I traipsed along the riverbank on our farm, sinking into the snow with each step. I carried my book and one of my dad's empty beer cans, now filled with gas, to a thicket of trees on a bluff overlooking the river. My Sorel boots were snug due to a recent growth spurt, but they kept my feet warm. I suppose all my winter gear could be replaced, but it served its purpose, and now wasn't the time. I carefully set the can in the snow and the book on a fallen tree while I gathered dried brush for a fire. Once I had piled the wood in front of a tree stump, I poured the gas on the stack and tossed a match into it, enjoying the ominous *"huff"* it made when it ignited. As the fire started, I stepped to the side and looked out at the river. The steep banks were covered with snow. The river was never safe to walk on in the winter. While much of it was covered with ice, it never froze over completely. I loved this farm. We were losing it, and

I imagined it would be bought up by some corporate farmer who would never walk these banks.

I had to get out of the house tonight. My older sister, Theresa, had apparently been caught in a state of undress with a firefighter in one of the trucks as the local volunteer force rushed into the station for a call, so she was now the talk of the town. Perhaps it's one of the perils of having the Pierz fire station next to Frosty's bar. When I left the house, Mom was kneeling in front of the couch, praying for her soul. Dad wasn't angry like he used to be. He'd given up and was now depressingly quiet. It didn't help that when confronted, Theresa never minimized her behavior. Instead, she embellished the story further by suggesting, "They had to turn the hose on us to get us to stop."

My older brother, Victor, struggled with schizophrenia and was convinced aliens were trying to communicate with us in Morse code through the flickering lights on our Christmas tree. Having a brother who tells tales of false inventions and declares people are trying to kill him casts a shadow on our family. I don't blame Vic. The delusions and paranoia are real and scary for him. Regardless of the stories, I love my family. I respect my parents, laugh with Theresa, and take care of Vic. But I'm alone and not loved in the manner I desire. I'm loved in the sense that I'm provided for. My parents aren't the 'Is something bothering you?' type. They're the 'Do you have your chores done?' parents. Theresa visits home as little as possible, and Vic is detached from the world. I had a good year in football, but not good enough for a scholarship. The same is true for my grades. Most of the kids in my grade are considerate, hardworking people trying to figure out life. Unlike the movies, the homecoming queen and king candidates are decent people.

I'm not in the selection as people have kept a safe distance from me ever since I assaulted an older boy for bullying my schizophrenic brother four years ago. Other than a bloody nose, the boy wasn't seriously hurt. My anger worked for Vic. The bullying ended. I, however, am viewed as someone with the potential to go off the rails. I probably should have explained myself since it happened in front of my class, and my peers weren't aware of the torture Vic had been through. I was too ashamed to desire sympathy, so I quietly took the consequences. I'll never forget the bus ride home. No one sat within two seats of me for the first couple of stops. Then, a courageous girl with flowing brunette locks and scintillating green eyes sat next to me. Serena Bell is the brightest and most beautiful girl in our school, but because she expressed her kindness without reservation, she also had her critics. It was consistent with my theory that there is nothing you can do to get everyone to like you. If you tried, someone would hate you just for that. But I didn't see Serena outside of school as she belonged to a ballet company and didn't date anyone around Pierz. I want someone to talk to who isn't going to judge me based on everything happening with my family—a girl who will at least try to understand me. I'm not sure that person exists.

I returned to the fire, picked up my book, and read forward from the bookmark:

> *"Heaven knows we need never be ashamed of our tears, for they are rain upon the blinding dust of earth, overlying our hard hearts. I was better after I had cried, than before—more sorry, more aware of my own ingratitude, more gentle."*

Charles Dickens wrote my thoughts so succinctly. I wanted to cry, but I couldn't. Tears had been beaten out of me years ago. Even if I couldn't participate, I felt Dickens' sentiment deeply. I returned to immersing myself in his written words.

"What are you doing?" an angel's voice asked.

I glanced up to see Serena approaching the fire. Her long brunette locks flowed from underneath her slouchy beige knit hat, and her body was covered by a forest green peacoat. My sixteen-year-old classmate only lived a mile down the road from me, but I never saw her around. God, if you could get her to love me, you could take my life at thirty, and I'd die a happy man.

Embarrassed, I held my book to the side, away from her. I stood up and offered her my stump. "Here. I was just sitting here thinking." Trying to make light of my family's misfortune, I quipped, "If you've heard the rumors about our farm, it's all we can afford to do."

"Where are you going to sit?"

I set my book on the ground and dragged a log over to the fire. "Here."

After I sat, Serena smiled at me and, instead of going to the stump, picked my book up out of the snow. "You wouldn't want people to know you're reading Great Expectations." She slipped her mittens off, opened the book, read the pages that embraced the bookmark, and then stepped in front of me.

"I just needed to get away," I explained.

"I've seen you here before. I finally had the courage to come and speak to you. I would have come sooner if I had realized you were reading Dickens. I mean, you never know what a teen boy might be looking at in the middle of the woods by himself at night."

I laughed. She sat close to me on the log. The warmth of her body made me pleasantly nervous. Her green eyes were mesmerizing.

She continued, "I heard you made the WCCO all-state team of the week in football. That's impressive."

"Thank you."

"I'm sorry, but I haven't been to a game."

"It's okay. I don't play because I expect people to watch. I play because it's like chess performed at one hundred miles per hour with all the pieces in motion during every move."

"Can you explain it to me in words I can understand?"

"I'm quarterback, so I can change the plays. If I can't figure out what the defense is doing, I send someone in motion." I stood up and pumped my right leg. "Let's say there's a defender covering the wide-out on the right side. When the wide-out sees my foot moving, he runs behind me to the other side of the field. After he crosses, I see the defender on the left side isn't picking him up. Then I know the defender is coming after me instead, on a blitz. More defenders are coming after me than I have blockers, so I have to change the play and get rid of the ball quickly." I laughed at the look of confusion on her face. I sat back down by her. "So, I guess the answer is 'no.' I can't really explain it in a manner you could understand."

She gripped my bicep with her mitten. "I promise I'll try to get to a game next year, even if I can't understand it."

"I went to your ballet."

Surprised, she leaned back. "With whom?"

"By myself."

"Why didn't you tell anyone?"

"It's not something football players brag about."

"You should have found me after." She leaned against me.

"I wasn't sure if you wanted me to."

"Of course, I wanted you to—goof. I have to get back home, or Mom will send the Sheriff, police, and fire department after me. I was at the end of my walk when I noticed you."

"My sister might be able to distract them."

Serena laughed knowingly. "That isn't on you." She stood. "Okay, read me a line from Great Expectations before I go."

"I don't have to read it." I stood facing her and recited, "I loved her against reason, against promise, against peace, against hope, against happiness, against all discouragement that could be."

Without hesitation, Serena kissed me. I will cherish that moment forever. It was a moment of warmth for a boy, lost in a blizzard, trying to find home. The night had split open, and the light revealed Serena's requited love for me for the first time. I was flabbergasted by the possibility that Serena could love me. It was a warm, loving kiss that continued while the endorphins in my brain danced in ecstasy. I felt bulletproof. She stepped back and said, "Tell me the next time you're coming out here so we can have a little more time."

"I can walk you back."

"No, you can't," she grinned. "If my parents see you, there won't be a next time."

I sat on the stump and watched her disappear into the night. It was the best moment of my life.

(3 DAYS LATER)
10:02 P.M., TUESDAY, DECEMBER 19, 2002

DAD WAS A RUGGED VETERAN who had a habit of calling me into the living room to view the bad news of the day. Tonight, we watched medics wheel three bodies out of a two-story farmhouse in South Troy, Minnesota. Dad turned to me and said, "The way the economy's destroying farm families, I'm surprised this isn't happening all over the state."

WCCO newscaster Frank Vascellaro turned to his wife, Amelia Santaniello, and said, "The family's sixteen-year-old son has been taken into custody."

Dad asked me, "How long do you think they'll keep a married couple on the news together? My bet is they don't make it a decade. She kept her maiden name."

Frank and Amelia looked like a happy couple to me. "What do you call the name a guy was born with?"

"I don't know. What?" Dad studied me skeptically.

"There's no word for it. It's just his name. In 1975, Kathleen Harney from Wisconsin wanted to keep her maiden name. She had to appeal her case to the state supreme court to do so. The circuit court ruled by common law she should take her husband's name." Common law refers to enforced practices because they are popular or common rather than by legal statute. "But the supreme court ruled, under English common law, her legal name is the name she has always been known as."

"Seems like a bad way to start out a marriage," Dad suggested.

"Her husband didn't care. Kathleen wanted to add her husband to her insurance, but the school she worked for told her she had to change to her husband's name to do so."

"Now she has me on her side. This is one more case of the government sticking its nose where it doesn't belong. Who the hell are they to tell her what her name should be?"

"Prior to that ruling, women couldn't get a credit card or a passport unless they did so in their husband's name."

"Do you see what's going on there?" Dad pointed to the TV. "That family was killed by their son, Richard Day. I have a friend who lives nine miles north, in Mazeppa, who gave me the scoop. Both parents and a brother are dead. Day's eight-year-old sister is in critical condition in the hospital."

"I saw. I'm not sure what I'm supposed to do about it. It's not the first tragedy in South Troy. That's where Laura Ingalls's only brother died before he reached a year." When he didn't respond, I added, "Did you know that Laura Ingalls Wilder refused to say 'obey' in her wedding vows?"

He shut the TV off. "Yeah, I should just leave the damn tube off."

This was as close as Dad came to apologizing. I appreciated his concession and told him, "It's all right. You can't change the world's problems if you're not aware of them.

Maybe someday I'll be in a position where I can do something about it."

In a calmer tone, Dad said, "I saw you talking to that Bell girl down by the river. Remember, you just take that thing out for pissin', and you put it back as soon as you're done."

"Sound advice," I remarked.

Dad shook his head, "Although, honestly, if you keep sharing that damn trivia, I'm never going to have to worry about you getting laid."

I elected not to respond. He might be right, but I can't help it.

Mom entered the room to let us know that the language being used was not acceptable. Instead of confronting Dad about it, she fixed her gaze on me. It was clear she wanted me to follow her into the kitchen, so I did.

"I like Serena," Mom smiled. "If you ever get a girl pregnant, you take responsibility for the child. I expect you to do what's right by the mother."

"I understand." I really didn't want to have this conversation.

Mom opened the refrigerator door and contemplated tomorrow's meals as she asked, "Have you ever thought about asking out that Golden girl? She's a saint."

Not from the TV show. The girl in question's last name was Golden. I wondered, "Isn't she my cousin?" And as much as I admired saints, I wasn't interested in dating one.

"Second cousin, so it's not a legal issue. What's going through that brain of yours, Jon?"

"I was considering the consequences of knocking up a saint."

"That's not funny."

It was a little funny. I stepped away. "Can this conversation be over?"

"I just don't want to have to hear who you're dating at Thielen's Meats again. Why don't you tell me yourself?" Mom was now facing me.

"Because I don't want you to think you have a say in it."

"That's mean." I knew Mom was frustrated about the state of our finances, and I didn't want to add to her distress.

"I'm sorry. I'm just tired." I was being honest, but I probably could have said it better.

"Understandable. You've got a lot going on. You can't afford to be in love. Girls today expect you to take them places and buy them things." The shame on her face was no less than what she was painting across mine. Having said enough, she nodded to me, indicating that she had accepted the apology. It was as affectionate as we got in our family.

"I have to end the conversation, Mom. If I don't shower, you'll never have to worry about a girl getting close to me." It may seem a little rude, but anyone who has been in a conversation with my mother understands. She continues to talk until you say something like, "I'm sorry, but I have to go."

2

TONY SHILETO

1:30 A.M., MONDAY, DECEMBER 22, 1997
21397 145TH AVENUE, WABASHA

I woke to my phone buzzing. Even after a good night's sleep, I never wake up in a good mood. As a Sheriff's Investigator, a late-night phone call is always bad news. I quickly grabbed the devil's pager off the nightstand, hoping to avoid waking Doris, and sat up.

My wife slowly rolled over to face me as I sat on the edge of the bed. Her baby blue silk cami revealed sinewy muscular arms and shoulders. At one time, we snuck away to revel in each other's company. Now, Doris and I were polite, but it felt like we were coworkers sharing the same bed. Politeness didn't come naturally, though. When we were in sync, we argued, each defending our opinions with humorous jabs at each other. Honestly, Doris is a bit of a bully, but I loved her self-assured toughness. A part of me wanted to remain lying in bed with her and not leave until everything was resolved. But when duty called, I answered.

The caller didn't waste any time delivering the message. "Richard Day escaped."

"You have to be feckin' kidding me. How the hell does Ricky Day escape?" I ran my hand through my thick black hair. Richard Day was a sixteen-year-old boy and a mass murderer. His father was an angry and abusive man who had pulled Ricky out of school to work on the farm. Ricky resented that his eighteen-year-old brother was still allowed to attend school while he was relegated to the status of farm-hand. On that fateful night, Ricky had asked to meet his girl at a dance, and when his dad didn't allow it, he went ballistic. Ricky was a seething ADHD kid with access to a hunting rifle. He put a four-bullet clip in his Remington rifle, and the slaughter at the house on Laura Ingalls Wilder Historic Highway was over in minutes. Among the dead were his father, August; his mother, Naomi; and his thirteen-year-old brother, Blake. Because she raised her arm in self-defense and because of some tremendous medical work, his eight-year-old niece, Halle, survived. Ricky had three older siblings who weren't at home at the time. The community would freak when they learned of his escape.

The jailer explained, "An inmate named Jimmy Watson was unloading boxes in the cargo bay. It was a big load, so he asked if Day could help. Day's a big, strong farm boy. They thought it would speed things up. When Day arrived, Watson attacked the night guard, and Ricky took off with him."

"Feckin' idiots! Why would you allow a mass killer in the loading bay?"

"Honestly, Watson is the more dangerous of the two."

"Maybe, but Richard Day is public enemy number one." Generally, someone who assaults family, like Richard, is less dangerous than someone who has offenses against strangers. But Day's escape was a publicity nightmare, and my task was to find him as soon as possible. I advised, "Pull any video you have of Day and Watson on the outdoor cameras and print their mugshots. I'll be right in."

Doris rubbed my bare back with her hand. As she sat up, the thin blue straps of her cami fell off her shoulders. She kindly offered, "I'll throw some coffee on." She pursed her lips and added, "It's Marcus's birthday party tomorrow. Please remember to take a few minutes off work and come home to celebrate with him."

Doris glanced at the photos of Jimmy and Ricky on my phone as she continued talking. "You could make payments on a new car with what you blow every month at Starbucks. I think you'd sleep better at night if you made fewer coffee trips."

I threw clothes into a duffle bag. *And you just keep thinkin' it. It ain't gonna hurt you any. Beats thinkin' about the possibility that some slimeball is going to put a bullet in me.* There was no point in arguing. It was my task to hunt down a mass killer. I wasn't going to be home until Ricky Day was dead or apprehended.

3

DORIS SHILETO

2:00 A.M., MONDAY, DECEMBER 22, 1997
HIGHWAY 61, WABASHA

Tony was off to work, and I couldn't sleep. Marcus had spent the night at a friend's house, so instead of sitting home alone, I decided to go for a drive. I threw on my winter jacket and slipped on some leather gloves. Tony needs to make time for us. The sad reality is that Tony is happiest at work.

After three days above freezing, the weather dropped to sixteen degrees tonight, and with the tempestuous wind, it was painfully cold. I cruised down the road in my new Mustang. As the car warmed up, I found myself singing the song Bob Dylan wrote about this very road: "Highway 61 Revisited."

There was a curly-haired man ahead, thumbing a ride. He was over six feet tall and weighed one-eighth of a ton. That silo of a man was going to have a hard time hitchhiking. I pulled over and called Tony. We promised to call each other anytime we picked up a rider.

He didn't answer. He was likely being briefed and momentarily had his phone off.

To be safe, I called a friend, Karla, who worked nearby, "Hey, there's a man on Highway 61 in orange pajamas, needing a ride. I'm going to pull over and see if I can help."

"Where are you?" Karla responded.

"Only one mile away from you, south on Highway 61. Just passed a blue Coffee Mill Inn exit."

"You don't have to pick him up."

"I'm good." I slowed down and studied the gargantuan man.

"Be careful, girl!" Karla hung up.

Seeing I was a lone woman cruising by at two in the morning elicited a sinister smile from the King Kong-like character.

I reconsidered picking up my friend and drove on for about a hundred feet before finally pulling over. I watched the large dude in the rearview mirror running to my car, breath steaming in the cold winter air. Taunting him, I slowly pulled ahead another hundred feet before coming to a complete stop. I could feel my devilish grin emerge. Tony says I shouldn't test people, but I think this guy deserved it. I could see the irritation on the man's face as he chased my car. I wasn't 100% sure I wanted him in my vehicle. I slid one hand under my winter jacket as I waited.

He pulled open the passenger door and, panting heavily, slid in. "I can't tell you how happy I am to see you. Colder than a penguin's pecker tonight."

"Colder than skinny-dipping in Lake Superior," I countered.

He nodded as he waited for me to put the car in gear. "We goin'?"

"I thought I'd let you warm up for a bit."

"I'm good to go."

When I hesitated, the large man pulled out a shiv. "Get'er movin' bitch."

I slid my Glock out from under my jacket. His eyes widened as I said, "I like my odds."

Jimmy Watson glanced down at the badge, now visible on my belt. Sirens descended on us, and the darkness lit up with blue squad car lights rushing in from every direction. "You picked the wrong jail to break out of, Jimmy. I called my friend Karla, who works nights at the 79th Military Police Academy, one mile west of here. The Wabasha County Sheriff's Department is one mile to the east. You can attack me, but even if you survive my bullets, they'll tenderize your body with lead in minutes."

As police officers surrounded us, he dropped his shiv on the floor of the car.

"Now tell me, where's Richard Day?"

"I split with him right outside the jail. They're bringing that boy back in a body bag. Not gonna be seen with him. He's a dead man walkin.'"

I believed him. "Get your ass out of my car. Put your hands on your head as you step out."

There had to be a dozen squad cars around us. I watched officers cuff Watson and lead him away. As a state trooper, I loved my unmarked Mustang. After listening to Tony's message from the Wabasha jail, confirming that he would not be coming home anytime soon, I decided to head to work. If these boys wanted out of town fast, Highway 61 was their ticket.

My phone buzzed, "Hi Tony. I got Watson, but he claims he and Day split after leaving the jail."

"Are you okay?"

"You just got to have the right touch," I teased. "Took him down without incident. When he saw my guns, he begged for mercy."

"I'll have to take a better look at you when I return home," Tony answered.

"Actually, it was just one gun." And yes, he should take a better look at me. He should see me and be present instead of thinking about work twenty-four-seven.

"Do you believe Watson doesn't know where Day is?"

"I do. He knows the community has a shoot-to-kill attitude about Richard Day, so he didn't want to be caught with him. I'm headed over to the jail to do the paperwork. Love you, Tone."

"Love you too. Great work! I'll meet you there."

I'm beginning to question the wisdom of being married to another law enforcement officer. I protect my family time. Tony doesn't. Sometimes, love isn't enough. Tony and I jab at each other enough when we get along. I can't imagine what a divorce would be like. But that's a conversation for another night.

Mimicking Bob Dylan's scratchy and whiney voice, I sang:

"We'll wait 'til this case is done,
and have it out, on Highway 61."

4

TONY SHILETO

10:00 P.M., FRIDAY, DECEMBER 26, 1997
WABASHA COUNTY SHERIFF'S OFFICE,
848 17TH STREET EAST, SUITE 1, WABASHA

It was the fourth day of searching for Ricky Day. Gun sales were skyrocketing, and I was afraid some innocent teen who happened to look a little like Day was going to get shot to death. Families in the area had someone sit up all night with a loaded gun, protecting their homes.

My phone buzzed. "Hey, are you that investigator looking for Richard Day?"

"I am. Who is this?"

"Danny Dietz. I've got a farm over here in Sleepy Eye. I don't know if this is anything, but I just noticed a guy walk into my barn. Whoever it was waited 'til I was done for the night. I shut off the lights and was about to go to bed when I saw him out the kitchen window."

"Did you get a good look at him?"

"Nah. Speculatin', I'd say guttersnipe and a bit of a gimp. Looked like he was limpin'."

"Sit tight. I'll come by and check it out. I'm a couple hours away. Please stay in the house."

"No worries. I got a six-pack of Schell's Deer Brand beer at my feet and a loaded 30.06 on my lap. I'll sit tight and wait for your word."

"Take it easy with the ale, all right? Give me your address." Sleepy Eye was over three hours away from Wabasha. I had already traveled an hour in that direction checking out a lead that didn't pan out, so I decided I might as well take this one on, too. It was common for homeless people to survive out here, on the edge of the earth, by sleeping in barns, so there was no reason to call for backup yet.

1:38 A.M., WEDNESDAY, DECEMBER 27, 1997
MINNESOTA RIVER VALLEY SCENIC BYWAY,
SLEEPY EYE

I DROVE DOWN THE DIRT driveway into the farmyard. The grange was dimly illuminated by a yard light on a post, stationed closer to the house than the barn. Nighttime is scary in rural Minnesota—lots of darkness to disappear into. My car rumbled and groaned a little after I shut it off. I knew exactly how it felt. I watched my breath wisp away into the night air as I approached the barn.

I opened the door and shined my Maglite along the barn wall to make sure it was safe to keep my back to it. *It's good.* I backed down the entire wall, staring at the asses of cows as I slunk along. There was no movement beyond the heavy breathing and occasional bellering of the bovine herd. This side was safe. I repeated the process on the other side. No one. This meant I had to climb into the hay loft and hope like hell that no one was at the entry waiting to crack me on the head.

Why do I do this? I love you, Doris. I love you, Marcus. I kissed the cross around my neck and climbed the wall ladder step by step. Before crawling through the opening, I shined the light in every direction to make certain it was safe. Then, I quickly climbed into the hayloft and hopped to my feet.

A young man was huddled in the corner in the fetal position, shaking. It was Richard Day.

I wondered what he had in store for me. Gun drawn, I approached carefully.

Day was shivering. His face was ghostly. His hands were red and his fingernails white—signs of frostbite.

"Do you have a weapon?" I asked.

"No." He shook his head.

I called 911. "I have Richard Day, and he's going to need an ambulance. This boy's a couple degrees from dead. Take your time. I'd hate for you to get into an accident saving this dirtball."

I looked down at the crumpled heap of a farm boy. "What did you do, kid? You killed your family, and now you're going to die. What was it all for?"

Ricky's voice quavered, "C-can you give me last rites?"

What's the point? If he can make it to heaven after what he did, I'm going to live differently. Realizing he was serious, I said, "Okay. I can do that." I knelt by the crying and dying boy and recited the psalm as best I could, using my own words. "The Lord is my shepherd; I shall not want. As I lie in green pastures, you lead me to still waters. You restore my soul and lead me to the path of righteousness. Though I walk through the valley of the shadow of death, I will fear no evil: for you are with me. For you prepare a table before me, in the presence of my enemies, and anoint me with a cup that runs over." I took his hand. "The first step is confession."

He roughly spat out, "Sins of envy, covetousness, and false pride."

This boy knew his sins. Jailhouse preachers frequently addressed sins of false pride since most inmates end up incarcerated as a result of their preoccupation with self-importance and possessions. As both an investigator and now a surrogate priest, I wanted details. "Why?"

"T-tired of being a slave. Why should I have to give up my life? I had n-no life."

I sensed the boy wanted to talk after days of isolation. And he was just a boy, in a brawny athlete's body. "Okay, I've heard that your dad would go on angry rampages. He'd even wake you up in the middle of the night to finish a chore. That might explain why you killed August. But why Naomi? What made you so angry that you shot your mom?"

"Don't you get it?" Richard stared at me. "They were all in it together. It was them against me. When Mom would get me alone, she'd pretend she understood, but then she'd just make excuses for Dad. It's the accident."

"What accident?"

"Dad's always been a bully. He had a snowmobile accident a couple years ago that put him in a coma. He was driving too fast at night and hit a field approach. After that, he was unbearable. He couldn't help with chores because of his vision. He complained of headaches all the time. He couldn't remember shit. If Dad would get upset that the hayloft wasn't closed, he'd bitch about it nonstop for hours, even if he was the one who'd left it open. And you couldn't change the conversation. He'd go on and on and on and on until he'd finally become tired of it."

All the behaviors Richard identified, including perseveration, were symptoms of a traumatic brain injury.

"I was the whipping post."

While I was piecing together a picture of a family with painful secrets, I couldn't get the images of the children lying in the basement out of my head. "Why shoot your brother Blake?"

Richard paused. "I don't remember shooting Blake or Halle." He didn't appear sad, but a tear slipped down his cheek.

"Why shoot Halle?" I wanted to see if I could find any emotional connection to his family.

"I don't remember." His breathing slowed. "I'm not saying I didn't. I just don't remember. I had made a list of what I had to do to end my imprisonment. All I can think of is that she was on the list."

Ricky's remorse was all self-centered. He was sorry he was caught. "You had to kill your family to be free?"

"Just the ones at home."

Memories of finding the thirteen-year-old brother and eight-year-old sister made me sick. "What type of rifle was used?"

"A Remington Model Four semiautomatic."

The Model Four is a heavy rifle that jams up but takes down its target.

Ricky continued, "I asked Dad for something new or even a lighter rifle—a Winchester Model 70 would have been perfect. Dad would tell me the Model Four is a man's gun. That damn Remington. They'd all still be alive if it had jammed up that night. If something would have just interrupted my train of thought—"

"Where's the rifle?" We didn't have the murder weapon.

Richard's body stilled. "You'll find it in the spring."

If he had hidden the rifle in the snow, we would have found it. We tracked the footprints in the yard. And then it occurred to me. The hayloft is filled with hay to get the cows through the winter. By the end of spring, it's empty. "The Remington's buried in the hayloft," I said softly.

He nodded.

I waited patiently before finally sharing, "There was a pile of wrapped Christmas presents in your parents' closet. There was one for you from your dad. The shape of it caught my eye, so I opened it."

"Was it a lump of coal?"

"No. It was a brand-new Winchester Model 70 deer hunting rifle. It's a classic. Hunters refer to it as a shooter's rifle."

Richard's head rested on the wooden hayloft floor as he sobbed.

The hunt for Richard Day had ended.

5

MELANIE PEARSON

(16 YEARS LATER)
6:30 P.M., THURSDAY, JUNE 7, 2018
HOPPY GIRL BREWING,136 BRIDGE AVENUE, WABASHA

I set my phone face down on the patio table and wanted to scream. I might have if I hadn't been sitting on this quaint taproom patio in the presence of strangers. Well, maybe if I wasn't so emotionally repressed. My landlord called and officially evicted me. When I explained that I hadn't seen any eviction warnings, he informed me that my former lover, Sebastian, had signed the lease and that his mail had been forwarded to New York. When he left town, Sebastian had agreed to pay the rent if I paid off our credit cards. Mind you, our credit card debt was slightly larger, but as a demonstration of blind love, I cheerfully assented. It meant fewer Caribou Coffee stops for the month and no random weekend escapes to the Brainerd Lakes. It was a testament to my unconditional love. Sebastian used to make these sarcastic comments that I was suffering from amnesia anytime I forgot something. Well, Sebastian, either you're the one with amnesia or—he burned me. The thought that he didn't forget saddened me further.

I know he loved me, at least for a moment, and I loved him. We lived in a penthouse apartment on Cathedral Hill with a great view of historic St. Paul. Our living quarters were overpriced, but he convinced me the two of us could pull it off together. Spring brought red and white cherry blossoms, red tulips, and Scilly White Narcissus flowers. It was breathtaking. The cascade of scarlet blooming flowers complimented my red hair, and I felt beautiful. Maybe I even was. For the first time, I was the center of someone's world. Then Sebastian took a trip to New York. There were calls at first, then texts, and then nights spent looking at my phone, waiting for a response. And now I can't stop snacking. Who am I kidding? In the end, Sebastian felt absent, even when he was home. The harder I tried, the more he pulled away.

Ugh, and did I mention I just lost my job? If anyone was betting her friends could help her out, they'd have lost. For one, I didn't have a lot of close friends. I feel like I'm "normal." I laugh at jokes at about the same time everybody else does. I like Taylor Swift and line up with the masses to order my vanilla lattes. I think Friends was better than Seinfeld, and my best friend, Sophie, agrees, so I don't consider myself to be too far off the beaten path.

High school was painful, less because of bullying and more because I went unnoticed. I would take a risk and wear something out of my comfort zone, and no one cared. Of course, I could have been more assertive, but I had to keep friends at a distance. If my "bestie" got too close, she might ask to come over, and my mom was always so dismally depressed I could barely stand it. If people met Mom, they wouldn't stand me. So, when prom came around, I anxiously waited to be asked for a date, and then sweated with naïve optimism as the days passed. It never happened. But even that was probably pretty normal. My best friend, Sophie, was randomly assigned as my roommate at Winona State

University. Perhaps that's a testament to how bad I am at choosing friends.

Sophie took a job at 3M in Maplewood after college and talked our entire cohort into working there one by one. It was like our college life, every day, except we were paid. I lived the millennial dream for five years: Red Rock concerts, tap room tours, and vacations to Monterey Bay and the Florida Keys.

On Monday, Attorney General Lori Swanson announced that the State of Minnesota is suing 3M over the release of fluorochemicals. Ms. Swanson is seeking $850 million to clean up Minnesota's drinking water. Evidently, my employer's research team told the powers that be that the "forever chemicals" they used in Scotchgard were "more toxic than anticipated" back in 1977. Still, 3M used the chemicals in firefighting foams sprayed at the Camp Ripley and Duluth airports. Eagles in the area tested positive for the chemicals, and so did their eaglets. In response, 3M is cutting costs. They announced that, technically, they're not firing people. Instead, "We're adjusting our workforce to a slowing economy." So, I wasn't fired. I was "adjusted" to the ranks of the unemployed. *That feels so much better.*

My closest friends have ghosted me. I get it. We can't share because we're all competing for the same jobs. We all worked together, so we all got laid off at the same time. The truth is that they were all closer to each other than they were to me. I was the one afraid to tell my most embarrassing stories out of fear I'd be rejected. Looking back, I wish I had taken that chance. It was what they had in common with each other, but not with me. I was the odd one out.

My phone buzzed again. What now? My interview better not have been canceled. I need this job. An Apple News Top Story flashed on my phone. "Ricky Day to be Released from Prison Tomorrow after 16 Years: Sole Massacre Survivor

Halle Day Speaks out in Support." Well, good for her. I had enough of my own crap to deal with.

It was a balmy 75 degrees outside tonight, and I sat at a table on the patio wearing a short shamrock green button-down dress with a white floral design. I wore black leggings underneath to make it business-appropriate. I had stopped at Hoppy Girl Brewing and selected a pale wheat ale called "Chubby Chipmunk." Friends had told me about this quaint little taproom in Wabasha with great beer just off the Mississippi. The brick patio was the perfect place to sit back and relax on this calm summer evening.

I had just driven sixty-seven miles to meet a man who was offering me a job eight miles from my home. I need this job! Single, unemployed, homeless, and to top it off, I'm thirty years old, and I haven't been laid in forever. Maybe tonight was my night. Wabasha is the perfect place to find a curmudgeonly guy. The movie *Grumpy Old Men* was based on a couple of Wabasha residents. It was a good movie, but I think I'd like more of the Jack Lemmon type in my old age rather than Walter Matthau.

Fortunately, the warm sun felt heavenly on my skin as I sat back, imbibing the cold, crisp beer. Should I settle for a couple of sips before my guest arrives, or should I drink the entire glass and get a second to sip on? It would look bad if my glass were empty, so I needed to either be content with a taste or go for it. I took a large swallow.

A handsome man with platinum blond hair and a silver Armani suit stopped at my table, lifted his dark sunglasses, and gave me a quick once-over. The man was in his mid-thirties and had a chiseled, muscular body. He grinned, "I'm Tug Grant, Esquire. I have some business to take care of, but stick around. I'd like to talk to you later."

I gave the ridiculous yuppie a decorous smile and watched him sit at an adjacent table. On a lighter day, he would be a possibility. He was cute, dressed to kill, and was clearly smitten with me. Perhaps another time.

The bartender, Brenda, guided an attractive thirty-ish man to the table directly in front of mine. Brenda studied his ID and said, "Jon Frederick. Welcome to Hoppy Girl. Have you looked at the tap list?"

"Yes, I'll have the Firebrick. This is a nice place."

"Thank you," she responded.

I closed my eyes and enjoyed the welcoming sun. I reopened my eyes to see Jon sitting alone, clicking away on his laptop. He had thick brown hair and was dressed in business casual. His teal button-down shirt had words embroidered in gold cursive along the bottom. I could only make out two of them: *Compassion* and *Faith.* He wore black jeans and black tennis shoes. My immediate analysis was that this man was intense and probably wouldn't stop working if a tornado went through. I decided to test my hypothesis and ask, "What are you drinking?"

He toasted his glass my way and said, "Schell's Firebrick. A Vienna-style amber named after the bricks that lined old boilers. What do you have?"

"Chubby Chipmunk." Trying to be funny, I added, "Named after an over-inflated marsupial."

"Tamias," he corrected.

"What?" Pointing out errors is a poor way to pick up women.

Unabashed, he continued, "A chipmunk isn't a marsupial. Tamias is the genus of chipmunks found in Minnesota. In Latin, Tamias means 'the collector.'" He stopped himself and politely offered, "Sorry for the rant." Head down, he went back to typing.

I wasn't wrong about him. My gaze shifted back to the sexy attorney on my left. Noticing that I glanced their way, the Italian-looking thug who had seated himself next to Tug eyeballed me. The ragazzo had to be about six and a half feet tall with matted, raven-black hair. I looked away and then glanced back.

The attorney attempted to redirect him, "Roan, focus here."

Still ogling me, Roan remarked, "Drunks and leggings tell the truth, and her leggings aren't all that kind to her."

Dick.

The attorney felt bad for me and responded, "Are you blind? A fair-skinned maiden with fiery red hair—she's beautiful. Before you criticize her, you should walk a mile in her shoes. Then, at least, she'd have the pleasure of knowing you're a mile away."

I forced a smile toward the attorney. I know he was trying to be kind, but his feeling sorry for me made me feel even more pathetic. I heard Roan say, "So Ricky Day is free man tomorrow. Cops got to be furious. Our justice system is just a big catch-and-release program, isn't it?"

"We've got your case coming up Monday," Tug said.

"Yeah, my case. I should have shot him with a paintball gun—just to watch him dye." Roan hit Tug on the shoulder and laughed gregariously. "Get it? D-Y-E."

Tug rolled his eyes. "I'm just glad it isn't contagious."

Their conversation reverted to arguing over the price of a car. Out of boredom, I leaned in their direction and listened in.

Roan grumbled, "I'm not paying more than four figures."

"I can get $12,000 for it, easy," Tug said.

"Maybe you can," Roan argued, "but I can give you $9000 cash right now."

"It would be an insult to the car to sell it for less than $12,000," Tug replied.

Do cars really feel insulted? Intending to head into the taproom, I picked up my beer and tried to slip by the back of Tug's chair.

Tug quickly slid his chair back, bumping into me.

I lost my grip and dumped my golden beverage down the front of his Armani suit. I started defensively, "If you wouldn't have backed into me—"

He cut me off and finished the sentence. "You wouldn't have poured beer all over my $3000 suit."

Of all people, it had to be a damn attorney. I'm sure he'll find a reason to find me liable. I am so broke I have less than zero. I'm going to have to borrow money from my dad for a deposit on a new apartment. People with no money have more money than I do.

Sensing my panic, he said, "Calm down. It's all good."

"You can't blame me—"

"Do you know how many times I hear that in a day?" Tug laughed, "Let me guess. You thought I was on fire. I might be hot, but not on fire."

When I stood speechless, he added, "I know my friend here is a pig, but you didn't have to take it out on me."

"I didn't intentionally drink slap you—"

"No worries." Tug removed his suit jacket, folded it, and set it over an empty chair. He glanced at his tie and noticed the beer in my glass had managed to splotch everything. He calmly removed his tie and laid it over his jacket. I couldn't help noticing he had a handgun in a shoulder holster beneath his shirt. He undid the top button of his white shirt and, with a pleasant grin, proposed, "Let's try this again. I'm Tug Grant, and I'm not upset. What are you drinking? I'll buy you another."

"Chubby Chipmunk."

"The Redford Red Ale is the bomb."

"I'm sticking with the over-inflated Tamias."

"Tamias?"

"It's a long story." Appreciating his calm response to the fiasco, I finally apologized. "I am so sorry."

"Would you care to join us?" Tug offered.

"I'm meeting someone here for work."

"Okay."

Like a true gentleman, he purchased my beer and left me to sit and sulk—as I preferred.

I watched a petite woman in a copper-colored dress stroll onto the patio with a cold glass of beer and a slice of pizza. The pretty brunette had long flowing curls and green eyes that glowed against her tan skin. She looked like she'd just come from a wedding. After looking over the tables, she strolled to my laptop neighbor, Jon, and asked, "Do you mind if I sit?"

I had to admire her—good choice, but good luck! To my surprise, he closed his laptop.

"I'm Serena." The woman drank in his attentiveness.

"Jon." He stood and pulled a chair out for her.

She set her beer and pizza down on his table and, with the tip of her tongue, seductively licked a drop of tomato sauce off her lavender nails. Serena's full lips left me envious. Her tone was so sultry I could have sworn she uttered a raunchy pick-up line when she said, "I need to do something with my hands." She stood and walked to the bar for napkins.

After she left the patio, a large seagull swooped down, clamped onto her slice of pizza, and flew off with it. I burst out laughing.

The shock on Jon's face was hilarious. He glanced over at me, "Did you see that?"

Serena returned and asked, "Where's my pizza?"

"A bird—" Jon attempted to explain. He pointed to the clear sky, "flew down and took it."

"I doubt it." She placed her hand on her hip and rocked it. "You men! It's not enough to eat it; you have to lie about it too."

Jon looked to me for support, but I turned away and ignored him. *This was too good!*

I heard him trying to explain, "I swear, a herring gull, to be exact. Most live near Duluth, but they nest along the Mississippi. White with gray wings."

"Look, I know what a seagull looks like," Serena interrupted. "You do understand that describing a seagull isn't evidence that this happened?"

"Yes." He nodded reluctantly.

"Have birds of any type taken anyone else's food?"

Giving up, Jon offered, "I'll buy you another slice."

"I wanted *that* one. The perfect garnishing of mushrooms, strategically placed to maximize the flavor in every bite."

The attorney's friend had left, so Tug slid his chair over to my table. "Did you see that?"

"I did." I grinned, "This is so entertaining!"

"And you're not bailing him out?"

"No way."

He nodded, colluding in the cover-up. "I like your style. I don't see him recovering from that start."

Serena sat by Jon with her legs crossed, slowly swinging one tanned leg as she sipped her beer. "What do you do, Jon, when you're not stealing pizza?"

With a sly grin, he said, "I breed horses."

"Personally?"

"Yes. You could say I'm up to my arms in the work."

I turned to Tug. "I wasn't expecting that."

Tug whispered, "I know him. He's bull-shitting her. That's Jon Frederick, an investigator for the Bureau of Criminal Apprehension. He's testifying at a case in town tomorrow."

Jon asked, "And what do you do?"

"I'm in town taking a break from raising a couple of little scientists. Motherhood is an extreme sport, which is why I wear workout clothes every day. I thought maybe tonight I could go out in a comfortable dress and just relax with a cold beer, a slice of pizza..." She let her voice trail off.

"I swear a herring gull took your pizza." Jon pled, "I'll buy you a whole damn pizza."

"I like pizza, but the slice wasn't my prurient interest. I was hoping for some adult conversation, but I think you're a little too extreme for me. Up to your arms and all."

I couldn't believe the forwardness of this woman. She started to rise, but Jon gently took her wrist and coolly told her, "I apologize for touching you without your consent." He let go. "I want you to hear me out. I can be as gentle as the situation calls for."

"Care to share?" Serena raised an eyebrow as she remained next to him.

"Have you ever returned a baby robin to its nest or relaced a leather glove? I can be gentle, and I can be bold."

Serena remarked, "The last time I said, 'I'll drink you under the table,' was to my tea when I was hiding from my daughter."

"I will always be respectful." Jon gave her a boyish grin. "Honestly, I'm an investigator in town for a court hearing tomorrow. I was asked when I was first interviewed for my job, 'What would you do if you had to arrest your mother?' I told them, 'Call for backup.'"

Serena's face lit up. "Mmmm, a man who respects women."

"I will tell you this. I perform best when the pressure is on." Jon grinned.

She leaned into him and softly purred, "Your shoe's untied." Serena slid off her chair and knelt in front of him.

Fully aware Jon was embarrassed, she took her time.

Both Tug and I leaned forward to watch. She was untying his other shoe.

Still kneeling, she looked up and said, "I thought I'd save you the trouble. Would you be interested in driving me home?"

"Yes. Where are you staying?" Jon responded eagerly.

Serena nodded to a house just thirty feet away from our table.

"You live here?" Jon asked.

"No. It's Turning Waters Bed and Breakfast, and they have a great bed." She paused. "And breakfast. This is my last night, and I really don't want to be alone."

Jon helped Serena to her feet.

Instead of taking his hand, she hooked her index finger into a belt loop in the front of his jeans and led him to the house. I swallowed hard as I felt my face warm. That was one of the most erotic things I'd ever witnessed. First, the gull took what she wanted, and then Serena swooped in right after and was no less impressive. I muttered out loud, "I should sit at that table."

"Who says it's the table?" Tug laughed. "Maybe luck runs through the entire patio."

I corrected myself. "I'm not a one-night stand sort of gal, but I am envious sometimes of people who are." I sighed, "Their lives seem so easy compared to mine. It's not even dark, and Serena's hit a home run." I wanted to leave, but I couldn't afford to depart without giving my potential employer the opportunity to show. I put my hand over Tug's. "Thank you for being so understanding about the spilled beer. Not getting assaulted or sued might be the high point of my day."

"It's still early." Tug smiled. "I find you intriguing." He turned his hand palm up and gave my hand a warm, gentle embrace as he told me, "I'm a great listener."

It was kind, but I was way beyond needing a friend to listen. I needed solutions.

At that moment, two men exited the taproom. A pastor-looking man in a light blue suit jacket glared at me. His ivory dress shirt was buttoned to the very top, and his eternal damnation stare ran a chill up my spine. Seeking comfort, my hand dropped down to Tug's leg.

The tight-wound, baby-faced man leered directly at me and spat out, "Two-bit whore."

Tug shot to his feet. "You owe this woman an apology."

Like a spoiled adolescent, the zealot responded, "You do." He turned away, reached back, and punched Tug, knocking him to the ground.

The bartender was on him in a second. Petite blonde Brenda made the pompous freak look her in the eyes as she told him, "You don't hit people in my bar."

When he opened his mouth, Brenda waved her hand in front of his face, "Shut up and leave. You've said enough." She was soon joined by her husband.

The zealot didn't want to move, but his friend grabbed him by the collar and yanked him backward. The fighter appeared to be waiting for someone to challenge him and call him back into the fray. No one did.

I helped Tug to his feet and wrapped an arm around him to stabilize him. A thin line of blood ran from his nose, but it didn't appear broken.

Brenda stepped over to examine Tug more closely. After seeing that he was okay, she sternly told him, "You should leave, too."

I argued on his behalf, "Tug didn't do anything. He was just defending me."

Brenda wasn't about to back down. "I don't want any trouble."

I turned to Tug, "I'll help you go somewhere and clean up. Did you know that guy?"

"No."

"Why did he hit you?"

Keeping his arm around me for balance, Tug steered me toward his suit jacket and tie. He folded them over his arm and said, "Blood in the water."

As we walked toward the parking lot, I asked, "What are you talking about?"

"You had a bad day. I don't mean to be insulting, but you're wearing misery like a fifty-pound tunic."

"I got fired and dumped. I'm losing my apartment in two weeks and got stood up for an interview by some guy named Tilmore. What the hell kind of a name is Tilmore, anyway? He doesn't even have his picture on his website, so I have no idea what he looks like. Hell, he might have been the guy who called me a whore. If I could trade lives with you, I'd take the punch." I ended my rant. We had arrived at a midnight blue Ford Mustang. "What year?"

"2010, but in mint condition." Tug unbuttoned his white shirt.

"What are you doing?" I couldn't help noticing his solid pecs and tight abs.

He removed his shoulder holster and handed his gun to me. "I'd love to talk further. But I wouldn't expect you to go anywhere with me while I'm carrying, so I'm giving you my gun. If I get out of hand, shoot me."

Dumbfounded, I was momentarily silenced. I pondered his effort to sell his car and asked, "Are you hurting for money?"

"No. I'm buying a Model S Tesla," he scoffed. "I could go for some ice cream. Do you want to take a drive down Great River Road? The drive between Wabasha and Red Wing might be the most scenic in the state."

Still holding his gun, I looked down at it and said, "Sure." I had nothing to lose. "Are you okay to drive?"

"Yeah. I'm good."

Like a nervous schoolgirl, I found my body slowly twisting as I said, "If you want to talk more, I have a place. A friend told me I could stay at her home on the Mississippi. She and her hubby are in Texas looking for work. It's by the National Eagle Center on Lawrence Boulevard."

Grinning, Tug got into the driver's seat and said, "I'll follow you."

8:40 P.M., LAWRENCE BOULEVARD EAST, WABASHA

WHAT AM I DOING? HE did take a punch for me. There's something to be said for that. I found the key hidden under the pipestone flower vase and opened the door. We kicked our shoes off and walked up the steps to a carpeted living room with a floor-to-ceiling window overlooking the Mississippi. The sun was starting to set, lighting up the sky in a glorious blaze of red and orange. The room had a large gas fireplace with a wide couch in front of it.

"Your friends do well," Tug said admiringly.

"We all did well until a couple of weeks ago."

"Do you mind if I go into the bathroom to clean up?" Tug asked. "I want to make sure I don't smear any blood in this beautiful home."

"Sure." Appreciating his respect for my friend's property, I pointed him down the hall and set my purse by the fireplace. I still had his gun. I carefully laid it on the mantle and started the fireplace.

Tug returned and joined me by the window. The home was on a cliff and featured a magnificent view of both the Minnesota and Wisconsin sides of the Mississippi.

I put my arm around his waist and tickled him.

His muscles tightened, and a scowl crossed his face.

I took a couple of steps back.

Tug closed his eyes for a second and took a couple of deep breaths. A calmness had returned when his eyes reopened. "Sorry about that. I'm hypersensitive to tactile stimulation. I'd like to think it makes me a better lover. I was bullied when I was a kid, so I can't stand being tickled."

"I'm sorry." I felt bad. The way he pulled himself back under control without lashing out was admirable.

"It's okay. It's my deal. Nothing you need to apologize for."

I took his hand and invited him to sit with me on the couch. "Tell me about it. Where are you from?"

"I was raised in Elmore, Minnesota. The town's ghosting out. When I left, Elmore had about seven hundred people, and its population is a little over five hundred now. The last census showed there is someone over age sixty-five living alone in one of every six homes in Elmore."

Not wanting to talk further about census statistics, I asked, "What would the bullies do?"

"I was small and, like I said—very tactilely sensitive. Bullies would tickle me until I passed out and then throw me into County Ditch 41 to bring me back to consciousness."

"County Ditch 41?"

"The water revived me. County Ditch 41 and the Middle Branch Blue Earth River are the two water sources in Elmore. My only escape was to lie and tell them Dad was looking for me."

"That sounds horrible. I'm so sorry." I pictured this little boy crawling out of the ditch crying, clothes dripping wet, wanting to go home while the kids stood around and laughed.

"Honestly, the physical torture wasn't near as bad as what my mom put me through." Tug continued, "At thirteen, Mom left the family and moved in with the father of the cruelest bully. My sister and I had to walk by Mommie Dearest's new home on our way to Elmore Academy every school day. That gorilla of a kid would tell us, "Heard your mom moaning in my dad's room last night. She loves it here. See ya, losers!"

"I'm sorry you had to go through that." My heart sank.

"Melanie, you are very kind." Tug now held my hand between both of his. "I didn't mean to dump this all on you tonight."

I had to hear more. "How did your sister handle the bullying?"

"There was nothing either of us could do. We were both petite and natural platinum blondes. The bully freak had been gifted a man's body at age thirteen. Meg and I responded by being honor roll students in high school and eventually college graduates. My dad called Meg "Golden Girl" and me "Cotton Top." I think she got the better of the nicknames." He held my hand between his and tenderly massaged my hand and wrist. Our faces naturally drifted closer. Tug remarked, "Enough about me; tell me about you."

I was afraid that if I started talking, he would never want to see me again. Still, he seemed so *right.* I shared, "I needed to be home to take care of my mom. She was always so depressed. And Dad worked all the time. I didn't have anyone. I'd come home, do my homework, and go online. Mom was there, but she wasn't there." I couldn't bring myself to tell him Mom eventually died by suicide. I felt so guilty for not trying harder to help her. "Would you mind just giving me a hug—Tug?" I made light of it, "Or is it Tug hug?"

His embrace was comforting. Our lips pressed against each other, and harmonious with our lips, our bodies followed suit. As crazy as it was, it felt so right. Maybe for tonight, I could forget about everything.

11:45 P.M.

I HEARD THE DOOR CLOSE and woke up covered by a blanket on the couch. I smiled at missing the awkward goodbye. The fireplace was still burning, and it was nice and warm. If only I didn't have to go back to the reality of my life. Tug was kind, and he made me realize I was going to get over Sebastian's leaving me for New York. Maybe I already was. There was nothing I wished was different about Tug. He knew how to please a woman, and I didn't even have to ask about a condom. I wondered how many times he'd been in this situation. I guess he could have left me a note. I walked down the steps to make sure the door was locked. Tug had locked it from the inside when he left—very responsible. When I returned to the living room, I noticed a note on the floor. It read:

> *Melanie,*
> *I am Tilmore Ulysses Grant, or "Tug." Tilmore means "charisma and dreams," and the name suggests a powerful presence. I am busy until Monday, but I'd love to discuss how I can help you with your employment situation. We will be a two-person office, and working for me involves clerical work and research. I promise to exceed your previous pay and benefits. When not performing clerical work, you will be looking up information on the people I interact with—even at times going to their work sites incognito to get a first-hand understanding of them. All your time and travel will be paid.*
>
> *Thank you for an awesome night! You're an amazing person and I look forward to knowing you better. By the way, I'm not controlling. I won't be asking about your personal life or checking up on you. Our relationship can be strictly professional, or it can go further, whichever you desire. This will work!*
>
> Sincerely,
> Tug

For a second, I was elated to have work, but just as quickly, unease settled in. If I had known he was going to be my employer, I would never have slept with him. It helped that we were a two-person office. There wouldn't be gossip from coworkers. Maybe it *would* work. My mind quickly relished dreamy thoughts of future intimacy and perhaps posterity with this handsome, fit, intelligent man.

6

JON FREDERICK

10:30 A.M. FRIDAY, JUNE 8, 2018
WABASHA COUNTY COURTHOUSE, 848
17TH STREET EAST, WABASHA

I was thankful for another passionate night with my wife, Serena (Bell) Frederick. She loves to go to communities where we're not known and pretend we've just met. The seagull stealing her pizza was a bonus to the drama. Serena and I enjoyed a wonderful quiche with sides of fresh fruit and sausage at Turning Waters Bed and Breakfast. I had an ice-cold glass of orange juice while she went with a hot mug of tea, and then she headed home to our children, Nora and Jackson.

Twenty-one years ago, Serena and I sat at a fire together on the bank of a river, contently contemplating literature. The baptism of fire adolescents experience from the anguish of self-degradation and poor communication lay just around the bend for us. As a young man in need of clarification, I asked Serena to officially date me. When she refused, I assumed it was because she was embarrassed to be seen in public with me. I would later find out she was afraid that if we changed to dating status, I'd waste money buying her items and taking her places when she felt what we had was already perfect. Feeling rejected, I stopped talking to her. The relationship I rebounded into landed me in my first murder book, but that's another story.

Today, after Serena left town, I remained in Wabasha to give Tony Shileto a ride. Tony has been in a wheelchair after being shot in the line of duty four years ago. He was divorced and only received occasional visits from his son. Vicki, the young woman who usually drove Tony's wheelchair-fitted van, was getting picked up by a friend for a "glamping" trip to Hidden Spring Hideaway, just northeast of Dodge Center. Vicki and Marshall will be snuggled in a warm double bed in the middle of the woods in a large white tent tall enough to stand in. It seems cheesy, but I'm not opposed to the idea. In practice, it's not much different than the Ice Castle fish houses people put on the lakes in the winter. From my point of view, there are times to camp rough and times to camp comfortable.

I parked in front of the Wabasha County Courthouse. In 2000, the county needed updated facilities and erected a rectangular courthouse that looked like it had been designed with Lego blocks. The old courthouse had been built in Romanesque Revival style with arched openings on the fourth floor that featured a tall, peaked roof with a bell tower. Personally, I preferred classic architectural beauty.

Richard Day was finishing up his testimony when Tony and I entered the courtroom. Richard was clean-shaven, and his brown hair was prematurely turning gray. At age thirty-two, he had spent half of his life in prison. Ricky was a little over six feet tall and still had an athlete's body, but his voice was soft and gentle. "I don't expect to be forgiven for what I did. I was an immature adolescent who couldn't see a way out of my misery. I made a terrible decision I will always regret. The loss my surviving siblings have experienced is heartbreaking. I robbed them of the unknown. They can only imagine what could have been. There is no forgiving what I did. I am facing an eternity in hell. A life is a half inch on a football field. Eternity is the rest of it. But I will never use my despair as an excuse to be hurtful again. I will live the remainder of my life in service to God, in an effort to earn God's forgiveness."

After Richard was dismissed from the stand, he returned to the defense table next to Tug Grant. Richard's older siblings, Mike and Misty, nodded in response to his testimony. In interviews, Tug had proclaimed that the surviving family members would be present to support Ricky's release, and most were. His sister Beth's absence was certainly forgivable once a person knew the inside story, but the public never hears the entire narrative investigators uncover.

At sixteen, Beth had been sent away for the summer to "help a widowed aunt in Woodbury." Beth had become pregnant, and when she told her parents, they informed her that she wouldn't be allowed to return home until after she was done breastfeeding. Beth returned at age seventeen, and her parents announced to everyone they had adopted an infant cousin. Beth was allowed to come home with baby Halle, provided Halle was raised as her sister. This is how it remained up to the point of the shooting when Halle was eight. Beth's failure to appear in court to support Richard implied that she wasn't able to forgive him for shooting her daughter.

Halle, now twenty-four years old, was present. Halle was thin and had long blonde hair and blue eyes. She sat by her aunt and uncle, less emotional than they were about Richard's release. Her presence was remarkable, considering that Ricky had attempted to kill her. I thank God Halle survived. Her only remaining physical injury was a scar on her right arm. How someone works through the emotional trauma of being home when your brother executes your family and then turns the gun on you and fires is beyond me. Maybe you don't. I've heard Halle is a therapist now.

Tony was called to testify and wheeled himself up the ramp to the stand. Wheelchair accessibility was a quick reminder of why they built new courthouses. Tony looked good in his old black suit. Proud of his Irish heritage, Tony insisted on wearing a green tie with it.

As Tony was being sworn in, I thought about the case. I was seventeen—one year older than Richard Day—when he shot his parents and two younger siblings in 2002. Ricky was now eligible for parole. He had been sentenced to life in prison, equal to thirty years in Minnesota, or twenty years with early release for "good time" credit. Ricky had received six additional months for his escape attempt but had four years deducted because of his juvenile status at the time of his crime. Minnesota has determinant sentencing, meaning that once Ricky served his time, he was released. There was no parole board to deny it. Today's hearing was about determining Ricky's conditions of supervision in the community.

The theme of the courtroom was bleak brown. The robed judge sat above the rest of us on his oak bench, which dropped down to the matching oak witness stand. A handful of people sat on the wooden oak benches in the gallery. The wood was surrounded by ash-colored carpeting and taupe walls. The silver-haired prosecutor and the blond defense attorney, Tug Grant, sat at white laminate tables.

When Richard was sentenced twenty years ago, the courthouse was packed. Today, his release was inglorious and unsubstantial. There were no protestors.

The prosecutor asked Tony, "Would you give a quick summary of what occurred on the fateful night in 1997?"

Forced into an early retirement, Tony loved talking about old cases. In a relaxed tone, he recounted, "On December 19,

2002, Richard Day had an argument with his parents. He grabbed his rifle, which he left uncovered in the mudroom, and exited out the back door. I believe the family assumed he was going to do chores, as he did every night. Instead, he walked around to the front of the house and shot his mother through the kitchen window while she was washing dishes. He then approached the living room window. His father had been sleeping on the couch. When his father jumped to his feet, Richard shot and killed him. Richard then entered the house and shot and killed his thirteen-year-old brother, who had run to his mother's aid. Then Richard chased his eight-year-old niece upstairs and found her hiding in a closet. Richard shot her, but it wasn't lethal, thanks to Halle raising her arm and some great medical work. Richard's rifle had a four-bullet clip, so after shooting each of his four family members who were home, his rifle was empty. It was the moment Richard Day became a mass murderer."

The prosecutor asked, "Was there any indication that one of the children may have begged to live?"

Tony answered, "The girl had raised her hands defensively, in front of her face, as if she was asking for her life to be spared."

At the defense table, Richard hung his head in shame.

The prosecutor asked, "What did Richard say about shooting Halle?"

Tony's dry voice cracked, "Richard said he didn't remember shooting Halle or his brother Blake. He didn't deny shooting them. Richard stated, 'I must have. I remember dragging their bodies in the basement.' He said killing his siblings was just a thing on his to-do list."

"Do you believe him?"

Tug Grant stood up. "Objection. The question calls for conjecture."

The judge agreed, "Sustained."

The prosecutor said, "No more questions," and casually walked back to his table.

The judge asked Tug, "Do you wish to cross?"

Tony was a hardened investigator and appeared hungry to have any of his testimony challenged.

Tug wisely said, "No, Your Honor. Richard has already been prosecuted and served his time."

I studied Richard Day. His words seemed genuine, but he was a man who had executed his parents and brother sixteen years ago, and he was now being released into the community. Richard could be standing in line at the store next to my wife and perhaps my children someday, and they'd have no clue about his history. As I get older, sixteen years doesn't seem that long. After spending adolescence to his thirties in a cage in prison, is Richard ready for freedom? Are we ready for his release?

7

MELANIE PEARSON

8:30 A.M. MONDAY, JUNE 11, 2018
HENNEPIN COUNTY GOVERNMENT CENTER,
300 SOUTH 6TH STREET
DOWNTOWN WEST, MINNEAPOLIS

Tug asked me to meet him at the Hennepin County Courthouse for an evidentiary hearing on a new case. In his crisp black suit and black-framed glasses, Tug paged through documents. I sat next to him at the defense table, waiting for the judge to arrive.

All business, Tug glanced at me and explained, "There are rules to the way evidence is gathered that must be applied to everyone, even if it means a degenerate occasionally walks free. If we don't stand up for the rights of every person, our society will become a military state."

Enjoying his intensity, I asked, "Who are you defending?"

"Roan Caruso."

"The same Roan who wanted to buy your car?"

"Yes." Tug paged through documents.

"He's optimistic if he wants to buy your car."

Tug turned to me with self-assured confidence. "He has me for an attorney."

The courtroom doors swung open, and Roan strolled in. With his straight, broad shoulders, six-and-a-half-foot stature, and matted black hair, he reminded me of a handsome Frankenstein.

"What did he do?"

"He's charged with first-degree murder for shooting a carjacker named Deondre Smith."

"How is he out on bail?"

"Bail was set at one and a half million dollars."

"Holy crap. That's a lot of money."

Tug explained, "You only need to come up with 10%. Remortgaging your house can cover it."

"Did he kill the man?"

"His guilt isn't relevant. Our job is to make certain proper procedures were followed."

Taken aback, I frowned.

Tug explained, "Roan and I went to college together. He's a smart guy—a good guy. He got wrapped up in a bad business deal and was framed for a murder."

"He looks like a thug."

"He didn't always." Tug put his arm around my shoulder in a comforting manner and said, "In this case, the murder weapon was found in his car, and if that evidence is accepted into court, he's screwed. Like I said, it isn't about guilt or innocence. The question is, 'Do they have enough legitimate evidence to convict him?'"

Prosecutor Bridget Bare walked into court and glared at Tug and me. *Why should it bother her if he puts his arm around my shoulder?*

"Were you ever in a relationship with her?" I asked.

I could feel his breath in my ear as he whispered, "Are you kidding? Horseface?"

Okay, her face was a little elongated but not unattractive. She had a knob in the middle of her thin nose. Bridget's long chestnut mane was pulled straight back with a barrette. There was no facial emotion. She was dead serious.

"I don't know what put the burr in her saddle. That hungry filly has been champing at the bit to leave me in the dust for years. I'm the sure bet, and she's Zippy."

"I'm not sure what that means."

"A sure bet is a horse that can't lose, and a Zippy is one you can't get out of the starting gate." He smiled.

My nervousness and excitement escalated as the judge entered.

"The race is on," Tug whispered.

Everyone stood, and Tug called a police officer to the stand. The officer was sworn in. Tug approached him and asked, "You are a Minneapolis police officer, correct?"

"Yes."

"Can you tell me why you pulled Roan Caruso over?"

The officer responded, "A homicide was committed up the street, and his car was bolting from the scene. Caruso has a very recognizable car—it's got to be over sixty years old."

"You said 'bolting.' Was he driving over the speed limit?"

"No."

"So, he was basically driving one of a number of cars going down the street."

The officer didn't respond.

Tug handed him a piece of paper and said, "This has been logged in as Evidence #19. Can you tell me what this is?"

The officer nodded, "It's a copy of the report I filed regarding the arrest of Roan Caruso."

"Can you read me the first line in the report?"

In a monotone, the officer read, "I pulled Roan Caruso over because he didn't have current tabs. Caruso had failed to put the blue 2018 license plate tabs on his car."

"What year were his tabs?"

"It was dark, and the plate wasn't well-lit. I just knew, beyond a shadow of a doubt, the blue wasn't there," the officer said.

Tug leaned into him, "You mentioned that his car was sixty years old. Roan's car has collector plates. Are you aware that you don't need tabs on collector plates?"

The officer cleared his throat. "Yes."

"So, you had no reason to pull over the car," Tug clarified.

The officer spewed, "I saw a gun sticking out from under the driver's seat when I approached the car."

"Stop," Tug directed.

"It proved to be the murder weapon," the officer blurted.

The judge pounded his gavel and turned to the officer. "You are only to answer questions you are asked. One more outburst like that, and I'll hold you in contempt of court."

Tug walked to the table, retrieved a picture, and said, "I want you to look at this evidence item marked #23." He handed the picture to the officer. "Please tell me what you see in this picture."

The officer snarled, "Nothing. It's just a black picture."

"It's a picture of the interior of Roan Caruso's car taken at the exact same time of night you claim to have seen a gun under his driver's seat."

The officer argued, "The dash lights aren't on in this picture."

"The dash lights don't work in Roan's car. As you mentioned, his car is sixty years old. You can't simply walk into an auto parts store and replace them. You can only see into the car when you open the door and the dome light comes on. Did you have a search warrant?"

The officer didn't respond.

Tug prompted, "I didn't hear you."

"No."

Tug looked at the judge when he asked the police officer his next question. "Are you aware that you violated the Fourth Amendment?"

The officer shook his head. "No."

Tug railed on, "The Fourth Amendment of the U.S. Constitution provides that it is the right of people to be secure in their persons, and it protects against unreasonable searches and seizures. It specifically states the amendment shall not be violated, and no Warrants shall be issued, but upon probable cause, supported by Oath or affirmation, and particularly describing the place to be searched, and the persons or things to be seized. Did Roan specifically state, 'I waive my Fourth Amendment rights'?"

"No."

Tug turned to the judge, "I ask that any items removed from Roan Caruso's car be ruled inadmissible."

"I'll take that under advisement," The judge responded.

"The case of Brendlin v. California in 2007 will be helpful," Tug added.

The judge turned to prosecutor Bridget Bare. "Do you wish for rebuttal?"

"Yes." Bridget stood and strolled toward the defendant. "Officer Macklin, you had just left a homicide scene. Was your concern about his tabs the primary reason you pulled over Roan Caruso? The standard is reasonable suspicion that he may have committed a crime."

"I heard gunshots, and while other officers rushed to the scene, I recognized Roan from previous dealings with him and suspected he may have fired the shots. I saw him through his driver's side window."

Prosecutor Bridget Bare smirked at Tug and then approached the officer. She asked, "So why did the form say you pulled him over for expired tabs?"

"You get in the habit of listing a reason, and he didn't

have current tabs. My real reason was that I knew he was a registered felon leaving a crime scene."

Tug shot to his feet. "Objection! Mr. Caruso is not a registered felon. His supervision ended years ago, and he doesn't register for anything. Mr. Macklin's testimony reflects his negative characterization of my client, which led to a violation of Mr. Caruso's constitutional rights."

The judge said, "Sustained." He turned to the officer. "Stick to testifying about what you know to be fact."

For the judge's benefit, Bridget said to the officer, "Are you aware that without the murder weapon, we have no case against Roan Caruso?" Bridget was basically begging the judge not to throw out the case.

The officer replied, "Yes."

Bridget turned to the judge, "No more questions, Your Honor."

The judge turned back to Tug, "Do you wish to cross?"

"Yes." Tug scratched his head. "Were you at the crime scene when you spotted Mr. Caruso driving that night?"

"Yes."

Tug took his time as he considered this. "Mmmm. So, every car driving away from you at an appropriate speed was 'bolting' from the crime scene. In all directions, that had to be at least twenty cars. Correct?"

The officer said, "Yes."

Tug paused for effect before adding, "And you had no evidence that Roan had indeed committed a crime, right?"

"Not at that point."

Tug tapped his chin, "And when you talk of previous dealings with Roan, you're simply speaking of times you've harassed him. Tug hasn't been convicted of a crime the entire time you've been a police officer, correct?"

The officer sighed. "Correct. He hasn't been *convicted* of a crime."

"No more questions." Tug looked directly at me with a grin as he returned to the table.

I found my attraction to this intelligent and powerful man growing.

As the judge left to take the evidence under advisement, Tug opened his laptop toward me and said, "After you read this, you'll realize I just won." The article on his laptop read:

BRENDLIN VS. CALIFORNIA (2007)
The police pulled over a vehicle to determine whether the driver was driving with expired tags. During the stop, an officer recognized the defendant, Bruce Brendlin, as a parole violator. The officer arrested the defendant and found methamphetamine on his person. The defendant was charged with parole violation and possession of narcotics. At his trial, he moved to suppress the narcotics, stating that the police lacked justification to stop the automobile in the first place. The defendant's argument was that the temporary plates indicated that an application for renewal of an expired license was pending. The State of California conceded, on appeal, that the stop was unjustified.

Tug explained, "Bridget and I will be battling for years. She's the Hennepin County Attorney, which makes her the prosecutor for the most heavily populated county in the state. And I'm the head of the bar and, as a defense attorney, her nemesis."

The judge stepped back into the courtroom, and everyone stood. Shortly after we sat, the judge declared, "Any items removed from Mr. Caruso's car in the search are inadmissible."

In frustration, the prosecutor announced, "We will be forced to dismiss the charges."

The judge turned to the officer, who was now in spectator seating. "Officer Macklin, learn the law." He then turned to

Roan Caruso and said, "You are free to go." He pounded the gavel, and everyone stood as he left.

I grinned from ear to ear. I love my new job!

Roan shook Tug's hand. Tug gave me a flirtatious grin and said, "I'll see you at our office."

I stood and walked to the door. My heart stopped when I saw Deondre's family crying in the back of the courtroom. I was so caught up in the brilliance of Tug's litigation skills that I hadn't considered that a young man was dead. A young man who was a son, a brother, and a father. There was a teen in tears, softly repeating to her baby, "We're gonna be all right."

When I glanced back at Tug and Roan, I thought I heard Roan ask, "Do I get my gun back?" I must have heard him wrong.

8

MELANIE PEARSON

3:00 P.M., FRIDAY, JUNE 15, 2018
EAST FRANKLIN AVENUE,
VENTURA VILLAGE, MINNEAPOLIS

I sat at a table at Maria's Café on East Franklin in Minneapolis, waiting for Tug. The quaint café was nestled into a red brick mini-mall, and the aroma of Columbian coffee was wonderful. I had never had a more enjoyable week of work. It was a rush to be in the middle of Tug's intense court cases. Sophie and I had put a deposit down on an apartment in St. Louis Park. I loved the shops and restaurants near the Blackstone neighborhood. Sophie was now working for the Target Corporation at Nicollet Mall in Minneapolis.

My phone buzzed, and worried about Tug's reason for running late, I answered it immediately. "Tug, are you okay?"

"Melanie? This is Sebastian."

Ugh. "Why are you calling?" After weeks of praying for a call, now that I'm finally over him, he calls. There was no way I'd take him back after the crap he pulled.

"My sister picked up my stuff. She said you were evicted from our apartment."

“I was, dickhead, because you didn’t pay the rent.”

“Melanieee.” The pitiful way he dragged out my name was irritating. “Are you okay?”

“I am now. My new employer gave me an advance so I could get an apartment. Sophie came through and found us a place to live.”

“I gave you a check for the rent,” Sebastian stated. “I asked that you hold it for a week to make sure I had enough money to cover it.”

Anxious beads of sweat formed on my forehead. I couldn’t remember.

“You put it in that small zipper inside your purse,” Sebastian said.

I never used that compartment. I grabbed my purse, opened the zipper, and there was the rent check. Shit! “I forgot.”

“You forget a lot.”

I had my memory checked after Sebastian left, and after an exhausting battery of tests, I was informed there was nothing physically wrong with me. I can’t be dissociating. I’ve never been beaten, never been raped. “What do you want me to do with the check?”

“The money is yours,” Sebastian offered kindly. The check was made out to you. Do with it what you wish.”

“I’m not interested in resuming our relationship. You ghosted me. And now I’ve met someone. I don’t know if it’s anything, but I’d like to find out.”

Silence. Finally, he said, “I’ve met someone too. His name is Huck. Well, when we first met, his name was Harmony, and he’s changing it to Huck. He’s a transgender man. We’re in love.”

I was trying to compute this in my brain. Was Sebastian gay? No—maybe? Fortunately, before I displayed my ignorance, Sebastian said, “Huck and I are starting a remodeling business called Home Transformations, working primarily in the Yonkers borough.”

I tuned out as he carried on. It felt weird to have my lover leave me for a woman who was morphing into a man. I have pansexual friends, so I have a rudimentary understanding of how all that works. The real issue was that it all made me wonder what Sebastian ever saw in me, and I felt uncomfortable about some of our last intimate moments. One night in particular, when he asked me to lower my voice and do something we hadn't done before, seemed to have new meaning now. But overall, the call gave me closure and a couple thousand dollars, so I couldn't complain.

Shortly after the call ended, Tug joined me at the table and apologized for his tardiness. We had a busy week, and time flew by. There wasn't any further romance between us. Honestly, I missed it, but I gave him credit for exercising healthy boundaries. At Maria's Café, I enjoyed Emilia's Empanadas con Aji, a savory pastry stuffed with beef and potatoes served with a broth dipping sauce. Tug went with the Bandeja Paisa Bowl. It was a layered dish with egg, avocado, and pinto beans. Maria's Columbian Hot Chocolate was the bomb. During a moment of laughter, I placed my hand on his leg, and he held it there. An intense warmth tingled throughout my body. Calm down, girl.

When we returned to the office, Tug locked the door behind us and said, "I think you need to come into my office and talk."

"Did I do something wrong?" I followed him, and he locked his door, too.

"You have done everything right." Tug loosened his tie and smiled, "Listen, I have no problem being professional at work, but if we could take an hour break, I would be forever indebted."

"I'm open to getting together after work." My heart quickened.

"I can't. I have a trainee I need to meet with after our workday ends." Tug stepped closer. "But you have my blood running hotter than lava."

He started to loosen his tie and I undid his top button, and then each descending one. The warmth of his kiss took me back to our night together. We frantically discarded our clothes, hungrily thrusting together on the couch.

4:30 P.M.

I LAY BACK IN EXHAUSTED elation and realized that, at this moment, my life was perfect! I had a fantastic lover and a great job. I had reconnected with my old friend, Sophie. My body tingled blissfully as I fell into a dreamy state. I closed my eyes and smirked about Tug having a private bathroom right off his office. I could fall asleep right here on the couch. It would be difficult to refocus on work.

Tug returned from the bathroom and casually told me, "You should get dressed. My wife will be here in fifteen minutes."

I was off the couch in seconds, scavenging for my clothes. I hurried to the restroom. Once dressed, I returned and confronted him. "Your wife!?"

"We've got four kids together." He couldn't even look at me when he responded, "It's not what you think."

"I haven't had time to think."

"I'm thirty-five," Tug murmured. "It never occurred to you that I might be married?"

"I didn't want to insult you by asking. You don't wear a ring."

"I told you I can't stand certain tactile touch."

"Do you live with her?"

"For the time being. Don't tell her we met at Hoppy Girl. I told her you interviewed Monday, and I hired you on the spot. There's no point in making *us* common knowledge until Deb and I are done."

Furious, I yelled, "You should have told me!"

Tug approached me tentatively, "I love you, Melanie. You're not like anyone I've ever met. We're a perfect team."

I heard the office door open and realized Tug had unlocked the doors when I was in the bathroom. I quickly double-checked my blouse to make sure it was buttoned correctly.

Tug called, "Deb, we're in my office."

Deb was an inch or two smaller than me, with mousy brown hair and no makeup. She looked strong and reminded me of a woman I'd expect to be working as a game warden. Deb would kick my skinny ass if she knew what just transpired. Mortified, it felt like the Cirque du Soleil was doing a show, complete with spinning wheels and flames, in my stomach.

After the introductions, I returned to my desk and got to work.

Deb closed the office door. There were no raised voices. It sounded like they were calmly discussing their children.

4:55 P.M.

DEB STOPPED IN FRONT OF my desk on her way out. "Tug says you have been a lifesaver. Thanks for stepping in and helping him out."

"You are very welcome." I felt slimy.

"Has Taytum been in the office yet?"

"No. Who's Taytum?"

"Taytum, with a *y*, is a law clerk who is studying—under Tug." The double entendre felt intentional. Deb took a Post-it off the desk and wrote down a phone number. "If you have any concerns about Taytum being here, or even if you just need to talk, give me a call."

After Deb departed, Tug strolled out of the office.

I made it clear, "This is a mess, Tug. Don't you think you should have told me you were married before you slept with me?"

"My marriage to Deb is platonic," Tug assured me. "Deb and I are navigating our separation." He leaned forward and, with his hands on my desk, begged, "I need you, Melanie."

"What happened to your last assistant?" I demanded.

"She had a baby and decided to stay home with her child."

"Your child?"

"No-no-no. Absolutely not my child. That would have been impossible." Tug stood. "She had the baby before I met her. Later, she decided she'd rather be a stay-at-home mom than work."

I didn't know what to say. I didn't even know what to think. I told Tug, "I need to finish typing your brief. When I'm done, I'd like to call it a week."

"All right," Tug conceded. "We had a great week working together, and my feelings for you are as strong as ever. I don't want to lose you."

After I finished typing the report, I shouted, "Goodbye!"

I packed quickly, but Tug caught me at the door. "Is there anything I can do to make this right?"

"Give me the weekend to think about it." When he backed away, I asked, "How late are you working?"

"I've got a couple of calls to return, and Taytum is stopping in for her weekly supervision."

Tears flowed as I sat in my car outside the office, fighting a war between feelings and thoughts, heart and head. *I couldn't give Tug up. I didn't want to.* I called Sophie and filled her in on the entire scenario. As I finished, I watched a leggy blonde wearing a Verde green blazer, matching knee-length skirt, and a white V-neck blouse march confidently to the office door. I told Sophie, "And now his Gwyneth Paltrow-looking understudy just sauntered into the office."

Sophie laughed., "You can't quit now. Don't you want to know if Tug's having an affair with her, too?"

"Wouldn't that be classic?" I laughed sadly.

"If you leave, what happens to our apartment?" Sophie asked.

She was right. I needed this job.

Being a true friend, Sophie added, "If he's harassing you, just leave. We'll figure it out."

"Nothing's happened that I didn't ask for. Honestly, I think I'm falling in love. How pathetic is that? Tug is a great attorney, and people throw money at him for his advice. He does work for the mob, politicians, and professional athletes. It's exciting coming to the office. And he's just as passionate for me. But there's that one thing—he's married."

"Do you think Tug and Deb are separating?"

"I listened to as much as I could of their conversation. There wasn't any romance between them. They just talked about the kids. Their son Lincoln spends too much time reading Marvel comics. Their daughter Audrey is too old to be wearing princess dresses. Tug tells me he's starving for affection. Honestly, I might just be naïve, but I believe him."

"Just don't let him use you, Mel. If you're going to make a commitment to him, he needs to make a commitment to you. You could keep your job and say there's no more lovin' till the separation's complete."

I thought back to the zealot calling me a whore at Hoppy Girl. I'd bet he was a friend of Deb's. "I wish I knew what I should do."

"Okay. Listen—you need the money, girl," Sophie said. "So, keep the paycheck for now, but apply for other jobs. And for damn sure, fill me in."

"Thank you, Sophie." After hanging up, I marched back to the office. If he were involved in a romantic relationship with Taytum with a *y*, that would be a deal-breaker. I quietly unlocked the door and snuck back in. Tug's office door was open.

I peered in and saw Taytum sitting properly on the couch, giving Tug her full attention as he paced and lectured.

Tug professed, "The rule against perpetuities is intended to limit the dead man's hand."

"The dead man's hand?" Taytum asked, "Isn't that a pair of eights and aces, like Wild Bill Hickock was holding when he was murdered in a Deadwood saloon?"

"In law, the dead man's hand refers to the ability of a dead person to still have a say in what happens to property." Tug explained further, "The rule against perpetuities is part of American common law that prevents people from exerting control over the ownership of private property long after they're dead. It forbids putting criteria in a deed that extends more than twenty-one years after the original owner is deceased. When you die, your property is turned over to a new owner...."

Tug was simply explaining law to her, as I had hoped. Her outrageous beauty made the situation less than ideal, but it wasn't terrible. I slid silently out of the office, hoping that Tug was truly as infatuated with me as I was with him.

9

TILMORE "TUG" ULYSSES GRANT

7:15 P.M., FRIDAY, JUNE 15, 2018
LONDONDERRY ROAD, PARKWOOD KNOLLS,
MINNETONKA

I pulled into the driveway and parked my Mustang. *What the hell is wrong with me? I love Deb.* I saw the suspicion in Deb's eyes when she looked at Melanie. Time to face my moment of reckoning.

Deb was waiting on the couch of our Minnetonka home. I was in serious trouble. She was a couple of inches shorter than me—not quite Melanie's height. Deb had fascinating green, brown, and gold in her eyes. While she was a little heavier than Melanie, she was physically stronger and had a superior strength of determination and morality. Deb told me, "I had Mom pick up the kids. Tug, please don't tell me this is starting over again."

That much I could do—not tell her. I hated myself for cheating on Deb. She was so sweet and kind. My honesty would destroy her. Deb had given up everything for me. The best course of action would be to suck it up and lie about it and then never do it again. I sat by Deb and took her hand. I needed to be aggressive. I couldn't afford to let her believe she was right. I started with, "I got rid of the last secretary because of your paranoia. Let's not start this over again."

"Melanie looked shell-shocked to see me." With tears in her eyes, she said, "I know that look."

Keeping my voice soft, I told her, "You may know that look, but that doesn't mean you're reading it right. What do you want me to say? I have no idea what was going on with Melanie. She might just be overwhelmed with the work."

Deb turned her hips and faced me. "Tug, stop! I can't do this. Who were you with at Hoppy Girl Brewing last Friday? How did you end up getting punched?"

"I already told you. Roan and I met to discuss his defense. Some loudmouth insulted a friend. I couldn't let it slide, and I ended up getting punched. After, we left and finished business at Rotary Beach Park."

Deb leaned into me, took a whiff, and stepped back. "You smell like women's perfume."

"I had Taytum's supervision after work. She wears a lot of perfume. Why do you always introduce her as y-Taytum?"

I could see the genuine pain in her eyes as she said, "Because I wonder why you spend time with her. Why am I not enough?"

"Deb, you are enough. Taytum provides legal assistance in exchange for my supervision, and that saves us a lot of money. I love you, Deb." I do. But after four kids, we'd become two people who shared a dwelling. We both came from conservative families and stepped into their expectations. I worked. She took care of the kids. I had no desire to change it, but the truth was we lived parallel lives.

"I'm serious," Deb said, "I can't do this anymore."

"Alright," I conceded. I couldn't afford to lose her. Deb runs the kids everywhere and attends every event. She's a

Scout troop leader for our daughters and our son. I offered, "I'll go to counseling. I'll do whatever you want. I need to shower, and then I'm yours for the rest of the evening. We could grab a bite at the 112 Eatery, come back here, and enjoy a glass of wine."

There was sadness in her pretty face, but she sighed and replied, "Okay. But this conversation isn't over."

I hated seeing Deb in pain, and I would never abandon my kids. Deb desperately needed hope. I took my phone into the bathroom and called Roan.

"What do you need?" Roan answered.

"If you want my Mustang for four figures, you need to do me a favor—tonight. Call my home landline and tell Deb you'll accept the deal I offered on the Mustang. Then tell her she would be proud of me if she saw what I did last Friday—okay? Tell her some guy called her a whore, and when I stood up to defend her, the miscreant sucker-punched me. Then, tell her we left to finish business at Rotary Park. If you can do that, the Mustang is yours for $9,999."

"You are a piece of work," Roan chuckled. "I can only imagine what happened. I'm doing this because you saved my ass, but I get the Mustang for $9,000. I hate lying to Deb for you."

I was being taken to the cleaners, but I agreed. "Alright, but you have to call right now, and you better be convincing."

"She'll believe me…"

When I stepped out of the bathroom, Deb was sitting on the bed. "I'm sorry, Tug, I just want you home more. Why did the guy at Hoppy Girl call me a whore?"

Feigning ignorance, I asked, "How did you find out?"

"Roan called. He said you stood up for my honor, and some grifter cold-cocked you."

This was an opportunity to find out who she talks to. "The jerk said something about seeing you talking to a guy."

"I don't know who he's talking about." Deb thought for a moment. "There's Carlos, who fixed the sprinkler system. He was claiming it worked fine when it randomly went on and soaked him. We were standing on the front lawn laughing, but it was nothing romantic."

"Do you think Carlos might have made some lewd comments about you to friends?"

"No, I can't imagine he would." She folded her hands, "Tug, you know I would never cheat on you."

I sat next to her and wrapped my arm around her. "I know. I love you, Deb. I do. I work, day and night, because I love you—and to support our family. We both have long days."

"We agreed this was best for the kids, Deb. I still believe it. I take the girls to dance lessons and Lincoln to jazz band and Knowledge Bowl like you want. Don't you think there are times I want to be something other than a maid and a taxi service? I can do with less. I make my own clothes to save money. All I ask is that you come home to me."

"I couldn't ask any more of you." I kissed her, and we embraced.

She asked softly, "Do you want to make love?"

"You don't have to ask me twice. But that accusation is going to cost you."

Flabbergasted, Deb leaned back on the bed. She raised an eyebrow and asked, "What do you have in mind?"

To make my lie believable, I needed to punish her for insulting me. An innocent man would expect a concession. I told her, "Let me spank you before we make love."

Uncertain, she studied me, "Why spanking?"

"I like the idea of having your bare ass on my lap. And it seems appropriate for being a bad girl."

"Okay. Open hand—no objects. You think I can't handle being spanked?" With a devilish grin, she nestled into me and taunted, "Even bad girls can be good."

Game on. Surprised that she agreed, my excitement quickly surged. I needed to reconsider the assumptions I had made about Deb. Maybe I wasn't giving her the fair chance she deserved.

Deb stood and, facing away from me, made a show of shimmying out of her tight jeans. Like the Callipygian statue of Venus, Deb exposed her perfect buttocks. Peeking over her shoulder, she simpered, "Hit that..."

10

MELANIE PEARSON

(9 MONTHS LATER)
FRIDAY, MARCH 15, 2019
EAST FRANKLIN AVENUE,
VENTURA VILLAGE, MINNEAPOLIS

Tug and I continued to work smoothly together. I had thought about keeping it platonic, as Sophie suggested, but couldn't. The successes were so emotional, and his passion for me was so intense. I had one weekend a month with Tug when he'd convince Deb he needed to be in the Brainerd Lakes area meeting with prospective clients. We'd stay at Grand View Lodge on Gull Lake and hit our favorite lake pubs, Bar Harbor and Roundhouse Brewery, on Friday and Saturday nights. The best was our nightly walks. In the winter, Bar Harbor had bonfires and a rink where people skated.

Snuggling next to Tug in the cool, smoky air kept all my senses in the moment's bliss. People in northern Minnesota assumed I was his wife. I loved being Tug's wife and looked forward to the day it would be a reality, but… The fact that he hadn't left Deb wormed through my brain like a terminal virus. While I relished our time together, I hated myself on the weekends when I was alone. I felt unloved, and it was getting old.

The end of another week was approaching, and I'd be alone until Monday. I needed resolution. I tried to speak with Tug about it this morning, and he sent me to St. Paul on a wild goose chase for records they could have simply scanned and emailed. Now, Tug was busy on a phone call, but I was going to hang around and finish this.

The front door swung open, and *y*-Taytum sauntered in, all blonde hair and tanned legs under a buffalo-plaid skirt topped off with a mouth painted in bold red lipstick. I immediately wanted to kill her. She was like an annoying, sexy schoolgirl Barbie who was always in the room. I forgot she had supervision with Tug. I was so envious. I hated her, and I didn't have a reason why. Well, other than she was a tall, slender blonde with a model-like figure.

Taytum started, "Can I give you a piece of advice?"

I sighed, stood up, smiled, and told her, "No." Feeling some satisfaction, I walked out the door.

After picking up groceries at Aldi, I cruised back to the office. In my haste to not be in the same room with Taytum, I had left my cell phone on my desk. No longer in the mood to talk to Tug, I was determined to rush in and out without being noticed.

I entered quietly. Tug's office door was open, and I could see his back. Tug's dress shirt was untucked and hung loose. He was pulling his pants up.

Taytum exited the private bathroom, fully dressed. Tug fondled her breast and gave her a quick kiss before he entered the bathroom and closed the door behind him. Taytum straightened her skirt and glanced at me as if my presence was insignificant.

I stared at her, frozen in place. The word "expunged" came to mind—to be erased.

Taytum stopped by my side on her way to the door and continued as though I had never left. "Here's my advice. I'm the only woman in Tug's life getting what she wants. Everyone else is trying to please Tug. You may feel like you're everything he desires, but the reality is that Tug only wants what he can't have. When this all ends, I'll be the one left standing."

"With Tug?"

With a sly grin, Taytum said, "Hell, no."

I had no idea what she meant by that.

After Taytum left, Tug stepped out of the bathroom and noticed me. "Melanie, I'm so glad you're here. You've been so distant this week."

Wrong thing to say, Tug. "Don't try to put this on me."

The wheels were spinning in his head. In a quandary over what I'd witnessed, he started, "I'm not sure what you think happened—"

"Go to hell! I quit." I slammed my keys on my desk and snatched up my phone.

"I love you, Melanie." He grabbed my arm.

"Then show some damn balls! Leave Deb. Stop spending time with Taytum." I jerked my arm free.

"Okay—okay," he said. Tug reached to me to hug me, but I backed away.

"When are you leaving Deb? You've been telling me the same thing for nine months. I need an exact date."

"I swear, in eleven months, I won't be living with Deb, and we'll have enough money to be set for life."

"Then call me in eleven months." I stormed out. "I'm done!"

11

MELANIE PEARSON

(6 MONTHS LATER)
FRIDAY, SEPTEMBER 13, 2019
BURNING BROTHERS BREWING, 1750
THOMAS AVENUE WEST,
HIGHLAND PARK, ST. PAUL

Since leaving Tug six months ago, I've fallen hard for a man named Darius Country. It's been a whirlwind romance, and we've already set a wedding date. To avoid the mistake I made with my last two lovers, I've clarified that Darius is both unmarried and attracted to women. My dad guessed by his name that he was either a black folk singer or a white hillbilly jug player. He was wrong on both counts. Darius is the fifth most common boys' name in Iran, the country where the surname "Country" is most common. Darius is small in stature and fit, like Tug, but has curly black hair and brown eyes. Darius works for Microsoft in Edina. I was now working with Sophie at the Target Headquarters on Nicollet Mall. My work doesn't have all the excitement and drama I had when I worked with Tug, but it's a good job, and I'm not alone on weekends.

Tonight, I was meeting Darius and his friends after work at Burning Brothers taproom in St. Paul. Burning Brothers is a completely gluten-free brewery, which is perfect for Darius. The bar was quaint but well-lit, with classic beer phrases painted on the walls. My favorite quote was Ben Franklin's, "God made beer because he loves us and wants us to be happy." I ordered the Pyro American Pale Ale. Darius and his friends were boisterously clinking glasses of the Scorched Coffee IPA. I wasn't sure what they were celebrating—maybe the Twins won, or somebody got a promotion. I felt uneasy. What could go wrong on Friday the 13th?

Darius's gluttonous friend, Trey, lumbered to his feet and held his glass up, offering a toast. Trey proudly wore a T-shirt that read, *I like Pig Butts* on the front and *Liquor Pig* on the back. I sat as far away as I could whenever he was around. "There's a place called Foxy's where the strippers have needle tracks and stab wounds."

"Yeah, we might want to avoid that one," Darius laughed and then declared, "Okay. In two weeks, we go."

Trey looked directly at me and said, "*The Hangover Part 4*, baby! Vegas. One last weekend unchained. And you both have to promise you will never bring it up to each other."

I did not like the idea of Trey planning a bachelor party weekend in Vegas with my fiancé. Darius knew I wasn't one for bachelorette parties. I hadn't known he'd be so into a weekend rager.

Catching my surprise, my mild-mannered Darius pulled me aside. "They want to take me to Las Vegas for my stag party. One last hurrah."

"Do you really want that?" We had been spending every night together for the past two months.

Darius hesitated and said, "Yeah. I think I do. It's just one weekend. We'll connect when I get back and have every day from then on together."

"And never speak of it again?" I questioned.

"Yeah. It's just two days. We have the rest of our lives to share stories."

I stood silently for a minute, but after concluding he wouldn't be dissuaded, I found myself saying, "Okay." Men are such dicks. "Don't bring back any diseases. Not everything that happens in Vegas stays in Vegas."

"No worries." Darius laughed, briefly kissed me, and returned to his friends.

Heartsick, I decided to leave. As I walked away, I could hear Trey yelling, "Who let the dogs out!?"

I hate Friday the 13th. By the time I arrived at my car, I was thinking, *what's good for the gander is good for the goose. Screw you, Darius. Have your weekend, and I'll have mine.* In anger, I grabbed my cell phone and dialed. I didn't receive an answer, but I left a message. "Tug, I'm getting married. In two weeks, I have my bachelorette weekend. If you're interested, I'd spend it with you at Grand View for my last hurrah. Anything you want all weekend. Call me."

After I hung up, I considered the stupidity of that call. Unfortunately, there was no taking it back.

On my way home, Tug called me from his office. "Melanie, I'm in." I could picture the smile on his face as he said, "You get the room, and I'll pay you cash for it. I can't have the room in my name. What made you change your mind?"

"Spontaneous recovery." It's a psychological concept that refers to the return of a behavior after the association (in this case, feelings) has been extinguished. "It's just a weekend, and then I'm gone for good." I challenged Tug, "It's your last shot, so bring your best."

Tug quipped, "When you have a chance to dance with Tug Grant's, it's off with the pants."

How can I still love this idiot?

12

DEBRA "DEB" GRANT

10:30 A.M., FRIDAY, OCTOBER 25, 2019
LONDONDERRY ROAD, PARKWOOD KNOLLS,
MINNETONKA

I discovered Carlos Garcia, our denizen gardener, was also an artist. He explained to me once that a denizen is legally in the country but does not have voting rights. It also means that if he gets into any sort of trouble, he risks deportation. He told me all this when I offered him an off-the-books bonus for doing such a nice job at our home. He wouldn't hear of it. Instead, Carlos offered to paint a commissioned portrait of our house with me looking out the window. I'm not sure what it meant to him, but I was open to the idea. Spending all my time caring for the children and attending Tug's social events made me feel invisible. The painting would give me the opportunity to see what I looked like through someone else's eyes. October of 2019 was on pace to be the third coldest October on record in Minnesota history, but in true unpredictable Minnesota fashion, today was 61 degrees and sunny, making it a perfect day for Carlos to take pictures outside.

Carlos had dark hair, thick dark eyebrows, and deep dimples that showed when he smiled. He wore a skintight white Huk fishing shirt, which accented his skin tone. Carlos strolled across the street, taking pictures of our house from various angles. I smiled at him out the window as he approached. He slipped off his shirt and wiped the sweat from his brow, revealing warm caramel skin and rippling abdominal muscles.

I laughed at the absurdity of the situation. Watching the forbidden inamorato stand shirtless in worn jeans had me sweating. *What are the neighbors going to think?* Perhaps *inamorato* was the wrong word since he wasn't actually my lover—he's more aptly a passing fantasy. I would never cheat on Tug, but I have had the occasional wicked thought about Carlos.

Tug and I were at a crossroads. I was tired of his affairs, but I loved my family. I know the statistics about single-parent kids. One-third of single moms have difficulties paying utility bills. Their kids are more likely to use drugs, get pregnant as teens, be arrested, and are less likely to graduate from college. But the truth is, I am single-parenting. Tug is never home. He had verbally committed to a change, and on Sunday, we were leaving on a vacation I badly needed—just the two of us.

Carlos knocked on the door. "Do you mind if I have a glass of water?"

I could use a cold shower myself. I said, "Sure." I looked him over and laughed, "But please put your shirt on."

"Are you offended?"

"No, but I probably should be. I'll pose for a couple of pictures, and then you need to be on your way. I can't be late to pick up the kids from school."

10:30 A.M., THURSDAY, OCTOBER 31, 2019
DECEPTION PASS, WHIDBEY ISLAND,
PUGET SOUND, WASHINGTON

TUG AND I STOOD ON the Deception Pass Bridge 180 feet above Skagit Bay, gazing out at the endless Pacific Ocean. The bridge connected the continental United States to Whidbey Island. It was 50 degrees, and being a tough Minnesotan, I wore a royal blue hoodie with a Macalester College logo. The ocean faded into the horizon in a combination of dark cyan and azure blues. We were flanked by evergreen forests featuring tall pines and occasional bigleaf maple trees on each side of the bridge. The view was majestic. As the celeste blue water of the bay swirled below us, I told Tug, "You need to have a special license to take a boat through this pass. The water's treacherous, and this pass has sunk a lot of ships."

He nodded, staring into the water below. Always managing to outdress me, Tug wore a cream cardigan knit sweater with his designer jeans. Tug's perfect blond hair was motionless, while loose strands of my hair kept blowing into my mouth. Tug wrapped his arm around me and asked, "How long do you want to stay up here?"

"Don't be such a worrywart. Do you think I'm just going to fall over the guardrail?" Tug has been so loving and clingy on this trip. Last night, when I wanted some egg rolls, he insisted he walk over to the restaurant by our hotel and get them himself out of fear someone might attack me.

Tug stopped peering below and faced me. "I love you, Deb. I've never been the man you deserve, and I'm sorry. I can't afford to lose you." There were tears in his eyes.

I leaned into him, kissed him, and said, "You're not losing me. We've never been better. We needed this."

"We did." A smile crept across his face. "Where can I take you to eat tonight? Do you want to head back to Seattle? We could try some fresh geoduck at Taylor Shellfish. It's in the Capitol Hill area with lots of artsy shops."

"That sounds nice, but I'm good with one more night in Oak Harbor. I was talking to one of the locals who told me to check out the Shrimp Shack. It's a little place in the middle of nowhere that sells fresh shrimp meals every day until they run out. There's no inside dining, so we either eat at a picnic table or in the Escalade."

He rubbed my nose with his. "Your face is cold."

"I'm favoring the Escalade." I pulled him into a tight squeeze and kissed him hard. "Thank you for this vacation." I pulled back from our embrace and waggled my eyebrows at him. "I can't wait to see what happens next."

13

DEBRA "DEB" GRANT

10:30 A.M., MONDAY, NOVEMBER 4, 2019
LONDONDERRY ROAD, PARKWOOD KNOLLS, MINNETONKA

Roan Caruso, an old friend from Macalester, was visiting today. Roan had been raised in the rugged Thomas-Dale neighborhood of Frogtown. Residents of Thomas-Dale have a one in fifteen chance of being the victim of a crime in any given year, making it the most dangerous neighborhood in St. Paul. A high school teacher had recognized that the trouble-some grade horse of a kid was a math prodigy and guided him through earning his diploma and getting accepted into college. Roan had fathered a baby girl at fourteen and was heartbroken when he wasn't allowed to see her.

I fell for the gifted, rugged man in college and may have been content with him if I hadn't met Tug. Tug was debonair, handsome, and spoke with words smooth as soft butter. Tug charmed the pants off me, and my parents loved him. Basically, he was the opposite of Roan.

Ironically, Tug was never jealous of Roan. If he would have criticized Roan, I would have stood up for him, for I knew the tender part of Roan. But Tug defended him. He understood that Roan could love me and befriended him. He even loaned Roan money. The class with which Tug handled this made it obvious that Tug was the right choice for me.

Roan asked to stop over today. The kids were all in school, so I had a little time to talk. Roan lurched through the doorway like a friendly monster, the way he does with his strong, bulky body. It was reported that Roan had killed a Disciples gang member after the teen jacked his car. Tug told me he defended Roan as a favor to me. Honestly, I felt if Roan did it, he should have been held accountable. As much as I valued our history and our friendship, I had decided it was time to sever the cord completely. Sometimes, letting someone down easy just prolongs their misery.

Roan had thick black hair and wore a black button-down dress shirt, black jeans, and black cowboy boots. He reminded me of the old alternative rocker Lou Reed. I found Reed's lyrics playing in my head, "Hey babe, take a walk on the wild side." In college, I was intrigued by Reed's song *The Halloween Parade.* Reed wrote a song about AIDS without mentioning it the entire song.

Roan looked at me hopefully, so I made it clear: "Tug and I are better than ever." Finally, Tug was looking at me with the fervor I sensed from Carlos and Roan. The blaze had dwindled to embers, but now, rekindled, we were making love like wildfire.

"Tug hits on all of your friends," Roan sneered.

"I can guarantee you, none of my friends are involved with Tug. He's like a dog chasing a car. He wouldn't know what to do if he caught one.'"

Roan studied me with warranted skepticism.

"Look, I'm not naïve," I added. I don't trust the women Tug works with, but I'm not going to accuse everybody of having an affair with him."

"Why don't you just divorce him?" Roan rumbled in his low baritone. "I understand the attraction he offers his strumpets. Tug is like a shiny new toy. But you're not like that. I don't get it. He's reckless. You're frugal. You make your own clothes while he walks around in suits that cost thousands of dollars. You gave up everything to make him a celebrity."

"I don't want a divorce. When Tug and I are alone together, it's magical."

"It's your mother, isn't it?" Roan wasn't about to let up. "Greta Scarpetta. No matter what you accomplish, it will never be quite good enough. The ornery bitch should have had more kids to dilute her controlling misery instead of concentrating it all on you. I remember her railing on you for wanting to be a Russian translator. You could have had a great career doing that. Hell, I could have had work for you, but Greta drilled into you that the most important job for a woman is to make her marriage work. Well, it was a hell of a lot easier for her; she had your pushover of a dad. You have Tug. You should get the Purple Heart for the misery he puts you through."

"Mom and I are better now."

Roan threw his hands up. "What a shocker—you're 'better' now that you fit the form she hammered you into."

"I'm okay, Roan. I'm busy, but I enjoy my life. The kids are doing great. Tug and I have just returned from wonderful vacations in Los Angeles and Washington."

He looked at me in disbelief.

It was time for me to deliver the bad news. "Roan, I know Tug has been lending you money. That stops today. We have Lincoln in a private school now, so money's tighter."

Roan was furious, but he looked away. I could feel his seething anger. It reinforced my reason for breaking up with him. When he really needed to talk, he didn't.

"I know Tug has made some poor choices. I think he tries to prove he's worthy of love over and over. How lonely it must be to constantly feel that need." I tried to soften the news. "You've been a good friend, but we're done. It's time for us to sever all ties. I hope you find your way back on track. I felt like when I chose Tug, you gave up."

"Everybody loves Tug," Roan snorted.

"I don't want you to hate me, but Tug and I need to move on without you."

"I don't hate you, Deb." Roan gave me a cursory glance. "That's what makes it so hard." He stood up. "Are you done?"

"I'm sorry, Roan. The heart wants what it wants." He was so hurt. As he walked out the door, I asked, "Why are you here, Roan? Why did you need to speak to me?"

"Open your eyes, Deb."

The way he said it chilled my spine. "Do I need to be afraid of you?"

With his back to me, he responded, "Yes," and left.

The phone rang, and it was the counselor at St. Paul Academy and Summit School. Lincoln was missing assignments in three of his classes. I immediately marched to his room. I threw the Marvel Comic sitting on his bed on the stack of comics in the corner. Night after night, I'd ask Lincoln, "Are you sure you don't have homework?" only to be told, "No," again and again. I was fuming. Lincoln could quote those damn comics word-for-word. The boy had so much potential, and it was all being wasted. Lincoln had his dad's genius, but he needed to begin applying it to school.

I lit a fire in the Weber grill on the deck and burned his entire stack of Marvel comics. I stood leery as I watched crackling flames blaze and destroy pages of superhero after superhero. *What level of rage would be unleashed in my reserved son?* Lincoln was quiet, but he was also a pubescent adolescent boy. *He was no Ricky Day.*

14

DEBRA "DEB" GRANT

7:35 A.M., WEDNESDAY, NOVEMBER 6, 2019
LONDONDERRY ROAD, PARKWOOD KNOLLS,
MINNETONKA

I made French toast this morning. The key was to add a touch of vanilla to the eggs and milk. Our three girls, ages six, eight, and ten, sat at the table, excited to have Tug eating with us again. Before our vacation, Tug had always gone to work before they woke up. Our thirteen-year-old son, Lincoln, wasn't talking to me this morning. He was sulking over my torching his comics. Parenting involves doing the right thing, even when it's unpopular. There was a nervous energy in our home this morning. The kids were still getting used to seeing Tug and me so affectionate and happy.

When I placed the heated syrup on the table, I shared, "This is from maple trees Lincoln tapped in Boy Scouts last fall. It's the best syrup I've ever tasted."

Lincoln sat silent.

Tug defended me, saying, "The decision to get rid of the comics was both of ours."

When Lincoln didn't respond, I decided to give him time to cool down. Being our oldest child and Tug's only son hasn't been easy for Lincoln. Tug needs to remember he wasn't perfect as an adolescent, either. I don't like the argument that Lincoln has it easier than Tug did. Tug's mom was absent, but Lincoln has had to put up with my mother's perfectionism. Mom made me, and now Lincoln, begin learning proper etiquette when we started speaking. Mom loved that I married Tug. It got her invited to major social events and allowed her to remind me over and over how important her lessons in proper manners were. I cleared my head of memories of getting swatted on the fingers with a ruler and focused my attention on sitting at the table and talking with my family.

Tug and the girls were in a great mood, and this brought me peace. We had a good life. After breakfast, I made sure the kids had their backpacks and all the girls had their hair done while Tug went upstairs and ran bathwater for me.

Once the girls were on the bus, Tug came back in and said, "I'll give Lincoln a ride to school." He turned to Lincoln, "Make sure the front door is locked and the chain's hooked." As Lincoln stepped away, Tug kissed me. "We'll leave out the back. Make sure you lock the door. I want you to be safe while you're enjoying a nice warm bath. The water's hot, so you need to let it cool a little."

"Thank you." I squeezed him tight and watched them leave. Tug and I had finally turned the corner in our relationship.

8:30 A.M.

I DECIDED TO TAKE A break and read the newspaper before I took my bath. I grabbed the *St. Paul Pioneer Press* off the counter and went upstairs. I had convinced Tug to stop our subscription to the Minneapolis Tribune until they began reviewing books written by independently published authors.

I want a newspaper that reports all the news. Ignoring independent publishers was like having a best beer contest but only allowing Coors and Budweiser to compete, missing out on all the great small breweries and taprooms. With paper in hand, I grabbed my reading glasses, sat on the bed, and read.

The landline phone rang, so I stepped into the office to answer it. The desk was cluttered with papers, and I couldn't find the handset, so I ran downstairs and answered the kitchen phone.

"Are you naked yet?" Tug asked.

"Not yet. But I will be soon. Interested in coming home?" I teased.

"Deb, I wish. Unfortunately, I have a meeting in thirty minutes."

"What do you need?"

"Does Rebecca have a concert tonight?"

"Yes, at 7:00."

"I promise I will be there."

"I appreciate that you've been attending the kids' events when you can. It's important family time." I drew a smiley face in my planner.

"I love you, Deb."

"Love you, too."

I returned to my bed and put on my glasses, determined to finish reading the article about how wolves have reduced the Minnesota moose population.

I heard a creak and looked up to see a stocky man with dark hair standing in the doorway, glaring at me. His black eyes were soulless. He aimed a gun at me and held a solid piece of black rubber in the other. At that moment, I realized my life was about to end. Staring down the barrel of a gun was terrifying.

"Stop starin' at me!" he shouted. Attempting to appear calm, he said, "Turn your head. Relax, and you won't get hurt. All I want is your money."

If I comply with his demands, he'll have no reason to kill me.

"Take your glasses off and lie face down."

I followed his orders. I felt a sudden thud on the back of my head and was out like a light.

When I came to, I was naked in the bathtub, and a hand was pushing my face beneath the water…

15

THE HITMAN

8:45 A.M., WEDNESDAY, NOVEMBER 6, 2019
LONDONDERRY ROAD, PARKWOOD KNOLLS,
MINNETONKA

I watched as Debra Grant answered the phone. I was supposed to strike her, but I froze. What am I doing? I had to do this. The man who hired me was not someone you let down. I was supposed to be here yesterday but couldn't get myself to do it. He suggested I either give him his money back or directly confess to Deb that I was paid to kill her. A confession would send me to prison. That's not happenin.' And the money's gone. Drugs are expensive.

The call ended, and Debra went upstairs.

I stood for a minute and then followed.

She looked up from her bed to see me holding a Luger. I waved the gun and yelled, "Stop starin' at me." I was so damn nervous my hands shook. "Turn your head. Relax, and you won't get hurt. All I want is your money." My face-to-face confrontations and bar fights never seem to turn out as planned. The contractor hadn't offered any guidance.

Fortunately, she complied, and for a moment, I thought this was going to be a piece of cake. I directed, "Take your glasses off and lie face down."

I struck her hard on the back of the head with the rubber truncheon I had brought, inspired by watching Robert Downey Jr. use a truncheon in the Sherlock Holmes movie. I couldn't believe it worked. She was out cold.

I stripped her body bare and realized Debra was an attractive woman. I wanted to—but I couldn't. I can't afford to leave a DNA trail. Plus, there's that piece where I was told if I rape Debra, I'm a dead man. I carried her to the bathtub. It would all be over quickly and cleanly.

I knelt by the tub and placed her body into it. With my open hand over her face, I pressed her head beneath the water.

Suddenly, she came alive with a vengeance. She rotated her body, forcing me to let go—Debra's naked body dove out of the tub, covering the floor with water. I couldn't get a grip on her as she slid by. When I attempted to stand, I slipped, hitting my head on the door jamb, almost knocking myself out.

When I got to my feet, I realized her modesty had led her to a fatal mistake. Instead of running out of the house naked, she ran to her bedroom to get a robe. I met her at the bedroom door with my Luger and pulled the trigger.

She flinched at the click.

The gun jammed. I shouldn't have used this old relic. These damn Lugers sometimes fail to feed because of worn recoil springs. I pistol-whipped her face hard, and I could feel the gun coming apart in my hand as I struck her.

Debra ducked and dove by me, scrambled to her feet, and raced down the stairs. I chased her like my life depended on it.

She made it to the front door, but I had hold of her hair by the time she unlocked it and slid the chain over.

I wrapped my arm around her neck and put her in a

headlock. She tried to scream, but I tightened my vice-like clamp, choking her. I dragged her, bent over, across the living room to the kitchen, and pulled a knife off a block on the counter.

She bit my arm hard and dropped to her knees.

I let go, and Debra quickly hopped to her feet.

But she found herself backed against the fridge. Debra faced me in her oversized white robe. She had blood dripping from a cut in her eyebrow and smeared around her nose. Her only way out was through me.

She put her head down and barreled into me.

I was holding the knife low. I drove it hard into her stomach. We tumbled to the floor, and as she wrenched in pain, I crawled onto her back and stabbed her again and again. Somehow, she found the strength to rock me off.

In the ruckus, I had cut my arm and dropped the knife.

Debra ran to the back door, which was also locked.

I caught up to her again as she tried to work the lock and pummeled her head and torso with my fists.

The crazy bitch turned and tore her nails into my face. I managed to keep them out of my eyes, but she still inflicted serious pain.

I landed a brutal gut punch in the area of her stab wound, and as she toppled forward, I kicked her in the head.

Debra fell to the floor.

Frustrated by my ineptness, I slammed the knife repeatedly through her robe and into her chest until the cotton began turning red. Exhausted, I buried the knife in her neck in a desperate attempt to make sure she was finally dead. When I tried to pull it out, the blade busted off.

I've been in some rugged barfights, but as I straddled her dying body, I realized Debra Grant was the toughest person I've ever fought. Feeling the hit was finally completed, I pushed myself to my feet and went to the bathroom to wash up.

I had a two-block walk to my car. In the mirror, I saw my blood-smeared face and shirt. I'd cut my arm with the knife; I had bite marks on my arm and scratch marks on my face. I'd wash my hands and face and hope to hell I didn't run into anyone. I was instructed to leave no DNA. My DNA was all over. On the upside, my DNA wasn't in the system yet. I just needed to stay out of trouble, and I'd be all right.

When I returned to the kitchen, Debra was gone. "UNBELIEVABLE!" I looked up to see the front door was open. I fled, hoping I could get out of the area before the police arrived.

16

LINCOLN GRANT

11:30 A.M., WEDNESDAY, NOVEMBER 6, 2019
SHADY OAK ROAD, HOPKINS

My sisters and I were pulled out of school at 10:30 this morning and told Mom was attacked. They found her bloody body lying on our neighbor's porch—Dad's at the hospital with her. We were brought to our aunt's home, and I was sitting with my three younger sisters in the living room watching TV while my aunts and uncles were in the kitchen nervously whispering.

My sisters were fair-skinned blondes, towheads like Dad, while I was brown-haired like Mom. The shame I felt for not speaking to my mother this morning made me sick. When I discovered she'd burned my Marvel comics, I'd told her, "I hate you." It was the very last thing I said, and I so wish I could take it back.

Our show was interrupted by the words "Breaking News" scrolling across the screen. We could see a helicopter view of our house. Across the bottom, it read, Attorney Tug Grant's wife in critical condition after being stabbed in Minneapolis home. They showed a clip of Mom being wheeled out on a stretcher and loaded into an ambulance.

My six-year-old sister, Audrey, announced, "Hey, she looks a lot like our mom."

The rest of us silently studied each other in shock, not sure how to respond.

Auntie Meg came to check on us, and when she saw what we were watching, she grabbed the remote and shut the TV off. Exasperated, she said, "What am I going to do with you?" Answering herself, she told us, "Get your shoes on. I'm bringing you all back to school until we figure this out."

2:00 P.M.
ST. PAUL ACADEMY AND SUMMIT SCHOOL
1712 RANDOLPH AVENUE, HIGHLAND PARK, ST. PAUL

I WAS SITTING IN CLASS but wasn't really hearing what Mr. Morris was rambling on about. What I wouldn't give to take back my last words to Mom. Finally, I realized Morris was calling my name.

"Yes?" My voice cracked as I responded.

"Principal Thompson is at the door and would like to speak to you."

When I stepped outside the classroom, Mr. Thompson didn't look angry. He looked incredibly sad as he told me, "I don't know how to say this, Lincoln. Your mom passed away. Let's go to your locker and collect your things. Then I'll have you wait in my office until someone picks you up. I'm so sorry…"

I stopped listening at that point. Even though I can't remember what was said, I'll never forget the principal was kind and caring. I fell into a haze that would take me years to break out of. I would never be able to tell Mom 'I love you' again. Never be able to say, 'I'm sorry.' *What would happen to us?* Dad would never let me go, but he never wanted much to do with the girls. I could see a custody battle between my dad and mom's parents coming. I lost my mom, and before this was over, I'd be separated from my sisters.

17

JON FREDERICK

10:00 P.M., FRIDAY, NOVEMBER 8, 2019
PIERZ

Serena and I had tucked Nora and Jackson into bed and grabbed a cold beverage while we snuggled under a blanket on the couch. Serena had a glass of nonalcoholic Coors Edge beer while I enjoyed cream ale from a Crowler of Red X a friend had dropped off from Bemidji Brewing. They brew a wonderfully smooth altbier. This amber ale is made with red wheat. The fireplace was on and the television off, so I was feeling good about the possibilities.

When Serena said, "We need to talk," my yearning plummeted. But when she came back with, "I think I'd like to have another baby," hope made an immediate recovery.

"You know I would." I kissed her.

"I'd like one semi-normal pregnancy," Serena smiled. "We weren't married yet when I was pregnant with Nora or Jackson, and I regret it. I would like to go through one pregnancy without all that drama—with you and me solid together."

"Sounds good. With a boy and a girl, we need a tie-breaker." I turned and faced her. "I'd like to be able to spend some time with the baby. I was so busy with work when Nora and Jackson were born; it was unfair to you."

"We need you to keep working," she reminded me.

"I know, but if I could earn some extra money before the baby's born, I could take a little more time off. I have an offer for some private work."

"What's the offer?" Serena raised an eyebrow.

"Tug Grant wants me to investigate his wife's murder."

"That's in Minneapolis," she said with disappointment.

"I'm not going to get a lucrative retainer from anyone around here."

Serena gazed down, "I know I'm talking out of both sides of my mouth, but I don't want you to go." She raised her eyes to mine. "If you go—make the retainer worth it. If it's not worth it, you walk away. We will find a way to be okay. We always do."

"I was thinking of asking for $30,000 plus $10,000 a month." I took a sip of my cold beer.

"If you can get that, you can go around the world on me," Serena teased.

Beer sprayed out of my mouth. Going around the world is a sex worker term for penetrating every orifice. After I finally stopped laughing, I said, "So, you've decided you want to try anal?"

"No. Absolutely not," she giggled. "That's how convinced I am I'm going to win this bet. Tug's a slick attorney. He'll find a way to talk you into waiting for his wife's insurance money, and we'll be waiting for years. If you can't get $30,000 up front, no deal."

"I'm generally a bit of a piker, only taking small bets, but I'm in. Okay, what do I have at stake if I don't get the deal?"

"You have to clean your closet—when I'm home. And I get to toss four T-shirts of my choosing. If I'm putting it out there, you've got to suffer a little too."

The last couple of times Serena asked me to clean out my closet, I made sure to do it while she was gone. I have no problem getting rid of the clothes I don't wear when she's gone, but when she's home, it's, 'But you look good in this color,' or 'I just bought you this,' or 'This is a Robert Graham.' She looks at me with sad eyes, and for the next two weeks, I'm wearing clothes I would have donated to Goodwill. I replied, "Okay, it only seems fair." I placed my arm around her, and we kissed. At first, it was a peck, as if we were signing an agreement. I pulled away momentarily, but I could feel the fire. Her emerald-green eyes glistened, and we slowly came back together, drawn by a tender force that was easy to surrender to.

We embraced and kissed until Serena got up and took my hand. "Let's go upstairs. Do you mind if I leave my winter socks on? My feet are cold."

"Minnesota lingerie," I remarked. "I can picture the Minnesota sock company, Hippy Feet, doing a fashion show. The curtains are pulled so all you can see is the women's stocking feet as they walk by. People cheer, while some whisper, 'That's so 2015,' and others ask, 'Are you going to the after-party?'"

We were now upstairs in our bedroom. I unbuttoned her pajama top, revealing her bare breasts. "Time for me to stop talking."

Serena gave me a devilish grin. "Stop talking and start walking." She laughed as she marched across the room in her stocking feet. "This year's theme."

8:30 P.M., SATURDAY, NOVEMBER 9, 2019
BEAVER ISLAND BREWING COMPANY, 216
6TH AVENUE SOUTH, ST. CLOUD

AS I LEFT THE HOUSE on my way to this meeting, I noticed four taproom T-shirts sitting on a folded garbage bag on the porch. Her selections were Austin Beerworks, Equal Parts

Brewing, True Anomaly, and Southern Star. They were great Texas breweries, but I had to admit the shirts were all worn thin. It was part of the reason I liked them. Serena was already gloating over her presumed victory.

Tilmore "Tug" Grant entered the pub wearing dark glasses, which were a stark contrast to his light blond hair. He was dressed for a GQ shoot in a crisp white Egyptian cotton dress shirt and designer jeans. They say you shouldn't judge a book by its cover, but I did. I had seen Tug and Debra at fundraising events in the past and disliked their Prince and the Pauper style. I had the sense that Deb wore bargain clothes so Tug could wear Armani suits. Tonight, Tug donned a black and blue Aragona suit jacket with a houndstooth design—estimated cost: $4,000. My price just went up, and the wolf in me liked my odds.

We made introductions and ordered, and the bartender, Holly, promptly delivered our beers. Tug ordered the '39 Red, a Scottish and Belgian dark roast malt. I prefer the crisp, smooth taste of the Blueberry Ripple made with hops from Spalt, Germany. The blueberry flavor is only a slight hint. I'm not much for fruity beers.

We sat at a high wooden table away from the other patrons at the bar.

"We've met before," Tug said. "I saw you with that hot brunette at Hoppy Girl."

I smiled and elected not to respond. Serena's voice in my head reminded me, *Your role as an investigator typically puts you at odds with defense attorneys, so it's not fair to judge by those interactions.*

Disappointed by my failure to talk about the night at Hoppy Girl, Tug furrowed his eyebrows and added, "There's no picture of a wife on your website."

Serena and I didn't hide our marriage in our small town, but we didn't advertise it online. Serena felt this was safer for our family, and it allowed her to do some undercover work on my cases as needed. I simply said, "There's a good reason for that."

He took a sip of his beer and reflected sadly, "Happier times."

"I'm sorry to hear about Debra. I didn't know her, but the people I've talked to said she was kind and compassionate."

"Deb was amazing." Tug looked away, removed his glasses, and wiped his eyes. "It will take five people to do what she did. I loved her. I have a hard time talking about her in the past tense. The whole thing was so senselessly brutal." Tug took a large swallow of beer. "I'm not sure how long I can hold it together, so I'm going to get right to the point. What's it going to take to get you to investigate Deb's murder?"

His phrase, "senselessly brutal," stuck in my craw. Maybe it means nothing. He didn't say Deb's murder was senseless. Instead, he said it was senselessly *brutal.* "I can start right away. I'm finishing up some private work, but it's work I can do anytime."

"I've heard you're the best," Tug told me.

"I'll work day and night if needed."

"Perfect. What's it going to cost me?"

"I'd need $50,000 upfront, nonrefundable, and $10,000 per month thereafter. I imagine my work will be completed in four months. Based on what I've heard about the murder scene, there is going to be DNA from the killer." Killers typically get cut in stabbings and leave their blood at the scene. If I don't solve this in four months, the crime scene techs will have the answer.

"I'll double that," Tug countered. "I'll pay you $200,000 if you agree to receive your full payment when you finish."

It was the offer Serena said he'd make. "I can't accept that." If he can afford a $4,000 suit coat, he can pay my $50,000 retainer. I responded, "I need the full advance, or I'm not taking the job. I take no financial risks with my work."

"Lucky for you." The wheels in Tug's head were spinning. He finally said, "I'm thinking $25,000 up front and $10,000 a month is reasonable. Look, I've got a custody battle going on here. My family's broken up. I've got my son, but my daughters are with my in-laws."

"If you can't do fifty, no hard feelings. My fee isn't negotiable."

"They say you're the best, and I want the best." Tug nodded, "Okay."

"My first workday in the field will be the day after the money is in my account. Now, explain to me why you need a private investigator." I took a swallow of ale and opened my planner to take notes.

Tug frowned. "People are already accusing me of committing the murder." He scrolled through his phone and showed me a picture someone posted online of him sitting in a restaurant with an attractive blonde woman, with the caption, Tug Grant's already out on the town. "That's my sister, Meg, with me. She was helping me make funeral arrangements. I didn't want to make those plans in front of the kids, so we went to a restaurant and sat in a private area. Of course, people assumed it was romantic."

"Do you have an alibi?"

"I have an iron-clad alibi. At 8:30, I had my secretary ring Deb. Lily spoke to my wife before I did. The murder happened shortly after that. My office is in Minneapolis, and Deb was at our home in Minnetonka. They're seventeen miles apart and a thirty-minute drive on a good day. And I have witnesses who will place me at a 9:00 a.m. meeting in Minneapolis."

"Did you usually call Deb in the morning?" I asked.

"Like clockwork. Check my phone records. Every day, right before my 9:00 appointments. Deb wanted to know that I made it to work safely, and I shared what I had on the docket. Deb suggested the idea of a daily call to bring us closer."

The money Tug was offering meant he seriously needed help. There was something he wasn't telling me. "You're anticipating some blowback. What did you have her insured for?"

"That's the kicker." He took a sip of his malt as he gauged my reaction. "Ten million dollars."

Holy crap. "Why so much?"

"The insurance was cheap because we're young." He ran his hand through his hair. "I don't know. I'm a wheeler-dealer. I'd have a few drinks with an insurance guy and say, 'Sure, sign me up for some more.'"

"When were these policies taken out?"

"Most in the last year—but none in the last six months. I swear, I didn't kill my Deb, and I have no idea who did. I'll take a polygraph on it if you want."

"Honestly?"

"Yes, absolutely. Like I said, this is going to look bad for me, but I didn't kill her."

"Were you having an affair?"

Tug gazed over the heads of the other bar patrons. "Not recently."

"Before you answer this next question, I want you to know that when you lie to me, it makes me less motivated to look for other suspects. How long ago did the affair end? Keep in mind, I'm going to find out."

Tug looked me in the eyes. "Nine months ago. I was having an affair with my secretary, Melanie Pearson. When she finally fathomed I wasn't going to leave Deb, she ended it." He took a sip of beer and shamefully added, "The truth is, for a second, Melanie and I were hotter than the hinges of Hades. Did you ever meet someone who thoroughly understood you and your work?"

"I have."

"We never separated the two—and that proved to be a mistake. Melanie would be taking care of business before

I even asked. She seemed to know what I needed—always." With some longing, he said, "For a moment, we were vibing in perfect synchrony."

"What did Melanie say when you told her you couldn't leave Deb?"

"I didn't tell her directly." He shrugged. "I've never been great at break-ups. She walked in when I was having sex with someone else at the office. Melanie threw her keys on the desk and quit. She was engaged, last I heard. She may even be married by now."

Melanie has apparently moved on. "Who was the woman you had sex with at the office?"

"Taytum Hanson. She was my law clerk. Taytum and I have no commitments to each other." He dug into his billfold and pulled out a business card. "Feel free to talk to her."

I studied him for a moment and said, "You orchestrated Deb's murder."

Tug hung his head. "I honestly thought about it. But it's a huge line to cross, and I forced myself to step back. And I'm damn glad I did. It was crazy. Looking back, I can't believe I allowed my thinking to go there."

I patiently waited for him to continue.

"I was on the verge of crossing a line I couldn't come back from." Tug took a large swallow of beer. "Out of fairness to Deb, I owed her one more chance. Deb gave up so much for me. And when I stepped back and looked at the big picture, I needed my family. Deb and I went on vacation to LA and Washington, and I remembered why I married her. I couldn't leave her. Talk to anyone who saw us out together, anywhere we went. There was no mistaking our love for each other. And then this happens."

I pondered the entire scenario—the insurance, the affairs. I concluded, "You were going to kill her."

"I went as far as taking out the insurance policies." Tug sat silently for a moment and reflected. "But I changed my mind. The law punishes us for what we do, not what we contemplate. I know I'm a terrible guy and not the type of person you'd typically work for. But I didn't kill her, and I don't know who did. Deb deserves justice." He finished his beer. "I'm ashamed, but I can't let my shame be an obstacle to finding justice for Deb."

This was going to be an interesting case. "Are you having an affair with the secretary you have now?"

"No." Tug smiled sardonically. "You know Lily Walker better than I do—Del's daughter. If I remember correctly, you worked on a case with Del. Lily's the one who recommended I hire you. After the whole thing with Melanie, I'm not mixing work and romance again."

Del Walker was an alcoholic in his later years but was a good officer once. He was shot and killed while helping me on the Lying Close investigation. God rest his soul. I know his daughters struggled with his death. I asked Tug, "Do you have suspects?"

Tug turned his hands palms up. "Richard Day was released from prison just before Deb's murder. Day's a mass murderer. You bring his name into the equation, and there's your reasonable doubt."

I made a note.

Tug continued, "And there was a guy named Carlos who was fond of Deb. She could have had a spurned admirer just as easily." He added as an afterthought, "The Disciples gang is furious that I got a guy off after he killed a gang member. There aren't a lot of people of color in my neighborhood. If somebody spotted a Black man that morning, it would be significant. Brutal beatings are the modus operandi for gangs."

I disliked his suggestion that if a Black man was seen, one should assume he was a gang member. There are a lot of very successful nonwhite Americans living in Minnetonka.

Eighteen percent of this lucrative suburb is not white. Tug was grieving and generating a lot of speculation, which is typical for his predicament. The worst parts of people's personalities emerge in tragedies.

He continued, "I was scheduled to be the keynote speaker at the Minnesota State Bar Association Convention this weekend. Obviously, I'm not doing that. My colleagues are yuckin' it up over at the Continuing Legal Education Conference Center at this very moment." He took a large swallow of beer, and when he set his glass on the table, there was sadness in his eyes. "I love arguing the law. Deb's gone. Opportunities lost." He pulled himself out of his morose state and asked, "Can I announce I hired you? It will counter the heat I'm going to get when people hear about the life insurance."

"Let's not announce it yet. The homicide investigators are less likely to share information with me if they know I'm working privately for you. Let me see what they have first."

"And have some influence on the investigation," Tug nodded. "That's good. My fear is they're going to put blinders on and hunt me while they let the real killer walk free."

10:30 P.M.

I CALLED SERENA ON THE way home and shared the agreement I'd reached with Tug.

"A $50,000 retainer! That's amazing!" The reality of losing her bet sank in slowly, and she murmured, "Hmmmm."

"I left a bottle of KY lube on the back porch."

"You didn't really, did you?"

"No. I didn't. I couldn't decide between the *Ohh Yess* for intense pleasure, *Turn up the Heat* for warming, or *Give Me Goosebumps* for tingling."

"I'm okay with just tingling."

"I'm kidding. I'm not holding you to it."

She laughed, "But you researched it."

"I research everything."

"Holding you to it is an odd expression," Serena quipped. "In this particular circumstance, what exactly does *it* refer to?

18

JON FREDERICK

8:35 A.M., MONDAY, NOVEMBER 11, 2019
LONDONDERRY ROAD, PARKWOOD KNOLLS,
MINNETONKA

I met Minneapolis Police Officer Xavier "Zave" Williams at Tug and Debra Grant's home in Minnetonka. Zave was a young Black officer in his early twenties who was thin and physically fit. Zave was new to the force and was on loan to the Hennepin County Sheriff's Department to help with this investigation. Against my wishes, Tug had leaked to the media that he'd hired me to solve Deb's murder. Being lowest in seniority, Zave got stuck with the task of escorting me through the murder scene.

Zave and I put our latex gloves on. We started in the kitchen, where a landline phone hung on the wall. He told me, "Tug called Debra at 8:30 on this phone. Both his secretary and Tug spoke to Debra, and both say she wasn't in distress at that time. But the assault on her had to start shortly after." Zave waved at me to follow him up the steps. He pointed into the bathroom but didn't enter. "There was water in the tub and all over the floor, but I don't believe the assault started here."

"She was only wearing a robe when the body was discovered, right?"

"Correct." Zave walked me into the primary bedroom. I immediately noticed a planner resting on the nightstand. Zave showed me a picture of the bedroom taken on the day of Deb's murder. A pair of jeans, with the underwear still in them, lay on the floor at the bed's foot. Her socks were lying four feet apart on the floor. Her shirt and bra were tossed on opposite sides of the bed. He asked, "Do you know any women who undress like this? I think he stripped her and tried to drown her."

"Was she raped?"

"No."

I looked around the room and noticed a Rolex on Tug's dresser. "And the place wasn't robbed?"

"No," Zave stated emphatically, "The intruder came here to kill Debra Grant."

"Why do you say that?"

Zave said with sad frustration, "You'll see. This was a brutal fight. The killer wasn't leaving until Deb was dead." Zave shrugged. "I'm new at this, so take what I'm sayin' with a grain of salt."

I wanted to hear his theory. Zave was privy to what the Hennepin County investigators were saying. "I'm listening."

Zave continued, "I think he stripped Deb in the bedroom and brought her to the bathtub to try to make it look like an accident, but then his plans went to hell."

In all homicides, a dozen things will happen that the killer never predicted—some in favor of the killer, and some not. Zave was implicating Tug without directly saying it. Who else would want Deb's death to look like an accident?

"Look at this." Zave showed me pictures of a busted-up gun handle. "The killer pistol-whipped her in the doorway here." Zave had pieced the handle back together in one image. There was a two-headed black eagle in the design.

"That's the symbol on the Albanian flag," I told Zave. "The two heads represent the emperor's dual authority over secular and religious concerns."

"Albanians—are you thinking the Mustafa mob?"

Seven members of the Mustafa family were arrested in the Twin Cities area in 2017 on organized crime charges. They had purchased thousands of cell phones obtained through theft and shoplifting and used them in identity theft schemes. They all served two years in prison. I thought out loud. "I don't know. It doesn't seem like the mob would brand a gun and leave it behind. There was a Mustafa killed in the Hawthorne neighborhood in Minneapolis last month."

"Not the same family," Zave pointed out. "That Mustafa was from the Somali Outlaws gang, and he was killed by a member of a rival gang, the 1627 Boys."

"Did you know Dua Lipa is Albanian?" The country triggered trivia about the pop star.

Zave smiled and remarked, "I'll keep that in mind the next time I'm levitating."

I followed Zave back downstairs to the kitchen, and we stood next to a large blood pool on the floor. He said, "I think this is where the fight ended. Deb's injuries indicate he punched her and stabbed her, breaking off a kitchen knife in her neck." Zave walked me to the front and back doors, pointing to blood on both. "At some point, Deb escaped long enough to get to both doors. Her bloody fingerprints are on the locks, indicating both sets of doors were locked, and there is no sign of a break-in."

I thought out loud, "The killer walked into the house through an open door. And the doors were locked behind him."

Zave interjected, "I spoke to the thirteen-year-old boy, Lincoln. Tug asked him to hook the chain on the front door before they left that morning. Lincoln saw his dad lock the back door when they left."

"Any idea why Deb might have unlocked a door? Grab the paper? Anything like that?"

"Maybe she didn't." Zave walked me to the basement door. "This was open. Maybe Tug let this guy in the house before he left."

"Serology is going to spend the vast amount of their time studying blood evidence on the lower level. Assuming she was bleeding the worst at the end, the fight started upstairs." If Deb didn't notice an intruder until he was upstairs, he entered the home without her awareness.

"We don't know if it happened before or after the killer left, but at some point, Deb got herself off the floor and escaped," Zave elaborated. "Her first neighbor didn't answer because he assumed it was a salesperson. The second two weren't home. She finally collapsed on the porch of the fourth house."

"Deb put up one hell of a fight against a man who had a gun and a knife."

"Got to give her credit for that," Zave agreed.

"With a brutal scene like this, you've got the killer's DNA. It's just a matter of how long it takes the lab to process it."

Zave said, "And in the meantime, people will be online claiming we don't have a clue. I'm going to put a picture of the gun handle online to see if anyone recognizes it. It looks like it was made in somebody's woodshop. If he's going to go through the work of making the design, he's going to show it to somebody."

"Do you mind if I look around?" I asked.

"You had a great rep with the BCA, so I'm going to trust you," Zave responded. "Don't leave your prints on anything, and share what you find."

"Understood." I returned upstairs to the bedroom. The planner sitting on the nightstand intrigued me. It surprised me that it hadn't been bagged and taken in as evidence. Careful to only touch the edge of pages, I skimmed through it. On the day of the murder, there were notes to meet with another

Scoutmaster that afternoon. Deb had the pick-up times for the children marked. Lincoln had a music lesson, and Rebecca had a concert at 7:00. Beneath the event, it was written, "Tug will be there," followed by a smiley face. *Was it the last thing she wrote?* I paged back. Deb was a busy woman. The note that caught my eye was at 10:00 a.m., two days before her murder. It read, *Roan Caruso-no more $.*

I called Zave into the room. "Look at this. Isn't Roan Caruso the guy who was acquitted of murdering the Disciples member?"

"Yeah," Zave nodded. "Tug Grant defended him."

"Did the autopsy say anything about Deb having black ink on the bottom of her right hand," I asked.

Zave smiled quizzically. "Yes, she did. Why do you ask?"

I pointed to the smudged smiley face. "This is the last thing she wrote: Tug will be there."

I paged through the planner, noticing no pages were torn out. Tug had to know Deb had a planner. If Tug had killed her, wouldn't he have taken it to make sure there wasn't anything written in it that could implicate him?

"I'll bag it," Zave said. He was holding an evidence bag that contained a DVD titled *Dial M for Murder.*

"Where did you find that?" I asked.

"The CSI crew found this in a garbage can outside. It should have been hauled away, but the driver was arrested for an outstanding warrant before he got here. They arrived to finish the route the next day, but I told them to leave the trash for now. An investigator found this in the garbage and thought it was interesting."

The presence of that specific movie tormented me. Still, weird coincidences occur in murder cases that can make innocent people appear guilty. It's not surprising a criminal attorney would enjoy a good murder mystery. I have that DVD at home myself.

19

JON FREDERICK

6:35 P.M., FRIDAY, NOVEMBER 15, 2019
PIERZ

I don't really know what makes a week of investigating productive until the case is solved. This week, Tug passed a polygraph indicating he didn't kill his wife, and he has no idea who did. I spoke to Deb's neighbors. At the moment the killer left, no one was in their front yard, and no one was looking out their window. No one witnessed the killer, or Deb leave the home. The neighbors were all now investing in security cameras, but at the time of Debra's murder, no one in the neighborhood had one. I heard over and over, "Before this, nothing bad ever happened here."

I'd spent the day on the phone talking to people in Washington and Los Angeles who interacted with Tug and Deb on their last vacation. So far, everyone has said they were in love, and if anything, Tug was overprotective of her. The guide who crossed Deception Pass with Deb and Tug in Washington said Tug was almost annoyingly worried about Deb.

My final call was to the concierge at the JW Marriott in Los Angeles. Deb and Tug had stayed near the Staples Center in the LA LIVE area. Large movie screens line the streets, and nighttime is an ongoing electric light show. Their hotel had a swimming pool on the roof.

The concierge told me, "I remember Tug and Debra Grant. Tug Grant was paranoid something was going to happen to his wife. He would be with Debra anytime she went anywhere, and if she wanted anything, Tug would run out and get it. When I asked him about it, Tug said, 'I can't afford to lose her.'"

"Thank you." Then it hit me. I thought about Zave's comment that Tug made sure the doors were locked before he left Deb that last morning. What if Tug had contracted the hit and was unable to call it off? It would explain his paranoia about leaving her alone. Who wouldn't want the hit called off? The hitman—especially if he'd already been paid. Tug's records indicated there was a payment of $100,000 made to Roan Caruso.

It was time for me to let it go for the weekend and enjoy my family. I would process my thoughts on the drive home.

10:05 P.M.

MY MOMENTS WITH SERENA MADE any struggles I had to endure worth it. Her demure style, a thin ivory drop-tail T-shirt tonight, fueled a desire in me. She doused a hundred small fires on the home front daily, and the grace with which she handled calamities was praise-worthy. After all this, she approached me tonight with glistening eyes and a charming, ready smile.

Serena bent down in front of me as I sat on the couch, and I raised my lips to hers. She pulled away, kissed my forehead, and whispered, "I want to taste you, be so close to you that we are one person, and never forget you."

Her warm body slid next to mine, and she gave me her sensuous smile. "But first, I need to hear about Tilmore Ulysses Grant."

"You're making it difficult to think about work."

"What are you going to call the new case?" Serena teased.

"'A Scandal of Vandals.' I needed to focus on some dry trivia for a moment. "The Vandals were an ancient Germanic people who senselessly destroyed Rome in 455. 'Desecration' is the word associated with them. People began using the word 'vandal' in the 1660s to refer to the destroyer of something beautiful or venerable, like Debra Grant."

"You don't hear the word venerable very often. From the news stories about Deb, I believe she was accorded a great deal of respect. Okay, but you used vandal*s*, not vandal singular."

"I think there was more than one person involved in Deb's death. It doesn't make sense that a thug would kill her without either robbing the place or trying to assault her sexually. The killer had to be paid or be part of a vendetta. Tug suspects the murder could have been retaliation by a gang. Tug got Roan Caruso out of a legal charge after he killed a Disciples member."

"It sounds like you don't believe Tug killed Deb."

"Tug has a rock-solid alibi. Lily Walker is working in his office now. I spoke to her, and she verified that she was with him at the time his wife was attacked."

"But ten million?" Serena asked, "Who insures their partner for ten million dollars?"

"There is no doubt in my mind that Tug intended to kill her. He claims he changed his mind. I found him believable, and he passed a polygraph indicating he doesn't know who killed Deb. Tug was scheduled to be the keynote speaker at the Minnesota State Bar Association Conference. He wasn't able to because of Deb's death. Wouldn't a narcissist revel in that opportunity?"

"That's a point in my favor. Narcissists love when others compliment them because they don't have to defend themselves. But they're also fearful that others will discover they're a fraud. With Deb's death, he doesn't take the risk, and all the attention will be on 'poor Tug.'" Serena paused. "The $50,000 is in our account." She smiled. "So, let's figure this out."

"Would you be interested in running a stakeout?" I inquired.

"Not in Minneapolis," Serena protested.

"No, at Volume 10 in Little Falls."

"With Julaine —hairstylist extraordinaire?" Serena laughed. "I could get into that."

"Tug's sister, Meg, gets her hair dyed by Julaine about every six weeks. Meg followed Julaine to her new place after she left St. Cloud. I'd like you to schedule after Meg's appointments, show up before hers, and sit with her."

"This will be hours of my day."

"I know. This is what stakeouts are like. I don't even know if anything will come out of it." I laughed at Serena's radiant smile. "What?"

"This means I get to get my hair done by Julaine."

"It does. I've already talked to Julaine about it. You will go by your maiden name. Don't bring up Tug, and if she brings up Tug, don't imply that you think he's guilty."

"Alright. I'm ready to get to work, but not tonight." Serena stood in front of me and slipped off her tee. "I have a debt to pay." With the tip of her index finger, she pushed my forehead back. "Relax, boy…"

MIDNIGHT

SERENA AND I WERE TRANQUIL, bodies glistening in the glow of the fireplace embers. With a tired smile, she purred, "I was supposed to be your servant. You didn't need to return the favor."

"It was the perfect build-up to the finale."

She blew out a slow breath. "Two down, one to go. The tingling lube is on the nightstand upstairs."

I laid on my back, and she rested her head on my chest. "You want to fall asleep." I ran my hands through her hair. "You should sleep."

"I'm a woman of my word."

"I appreciate that. But as your lover, I have a pretty good idea of what you like and an even better idea of what you don't like. I'm not putting you through it."

Serena opened one eye and looked at me, "I want to be everything to you."

"You are. I love how we make love. You kiss me like you can't get enough, and I feel the same. I don't ever want to lose that. If I start asking you to do things you don't enjoy, we will lose that."

"I don't want you ever to think about anyone else."

"I don't. You're my lover." I teased, "You could write a Kama Sutra book on how to make love to an injured man. We have had periods where it had to be only in certain positions, and it's always been great."

"It has." Serena closed her eyes and smiled.

"And I love that you spoon against me and even rub that perfect ass against me in playful love." I imitated the way she dragged out the Malaysian word for it, "mannnnja. I can't separate the act from you, and I don't do things that intentionally hurt you. I never want to." Her warmth and tenderness immersed me in a delightful peace.

In exhausted gratification, she fell asleep on my chest. I cherished the warmth of her body, knowing it contained her spirit, her love. I am at peace, Serena. This is how I know you indeed love me, as you profess.

20

JON FREDERICK

11:30 A.M., MONDAY, NOVEMBER 18, 2019
15TH AVENUE, SOUTH & 6TH STREET SOUTH
CEDAR-RIVERSIDE (WEST BANK), MINNEAPOLIS

I walked along the eighty-plus tents that made Cedar-Riverside the largest homeless encampment in Minnesota. This is where Richard Day's supervised release agent told me I'd find him. In Minnesota, there isn't "parole." Instead, it's called "supervised release." I spotted Richard carrying a box a hundred feet ahead of me. He was approaching the encampment residents, reaching into the box and handing the eager recipients a Styrofoam food container. Some waved him off, but the majority appreciated him. I stood back and quietly observed his act of goodwill.

Suddenly, a large, angry, scraggily-haired man ran at Richard and knocked the box out of his hand. The man began stomping on the food containers. He yelled, "I know who you are. We don't need psychopaths here. Get the fuck out of here!" The man spat at Richard.

Richard penitently knelt, put his head down, and offered no resistance.

I sprinted toward the duo before the miscreant annihilated Richard. When the attacker saw me coming, he retreated to his tent.

Without saying a word, Richard crawled on the frozen ground, gathering the destroyed containers and putting them back into the box.

I went to Richard and helped him clean up the mess. "Don't let people beat the hell out of you. That doesn't make the world better. No self-flagellation or wearing the cilice. All that crap is for masochists."

"Cilice?" Richard glanced curiously at me.

"A cilice is a cloth made from coarse animal hair intended to irritate the skin. It was worn to repent for sin. In the bible, it's referred to as sackcloth. Jesus never meant for people to hurt. Going into dangerous neighborhoods and trying to help is respectful because someone benefits. Self-injury is narcissistic."

Richard told me as we cleaned up, "It's hard to get decent produce because of all the shipping issues. I went through the broccoli and cauliflower and saved all the good pieces for the meals, just as I selected the good cuts of meat. I ate the less desirable leftovers so nothing would be wasted."

"The combination of record rainfalls in the Midwest, flooding, and a simple lack of truck drivers has food prices rising. Vegetables have increased in price at a rate more than four times that of other foods." I dirtied my hands, picking up chunks of the stir-fry as I said, "What you did is commendable. He was just being an ass."

Richard didn't look at me, "You don't have to help. I created this mess."

"And you didn't have to make a great meal for people in need, but still you did." When we were done, I showed him my investigator's badge. "I need to know if you have an alibi for the morning Debra Grant was killed."

"I was sorry to hear about that. But as for me, you can see exactly where I'm at any time of the day." He lifted his pants leg and showed me his ankle bracelet. "If it was a weekday, I was at work at General Mills."

I'd already checked his GPS data, and it placed him at work. "Any idea who would have killed Tug Grant's wife?"

He didn't appear surprised that he was being questioned. Richard left the box on the ground and stood as he casually replied, "None. I feel bad for Tug and his family. We weren't particularly close, but still, he helped me. Maybe his job's easier if you keep folks at a distance. I'm thankful to Tug. I wouldn't be out here if it weren't for him."

"You have no animosity toward him?"

"No. None. Why would I?"

"You went to prison," I countered. "And when Tug took over as your attorney, you lost your appeal."

"Tug tried to argue I didn't realize my plea involved a life sentence. I lost my appeal when the judge asked me directly if that was true and I told him I knew I could get life. I just wanted to end the media frenzy, for my families sake."

He looked down the street at a slowly approaching car. "I went to prison for killing my parents and brother and almost killing my niece. Tug was the reason I was released. What happened to the investigator who found me in the barn and saved me? I saw him in a wheelchair in court."

I think Tony Shileto would consider hunting Richard down rather than saving him. "He was shot by a man he was investigating. It's heartbreaking to see a once active man incapacitated. Tony still helps with investigations."

"I pray for him. Tony gave me my last rites in the hayloft that night. It was incredibly kind of him."

Tony never ceases to surprise me.

A 1959 black Cadillac Eldorado with tinted windows slowly pulled up. I recognized the year because it was my dad's dream car. The '59 Eldorado had the highest tail fins ever built on an American car on the rear fenders. My immediate thought was drive-by. I unbuttoned my shirt and pulled my gun out of the shoulder holster. I pulled Richard away from the street, and we stepped back to the tents.

The car stopped across from us for thirty seconds and then drove on. As it pulled away, I ran to the street and jotted down the license plate number. It was a collector's plate. "Have you seen this car before?" I asked.

Richard nodded grimly. "A few times since my release. I understand if someone kills me, but I'm not ready to die. I need time to show I can be a decent man. Every day, I live my life looking for opportunities to help others, hoping I don't end up spending an eternity in hell. People are going to sabotage my efforts, but I deserve that, and it challenges me to keep the faith. I don't have extra money, but I can work. I've helped people clean up after a fire and vandalism. My corrections agent's skeptical, but she should be. That's her job."

"I'd shake your hand, but—" I held up my sticky, food-covered hand. "I wish you well, Richard. Take care."

I wiped my hands clean in the snow and called a former BCA colleague, Paula Fineday.

"Jon, what's up?"

"I need a favor. I'm in Minneapolis checking on Richard Day for a private client, and an old Cadillac rolled up on us. I know I'm no longer working for the BCA, but I'm assuming the BCA doesn't want Day executed. Would you mind running a plate for me? It's a collector plate—349 386."

"It piques my curiosity." I could hear her clicking away on her computer.

"Richard said the car's cruised by a few times since he's been released."

Paula paused. "It belongs to one Roan Caruso from Minneapolis…"

4:00 P.M.
51ST STREET & WASHBURN AVENUE
SOUTH, FULTON, MINNEAPOLIS

I STOPPED AT AGNES SCHRAUT'S home. Agnes was a cantankerous woman in her eighties who gave me an open invitation to stay when I was in the metro. Minneapolis was scary, and she reveled in having an armed ally in her house. Fortunately, for my sake, Agnes had gone to bingo when I arrived, which allowed me to work in peace. *What was Roan Caruso's connection to Richard Day?* I'd need to come back to that. I got on my laptop and looked up the Grants' gardener, Carlos Garcia. His criminal history revealed nothing. I pondered for a minute and then called Tug Grant. Call it a hunch, but I felt he knew more about Carlos than he had let on.

"What do you need, Jon?" Tug answered.

"I couldn't find anything in Carlos's criminal history. I thought maybe you'd have something."

Tug got serious. "I do. In 2017 Carlos was charged with Interference with Privacy: Surreptitious intrusion; observation device. Carlos came into the courtroom intending to plead guilty, but I was his attorney, and I talked him into withdrawing his plea. I got the charge dismissed. I did it because I thought he was a guy who made a stupid blunder. Now I wonder if I made a mistake."

"Exactly what did Carlos do?"

Tug explained, "Carlos had gone on a first date with a woman. A blizzard began while they were in the theater, and when Carlos drove her home, she let Carlos sleep on her couch instead of making a treacherous drive home. During the night, Carlos entered her bedroom while she was lying in bed asleep. He took a picture of her lying topless without her consent. When the police confronted him, he admitted it."

"How did you get the charge dismissed?"

Tug laughed, "The wording of the law is that a person is guilty of a gross misdemeanor if he/she/they enter another's property and surreptitiously gazes, stares, or peeps in the window or any aperture of a dwelling; with the intent to intrude upon the privacy of a household member." Tug pointed out, "By the letter of the law, Carlos wasn't guilty of a crime. Carlos hadn't taken the picture through a window or a hole in the wall, as the law states. The judge dismissed the charge, and the Minnesota legislature is now changing the law to state that invasion of privacy involves viewing someone "in an area where a reasonable person would have an expectation of privacy."

"And then you hired him to work on your lawn?"

"I ran into him about eleven months ago. He was in a stable relationship and picking up odd jobs where he could. When I told Deb about it, she insisted we give Carlos a chance." He paused. "It bothers me that Deb was naked. Did he take a picture of her?"

"I'll look into it."

"Carlos painted a picture of Deb..." Tug trailed off.

I wasn't sure what to think about that. It certainly went beyond landscaping.

7:00 P.M.

SEMINOLE AVENUE, WEST ST. PAUL

I FOUND MYSELF SITTING OUTSIDE Carlos Garcia's home. From the street, I could see him sitting on a couch with his arm around an ebony-haired Hispanic woman, watching television. They laughed about something and then caressed lovingly.

I went to the house and knocked. When Carlos answered, I showed him my private investigator's badge. I told him, "I'd like to ask you some questions about Debra Grant."

Carlos was in his forties and had a couple days' growth of dark facial hair. He rubbed his neck. "I liked Debra. She was a good, hard-working woman."

"Can you tell me where you were on the morning she was murdered?"

"Yeah, exactly where I was. I was at the Jacobses' home one block away—on film. They have a camera system. I'm on TV all day long, so I'm covered if anyone makes allegations."

"I have to ask about your criminal charge."

"I was stupid." Carlos reluctantly disclosed, "A kind woman let me sleep on her couch because the roads were bad. I couldn't sleep. When the snow let up, I decided to head home. I went to knock on her bedroom door and saw it was partially open. She was lying naked in bed. She looked good, and I was holding my phone. I walked in and took a picture. It was stupid. I deleted the photo before I got home." His active hands emphasized his words. I couldn't help noticing scratches on his wrists. "She must have been awake and called the cops. I never denied what I did. And I would never do it again!" Carlos added.

"How did you get those scratches?"

"Trimming prickly trees." He glanced at his wrists. "You have to trim oak trees in Minnesota between November and April to prevent oak wilt."

"Did you hire Tug Grant to be your attorney?" I asked.

"No. He was assigned to me. I would have taken the plea if I didn't have to worry about getting deported. I made a bad choice. Now I'm with Luciana. All is good."

All attorneys are strongly encouraged to provide fifty hours of pro bono work a year, so it made sense that Tug would take on a relatively easy case like Carlos's to fill his quota.

Luciana joined us in the entryway. "This is my wife, Luciana."

"Jon Frederick." I nodded toward a painting on the wall of a saint who bore a strong resemblance to Paul Bunyan. "St.

James the Great—patron saint of Spain. Brother of St. John the Apostle. Jesus referred to the two brothers as the "sons of thunder." They weren't afraid to speak up when someone was making bad choices."

"Catholic?" Luciana smiled.

"Yes." I smiled back at her. "St. James was the first apostle to be martyred, in the year 44, and the only apostle whose martyrdom is noted in the New Testament. James stated, 'The one who does not practice mercy will have his judgment without mercy.'"

Luciana took my hand again and patted it in appreciation.

I redirected my attention to Carlos. "Do you have any idea who would want to kill Debra?" I asked.

"No." Carlos shook his head. "None. The Grants were always good to me."

"How long have you worked for the Grants?"

Carlos asked Luciana, "I've been working for the Grants for about a year now, right?"

"Maybe a little less, but close to a year now," she agreed. "Because Tug interviewed you for the job on the morning of Valeria's birthday."

"Tug hired you?" I questioned.

"Yeah," Carlos responded. "After the interview, almost all my dealings were with Debra. She was one who was always home."

"Did you see anyone unusual in the neighborhood on the morning of Debra's murder?"

"No, but I'm looking at the ground when I work. That's where my work is. I didn't even hear a gunshot."

"The killer had a gun, but it never fired."

Luciana leaned into Carlos and said, "It's so sad—those four kids without a mom."

"It doesn't make sense." Carlos shook his head again. "Everyone I work for says Debra was a saint."

"Luciana, could you step away for a minute? I have a question for Carlos."

"Okay." Luciana looked worried as she reluctantly stepped away.

"What can't you ask in front of Luciana?" Carlos asked.

"You painted a picture of Debra Grant. I need to see it."

"What are you going to do if I refuse?"

"Talk to law enforcement." His denizen status made him deportable, and that gave me leverage to garner his cooperation.

"Okay. Follow me."

I followed Carlos into the basement, watching him carefully in case he suddenly pulled out a weapon. Boxes of paintings were piled up in rows. Carlos stopped and carefully slid one out. He took a deep breath and handed me the picture. "Here. Keep it."

I took it. "If you don't mind, I'll give it to her family. Why didn't you give it to Debra?" I asked.

"She didn't want it."

When I looked closer at the picture, I could see why. Deb looked troubled. Still, she was beautiful, standing in the kitchen, wearing jeans and a pink tank top that faded to orange with a classy floral design. The room around Deb had warm golden lighting. As the picture drifted away from her, the bricks morphed into large cement blocks, and the windows farthest away from her had bars on them. I commented, "You felt the home was a prison for Deb?"

"I painted what I felt at the time."

Looking at the painting, I could sense that Carlos loved her. "Were you having an affair with Deb?"

"No," he replied immediately.

Luciana came downstairs, sat on the basement steps, and listened.

"Was Roan Caruso having an affair with her?" I asked.

"It would surprise me," Carlos responded. "Deb was a good woman."

I studied the picture. "With a deep secret."

"Tortured," Carlos remarked.

"By what?" I asked.

"Have you met her husband?" Carlos asked.

"What did you think of Tug?"

"I didn't really know him personally." Carlos retreated. "He's a great attorney."

He didn't want to render an opinion. I wondered if he was jealous. "Can I see some of your other paintings?"

Carlos pulled out a painting of Hispanic men working in chains in a field, a painting of gun-wielding Black teens standing on the corner while their mothers wept on the curb, and a painting of five white men nailed to crosses made of rifles. All his paintings had *people* in various states of pain, except for one. Deb was the only lone person in his paintings. Was Deb the tortured soul, or was Carlos?

11:30 A.M., TUESDAY, NOVEMBER 19, 2019
PIERCE STREET NORTHEAST, BELTRAMI, MINNEAPOLIS

I WATCHED A VIDEO OF Carlos Garcia this morning. On the day of Debra Grant's murder, he planted shrubs along the fence in the Jacobs' backyard until 8:40 a.m. A call came in on his cell phone, and he left the screen. At 8:55 a.m. Carlos returned and finished his planting. Carlos was wearing a gray hoodie when he left but no longer wearing it when he returned. *Was this enough time to kill Debra and return?* Possibly. She was only one block away. Deb hadn't been sexually assaulted but was naked except for her robe. *Had her assailant snapped a picture of her?* It would have been Carlos's modus operandi.

I called Zave and shared the information with him, including the scratches I noticed on Carlos's wrists. Zave told me he wanted to speak to Carlos before I confronted him again, and I agreed. I had to. The homicide was his case.

After being instructed to back off, I called Tony Shileto. "How's it going, Tony?"

"Boring as dishwater," Tony remarked. "What do you have?"

"The police are locking me out of investigating Carlos Garcia. Carlos has no criminal charges, but I know a police report was completed on an invasion of privacy charge. I'd like to know what was in that report."

"I'll see what I can do. What city?"

"Minneapolis."

"Alright. I'll call you back as soon as I have news."

I considered my options. My phone buzzed. *That was quick.* "Hello?"

"Hi, this is Luciana. I've been thinking about what you said. I have mercy for Debra Grant." She paused and said, "There was another picture. A naked picture of Deb…"

When the call ended, I realized I was stuck. *How could I get more information on Carlos Garcia without talking to him?* He's not a legal citizen, so he has no paper trail. I'd back off for the moment to give the Hennepin County Sheriff's Department time to investigate him, but if they didn't find anything, I'd circle back.

Tony called. "Carlos Garcia had pictures of naked women on his phone. Several were sleeping. But after he escaped prosecution by a loophole in the law on one case, there was no point in trying to prosecute the others."

"Thank you, Tony." Carlos had lied to me. He hadn't deleted the picture.

21

SERENA FREDERICK

11:30 A.M., THURSDAY, NOVEMBER 21, 2019
LYNDALE AVENUE EAST, NORTH LOOP, MINNEAPOLIS

Jon and I ate supper with Zave Williams and Lauren Harold at Masu Sushi in Northeast Minneapolis and then headed to Zave's home in the North Loop for a nightcap. After discovering Zave was single, the matchmaker in me knew Zave had to meet Lauren. She was a former dairy princess with flowing blonde hair who grew up in our neck of the woods. Lauren worked as a sketch artist for the Bureau of Criminal Apprehension.

Zave had picked up a six pack of Red Squirrel Amber Ale from Jack Pine Brewery in Baxter and he and Jon were enjoying a glass. Jon referred to the beverage as an "expertly malted amber." Lauren had brought a four-pack of aluminum bottles of Stella Rosa Black, a red blend. Knowing I was picking her up and dropping her off, Lauren relaxed and enjoyed a couple. Lauren seemed to have a little bit of a dreamy buzz going. As a woman in hot pursuit of pregnancy and our sober driver, I drank Diet Pepsi.

Zave ditched his dress shirt and returned to the living room in a black Ripsaw band T-shirt. He plunked down next to Lauren on the couch. They were both polite, and they flirted a little, but I sensed that this would end with neither being willing to take the next step.

Jon offered me the lounge chair and sat at the end of the couch closest to me.

"Do you want to talk work first?" Zave asked.

"Absolutely," Jon responded immediately. "What do you have?"

"Aren't you working for Tug?" Lauren queried Jon.

"I am. I plan on finding the person who killed Deb. I'm not protecting her killer, even if it's Tug."

Zave smiled at Lauren, as if to imply he'd already had this conversation with Jon, and said, "I've got a response to the post I placed online with the picture of the gun grip. The wooden grip was made in a shop class at Fridley High School. Obviously, they never had the gun there. It was a Father's Day present. Unfortunately, it was stolen from the owner's home six months ago. A report was filed at the time. No news about it since."

Jon said, "I was checking on Richard Day to rule him out as a suspect and a '59 black Cadillac slowly cruised by. I ran the plates, and the car belongs to Roan Caruso."

Lauren interjected, "Isn't he the guy who killed the Disciples kid?"

Jon clarified, "Yes, but Deondre was nineteen." Jon took his glass of beer and walked over to the window. "I need to know more about this Caruso guy."

I joined him. The Mississippi was inky and ominous at night. The mighty mass of water reminded me of a black anaconda slowly putting a stranglehold on the city.

"Did you talk to Carlos Garcia?" Jon asked.

Zave nodded, "Yeah. The DA sealed him up. He's not available to talk to anymore. It wasn't Carlos who killed Deb."

"How do you know?" Jon wondered.

"We got the DNA evidence back."

Zave's relaxed state was trying Jon's patience. Jon asked, "Well, who does it belong to?"

"The DNA belongs to a guy named Dick Doden who lives over in Little Italy."

Little Italy was a reference to the Italian neighborhood, Beltrami, in Minneapolis.

Zave continued, "It's classic. His DNA wasn't in the system, but his sister had posted hers on Ancestry.com, looking for relatives a year ago. When we shared our sample, we had a hit on a first-degree relative. We followed Doden and picked up a cup he discarded with his DNA on it. It provided a 99% match. The shoes we took from his home matched the footprints in Deb's home. His fingerprints are in the home. Dick Doden killed Deb Grant. The question is, who hired him?"

"So, is Dick talking?" I wondered.

"I'm sorry, that just sounded funny." Lauren giggled.

Zave leaned toward Lauren and softly shoulder-bumped her as he answered, "He met with his lawyer today. They want some time to discuss it, and said they'll come back and talk when they're ready. Prosecutor Bare told him there will be no deal that doesn't include a sentence of life in prison for the beating he gave Deb."

"You should know that Tug passed a polygraph examination indicating he didn't kill Deb and he doesn't know who did," Jon said.

"Occam's Razor," Zave remarked.

Occam's Razor is a scientific term that refers to shaving away the long shots and focusing on what's obvious. In this case, ten million dollars in life insurance and an affair make Tug the obvious suspect. Zave could be right, but at this point, I had too many unanswered questions, with the most obvious being, *how does Tug Grant know Dick Doden?*

22

JON FREDERICK

11:30 A.M., FRIDAY, NOVEMBER 22, 2019
LUCELINE BREWING 12901 16TH
AVENUE NORTH, PLYMOUTH

Tug Grant was sitting at a wooden table when I entered. I went to the bar and ordered a Minnesota Ice, a German Kolsch served extra cold. As I approached Tug with my glass, he held his up for a somber toast, "Mele Kalikimaka Tropical Blonde Ale."

After our glasses clinked, I sat down and asked, "Why did you release to the press that you'd hired me to investigate the murder? I asked you not to."

"I had to." Tug pinched his nose. "After Jada Anderson announced on the news that I had ten million dollars in life insurance for Deb, my kids' friends stopped talking to them. I needed to announce I want this solved for my kids' sake. The impact of Deb's murder has been like an atomic bomb on my life. My son, Lincoln, is living with me, but my mother-in-law, Greta, has claimed my three daughters. And Greta has connections."

"Her connections are irrelevant. The girls are legally yours. You could take custody of them."

"With all the crap that's online, the girls don't want to be seen with me." Tug blew out a long breath. "Just what I need—some reporter filming me dragging my crying girls home. That wolf bitch says if I claim my rights to them, she's coming after Lincoln, too."

I could understand trying to protect his children. "Is there any possibility Greta could have paid someone to murder Deb? From the people I've spoken to, Deb tolerated her mother, but they didn't have a great relationship."

"Please investigate that." Tug busted out laughing. "And let me announce it."

"No announcing anything until I have some solid evidence. Right now, Greta has a reason to get along with you. If you go after her and she's connected, she could bury you. Deb was her only child. Assume Greta has a lot of information about you."

"You're right." Disgruntled, Tug slammed down his beer. "I really wish I wouldn't have been such a horseshit husband."

I thought, *me too*, but I asked, "Do you know a man named Dick Doden? Doden's Scandinavian, but his mugshot looks Italian. His mother's maiden name is Russo."

"No. Never heard of the guy. Why?"

Tug's response appeared genuine. "Dick Doden killed Deb."

Tug threw his hands in the air. "Why didn't you start with that? I'm off the hook."

"Because you're not. The investigators are convinced somebody hired Doden. This wasn't a robbery gone wrong. It was a hit."

"That doesn't make sense. Why?"

"This is what I've uncovered so far. There was no evidence of a break-in at the home. There was no evidence Deb had been sexually assaulted. The home wasn't robbed. Richard Day didn't have anything to do with Debra's murder. He isn't the type of killer who pays other people to kill. Richard appreciates what you did for him and expressed sincere sadness for you and your family."

"And you believed him?" Tug questioned.

"Yes."

"Anything else?" Tug tapped on the table.

"The piece I struggle with is that the killer initially appeared to try and make it look like an accident."

Tug considered this. "Do you think it was a paramour?" He paused, thoughtful. "It had never occurred to me that mending my relationship with Deb might have infuriated a suitor on her end."

"Anyone you suspect?"

"I've always wondered about Carlos Garcia. Deb seemed to have a twinkle in her eye when she talked to him, and that always unnerved me. You see the immigrants landscaping all around the Twin Cities. We don't know their criminal history."

"I'll check into it. Why did Deb meet with Roan Caruso two days before she was murdered?"

"I didn't know she did." Tug looked surprised.

"There was a note in her planner. It said something about the money you gave Roan. Did you know Deb had a planner?"

"Yeah," he nodded.

I didn't know that he'd paid Roan. It was a hunch. Considering the way the couple dressed, Deb seemed tighter with the money. I continued, "What was the money for?"

"Roan always has some new business venture going. He was a good investment. He always paid me back with interest," Tug admitted. "You need to understand our history. Roan and I were friends in college. We were both smart but a little misguided. Roan told me he was dating the most amazing woman on earth, and when I met her, I realized he was right. Not long after that, Deb left Roan to be with me. I've always felt guilty about that. But not so much that I'd ever give up Deb. The guy who ended up with her would have a great life, and Deb would make it happen. Deb was a caretaker and wouldn't hesitate to use her mom's connections to help her man. I know it broke his heart to lose her, but I don't see Roan killing Deb. He would have sooner killed me."

"Whoever did this set you up to take the fall. They may have been close enough to you to know that with the affair and the insurance, you had already made yourself look guilty. Does Roan know you that well?" I asked.

Tug nodded, "I check in on him periodically, and we have a beer or two together."

I considered another angle. "Who benefits from you being sent away?"

"I don't think it's so much that someone benefits. I'm convinced it was payback, okay?" Tug argued.

"For what?"

"Do you have any idea how much people hate attorneys? We're expensive, and the cases are emotionally charged. When they lose, they never consider that their unscrupulous transgressions created the mess. It's 'you lost the case for me!'" Tug patted his brow with a napkin. "Think about the intense beating Deb took. The killer either loved Deb or hated me. That's who you're looking for."

23

JON FREDERICK

4:00 P.M., SATURDAY, NOVEMBER 23, 2019
PIERCE STREET NORTHEAST, BELTRAMI, MINNEAPOLIS

Roan Caruso lived in the Beltrami neighborhood in Minneapolis, just east of St. Anthony, which was settled primarily by Italians. His large rose brick house was on the block behind Our Lady of Mount Carmel Catholic Church. The Blessed Virgin Mary was the patroness of the Carmelites, who had lived on Mount Carmel in the Holy Land. They were contemplative and cloistered hermits who said nothing during meals. The scapular, given to Catholics at first communion, was a signal of grace for the Carmelite order. Mary promised that whoever died wearing it would not suffer everlasting punishment. As a Roman Catholic, I wore a brown scapular at my first communion and confirmation. It had thin cloth straps worn over the shoulders and a picture of Mary that hung over the heart. It was intentionally inexpensive and was not jewelry.

As I approached the house, I heard a man and a woman arguing inside. The woman yelled, "Why does she have to stay over? Why can't you just meet her once a month like most guys do with their bastard kids?"

The man yelled back, "Because I said she could. That's the only answer you need."

It didn't appear that Roan benefited from his home's proximity to the church. I stood on the steps debating how to start the conversation. *What did Roan intend to achieve by visiting Deb just days before her murder?* Roan was a former boyfriend—*perhaps a spurned lover?*

The door swung open, and a buff man about six and a half feet tall with thick, matted black hair confronted me, "What do you want?"

When I glanced up at him, I noticed a camera mounted under the soffit and realized he had seen me on the security system. I showed him my private investigator's badge. "I want to know what you and Debra Grant met about two days before she was murdered."

Roan didn't even glance at my badge. Assuming I was law enforcement, he stood in the doorway and scoffed. "You think I came to tell her, 'Be home on Wednesday, I'm comin' to kill you?' Deb was a friend. Not a friend with benefits—just a friend. Catania and I were eating brunch at the Handsome Hog in St. Paul the morning Deb Grant was murdered."

"Do you go out and eat brunches often during the week?" I asked.

"What difference does it make? We were that morning."

A woman with long dark hair partially hanging over one eye and no makeup came to Roan's side. I knew her from my work at the BCA. Roan was living with Catania Turrisi—the great-granddaughter of Giuseppe "Don Pepé" Turrisi. Don Pepe was the head of The Minneapolis Combination, or the La Cosa Nostra, in the Twin Cities. Catania was named after Don Pepe's hometown in Sicily. The Italian mob didn't have the power they once yielded in the metro, but they were still a force to be reckoned with, so the BCA kept track of them generation after generation. Catania's first words to me were, "Who the fuck are you?"

"Jon Frederick. I'm here asking about the money Roan received from Tug Grant."

Catania cut in, "You gotta warrant?" Her thick Italian accent made the "r's" disappear. If Roan was living with Catania Turrisi, he didn't need to borrow money.

Before I could respond, she looked over my shoulder and said, "For fuck's sake. Whadda they think we are, a petting zoo?"

I turned to the road and watched Halle Day get out of a car and walk toward the house. At that moment, the combined synergy of Halle's confident demeanor, soul-piercing eyes, and long blonde hair reminded me of Taylor Swift. *What was Halle Day doing here?*

"I'm goin' for a walk," Catania murmured and left.

"This is a bad time. Can we talk later? My daughter's visiting," Roan said.

When Halle approached us, I introduced myself. "I'm Jon Frederick."

With a shy smile, she offered, "Halle Day."

I turned back to Roan. "Can you tell me why you're following Richard Day?"

Halle looked concerned.

"Just making sure my girl here's okay." Roan put his arm around Halle.

"Leave him alone," Halle told Roan. "Ricky's a different person now."

"Leopards don't change their spots." Roan said, "We are just what we are. Nobody's different."

"He is," Halle countered. "Leave him alone."

Roan kissed her head and looked at me. "You still here?"

"We'll talk another time." I stepped away. This was a morning of surprises. Roan Caruso has mob connections and is the father of Richard Day's niece. Halle was the sole survivor of Day's mass shooting. Tug's connection to Roan had to have something to do with Tug becoming Richard Day's attorney.

I called Tug as I drove away. "I just met Roan Caruso, his daughter Halle Day, and Catania Turrisi."

"Now that's an assortment of misfits." Tug laughed, "Cat, the moon-bat plutocrat."

I cringed. 'Moon-bat' is a derogatory term for a liberal, and a 'plutocrat' refers to power deriving from wealth.

Tug continued, "Roan says Cat has PMS, but it seems like someone with PMS would have days where they're not rancorous. I think she's PB and J—permanently bitchy and jealous."

"Halle seems pretty normal."

"If Halle's normal, it's only because of her mother."

"Why did you defend Richard Day?"

"I only defended Day regarding his release." The line was quiet for a moment before he continued. "Okay, here's the truth. Roan asked me to pretend to defend Day. He wanted me to find a way to keep Ricky locked up. The case intrigued me, and if I was going to defend Day, I was going to defend him. My reputation was at stake. Day was given four life sentences to run concurrently, which is the same as one life sentence.

If a person has committed more than one crime, a judge can run the sentences consecutively or concurrently. Richard was sentenced concurrently, meaning every year served was one year on four charges. Richard was convicted of three counts of Murder in the First Degree and one count of Attempted Murder. Each murder charge is thirty years to life, and the attempted murder carries a maximum sentence of fifteen years. After fifteen years, Richard had served half of his sentence for three murders and his complete sentence for the attempted murder.

Offenders can have one-third of their sentence reduced for 'good time,' which means they did not have any violations during their incarceration. Consequently, Richard Day was set to be released after twenty years of good behavior. Richard's sentence was reduced further due to the M'Naghten Rule, which considers the individual's understanding of the wrongfulness of their conduct. Since Richard was a juvenile, he was considered less responsible and was subsequently released after sixteen years, with an expectation of lifetime supervision—probation. The judge must have thought that someday there would be hope for the boy."

In 1843, Daniel M'Naghten had paranoid delusions that the Prime Minister of England was going to kill him. M'Naghten attempted to kill Sir Robert Peel, but instead, the bullet he fired killed Peel's secretary. M'Naghten was found not guilty because of his "defect of reason." M'Naghten became the standard for insanity pleas. Only four states, Montana, Utah, Idaho, and Kansas, do not consider insanity to be a defense.

"Was Roan angry that Day only served sixteen years?" I asked.

"Yeah. He harangued me about it for a bit but eventually seemed to let it go."

"I feel like Roan is the key to solving Deb's murder."

"Roan is tough, and he lives by a code of secrecy. Right out of college, he could have walked on his felony theft charge. I begged him to give up just one name, but he refused. Roan isn't going to give you anything. He'll mess with your head, and it will be time lost that could have been used productively. And he has an alibi, doesn't he?"

"Yes. Roan and Cat just happened to be eating about as far away as he could get from your home and still be in the metro area. It feels planned. What's the story behind Roan shooting a Disciples gang member?"

"We didn't get into details about it." Tug yawned. "I think the guy tried to jack his car, and Roan loves that old Caddy more than sex. The alleged murder weapon was obtained by an illegal search of his car, and that was that."

My next call was to Zave Williams.

5:45 P.M.
1249 FREMONT AVENUE, NEAR NORTH, MINNEAPOLIS

ZAVE AGREED TO JOIN ME at a Disciples home in one of the most dangerous neighborhoods in Minneapolis. We were meeting with Wesley Washington. Wes was a Disciples gang member who, for obvious reasons, was referred to as "Dreads." Wes moseyed his lanky six-foot two-inch frame to the driver's side by Zave.

Two bulked-up men built like defensive tackles for the Vikings stood guard on the porch of the house. After Zave and Dreads maneuvered a complicated handshake, Dreads said, "Another brother dead at the hands of a fuckin' cracker."

"I don't like it any more than you do." Zave nodded in support.

Dreads asked pessimistically, "Now that Caruso's free, whatta you boys gonna do?"

Feeling I'd finally been invited into the conversation, I pointed out, "We might not get Roan for the murder of Deondre, but we might still get him for another murder. What was the argument between Deondre and Roan Caruso about?"

Dreads studied me skeptically and then spoke directly to Zave. "Deondre jacked his car." Dreads glanced at two boys throwing a football under the streetlight. He nodded toward the taller boy. "That's Deshaun Hill, man. Remember that name. That kid's going to be a superstar."

I watched a young teen throw a long pass with a perfect spiral to his friend.

"Deondre messed up," Dreads said. "You can't jack a collector. The parts are too easy to trace. And people have an attachment to that shit—like it's one of their babies. He got orders from Fox to give the car back. Fox said we don't need a war with Minneapolis Combination, so return it. That's the 'zact fact."

"What went wrong?" Zave asked.

Dreads said, "Nothin' on our end. Deondre gave him his car and stuff. Caruso shot Deondre dead. And the Guinea gets out of the charges on an illegal search—bullshit! Makes a man wonder if the cop was in on it."

"That doesn't make sense," Zave quickly interjected. "If the cop were in on it, he would have let Caruso drive away. The cop hears shots and sees Caruso driving away in his Caddy. He knew what happened, and there wasn't a damn thing he could do about it. He pulled Caruso over anyway so the world would know Roan Caruso killed this kid. I know the cop. He was hoping the judge would find a way to allow the search."

"Okay." Dreads nodded.

"You said Deondre agreed to return his items." I asked, "What were the items?"

Dreads said, "A leather folder with a signature in it. Caruso told Fox the signature represented an important agreement between Italians."

"You wouldn't, by chance, remember the name? I asked.

Dreads gave a sly grin, "I can't read it, but I got a picture of it." He took out his phone and showed us a signature on parchment paper inside a protective plastic cover.

"Does that say Button Gwinnett?" Zave smiled.

I looked closely. "Sure as hell."

Zave turned to Dreads, "Button Gwinnett is one of the most valuable signatures in the U.S. He signed the Declaration of Independence."

"If nobody knows BG, why is the sig valuable?" Dreads wondered.

I wanted to say, "He was the original Bee Gee." *You can tell by the way he uses his walk he's a woman's man. No time to talk... Stayin' alive.* But my white humor would have gone unappreciated. Instead, I explained, "There are collectors who try to get the signatures of everyone who signed the Declaration of Independence. Gwinnett's is the rarest since he died in a duel ten months after signing, and the British burned his house down. There are only seven of his signatures known, and four are in the New York Public Library."

Dreads asked, "How much?"

"My guess—at least half a million," Zave responded.

"The last sold for $722,000," I told them.

"The shit white people pay for. We should have hung onto it," Dreads said. "Caruso must have been in the middle of a deal when his car was jacked. I could understand givin' Deondre a beatdown—but executing him is bullshit. This ain't over."

6:30 P.M.

NORTH IRVING AVENUE, CAMDEN, MINNEAPOLIS

ZAVE TOLD ME THAT DEONDRE had a lover named Latrice Johnson, so I followed Zave to Latrice's home to hear what she had to say. As we waited on the porch for someone to answer the doorbell, Zave told me, "Let me take the lead on this."

"Sure." I had planned on it. After all, it was his case. I was fortunate to be invited along. The shortage of police officers in Minneapolis proved to be to my benefit since I doubt Zave would have invited me if he had backup.

We entered a small home in the Camden neighborhood in Minneapolis where Latrice Johnson lived with her parents. Through Zave's polite niceties, we discovered that Latrice had just turned eighteen. She held a one-year-old baby girl as she spoke to us.

Zave explained, "We are investigating Roan Caruso. I know you'd like him to experience some consequences, and we're trying to help. I'd appreciate it if you could answer some questions. Did Deondre tell you about any of the conversations he had with Roan Caruso?"

Latrice gave her leg a slight bounce to keep the baby content. "Is Roan coming after me?"

"Have you ever met him?" Zave asked.

"No. Deondre swore he'd never mention us to Roan to keep us safe."

Zave told her, "I don't know anything that would suggest he knew about you."

Latrice nervously looked at me and then back to Zave again. "Is Roan a made guy—like mob-connected?"

Zave answered, "My sense is he's just a thug, and we're trying to get him locked up."

I wanted to intervene, but I had promised to be a sidekick. I personally think Roan is a made man. I wish I would have shared more of my earlier meeting with Zave. I interjected, "We may not get him on Deondre's murder, but we might get him on another."

I was trying to think of a way to warn Latrice when she turned to me and said, "Roan asked Deondre to kill Debra Grant. He told Deondre he wanted a Black man to kill her. When Deondre asked what she did, he said 'nothin'.' She didn't do nothin.' It was an insurance thing. Deondre's not a killer. He told him, 'I won't do it.'" Latrice hesitated. "You're not going to make me testify, are you?"

"No." I explained, "What you have is hearsay evidence. It's not admissible in court. But please don't share what you just told us with anyone."

"It's important to our investigation, and we want to keep you safe," Zave added.

I couldn't help but think that it's very possible Roan killed

Deondre to cover his tracks. Once Deondre turned him down, Roan had a loose end. By killing Deondre, he would have eliminated the possibility that anyone could testify Roan had offered the hit to him.

7:05 P.M.

WE RETURNED TO ZAVE'S TRUCK, and I told him, "Roan is living with Catania Turrisi. He's probably a made guy."

"Holy shit."

"We need to forget about Latrice. We can't give her name to anyone."

"Yeah," Zave agreed. "We never mention Latrice's name again. They'd kill her if they knew what she told us. I would have handled that differently if I had known what you knew." Zave considered, "Okay. If it's an insurance thing, then Tug Grant's behind it."

Playing devil's advocate, I suggested, "Or, it's all Roan, and he's covering his ass. By telling Deondre it's about insurance, he makes it look like he's working for Tug. It could be a well-thought-out setup. Caruso looks like a thug, but he got a full ride in college because he was a math prodigy."

"He murdered Deondre in cold blood." Zave said with frustration, "It was completely unnecessary. I once heard Roan tell his underlings, 'There are two opinions, mine and wrong.'"

"I'm always up for a challenge. I'm no Einstein, but I like his quote: 'It's not that I'm smart. I just stay with questions longer.' Persistence trumps cleverness."

24

HALLE DAY

8:35 A.M. SUNDAY, NOVEMBER 24, 2019
PIERCE STREET NORTHEAST, BELTRAMI, MINNEAPOLIS

I dragged myself out of bed and slipped on some sweats. I pulled my hair into a ponytail and brushed my teeth. It was so weird staying at Dad's house, but I wanted to get to know him.

Roan and Catania were at the breakfast table when I entered the kitchen. Catania got up and kissed Roan on the head. She told him, "I've got a meeting," and left. Cat said nothing to me. She maintained her maiden name, Turrisi, out of respect for her father, so she should understand my desire to know mine.

Dad handed me a plate of eggs. "I'm proud of you, Halle. My daughter has a graduate degree. Do they call you 'Doctor'?"

"No, I have a master's in clinical psychology."

"Why be a therapist after all you've been through?"

"That's exactly why. I needed to understand all I've been through."

"Diagnose me," Roan challenged.

"We don't diagnose family."

"Sure, you do," he laughed. "You just don't tell 'em."

I hesitated and said, "Imposter syndrome. Even though you were a math prodigy, and you know more than most of your counterparts, you question if you belong. It happens to most people who come out of poverty."

"Yeah, that's bullshit."

A piece of toast smothered in butter sat on a plate. I asked, "Can I have it?"

"That's why it's there." Roan took a sip of coffee. "I don't know how you can forgive your uncle for trying to kill you."

"Forgiveness is freeing. My childhood was so crazy. I had to step away from it. Cut all the apron strings. Grandpa August was angry and scary, and my brother Blake was becoming just like him."

"Blake wasn't your brother," Roan interrupted. "You have one brother, my son Lorenzo."

"Blake was my brother when he died, and I'll always refer to him that way. It wasn't until after the murders that I found out the people I thought were my parents weren't. Instead, the person who I thought was my sister was my mother. That was good news because I loved Beth. And my mom was still alive. It doesn't diminish Grandma's death, but there's something about still having Mom around. And then Beth raised me. I couldn't have asked for a better mom. But anytime I asked about you, she'd tell me I had to forget about you—you're a gangster."

"It's like I was telling you last night. That's just parental alienation bullshit—to keep me away." Roan put his hand on mine for a moment. "Let me tell you something. Regardless of what she thinks about me, I'm not bad-mouthin' your mom. I wanted to parent you, but Beth's parents shut me out. If I would have raised a stink over it, I could have got your mom charged with Criminal Sexual Conduct for having sex with me. Beth was sixteen, and I was fourteen. She was a little more than two years older than me, and the law says more than two years' difference for juvies is statutory rape. But I'm not about the letter of the law. I'm about what's right. I was fourteen going on twenty-five, and I was the one who pressured her to have sex. Beth was a naïve farm girl stuck in St. Paul for the summer without friends."

I appreciated Dad taking responsibility for his behavior, but it didn't answer all my concerns. "People say you killed Deondre Smith. Why? What do you have going with the Disciples?"

"First of all, I wasn't the only one who wanted Deondre dead." Roan leaned back in his chair. "I have the right to defend my property. If you're going to take something important to me, you better understand that it might cost you your life. Natural consequences."

I wasn't sure how to respond to that. "It bothers me that every time you refer to Blacks, you talk about criminals. The vast majority of African Americans in Minneapolis are decent, law-abiding citizens who want their children to be safe and have an opportunity to be successful."

"I know," Roan nodded. "But they aren't the people I do business with. And I'm not just talking about Blacks; I've dealt with the worst of every race. The whites were no better."

I offered, "Mom says people think the Italian mafia died with Scarface, but the 'Ndrangheta Mafia, out of Calabria, Italy, is still one of the most powerful distributors of illegal drugs in the world."

Roan stood up and, with his back to me, poured his coffee into a throwaway cup. "I wouldn't know about that. That's all in my past now. Today, I manage wind energy contracts—trying to save the only planet that has beer."

"Honestly? If that's true, it's great!"

"It's true." Dad grinned. "And thank you, Halle, for giving me the benefit of the doubt!"

"Okay." I was still confused. "But how does that work when Catania is clearly connected?"

"Cat runs a restaurant and takes advantage of the hype. Why deny it when people will swarm to mob-owned Italian restaurants?"

"But wouldn't a restaurant be an easy venue to launder money?"

"I wouldn't say *easy*," Roan laughed. "Just kidding—you've been listening to your mom too much. I'm tryin' to be a good man. Despite being a consigliere for the Minneapolis Combination, I don't hang out in strip clubs or spend time with sex workers. I'm a faithful, straight-up guy, and I want to be a good dad." He bent down and kissed my forehead. "Okay, get settled into your room. I've got to pick your brother up from the airport. You finally get to meet him in person. Lorenzo lives here, but honestly, he isn't here much—between vacations and time with Aurora."

My brother, Lorenzo Turissi Caruso, is twenty-three and engaged, and about to return from a trip with friends to Miami Beach. I'm twenty-eight, single, and childless. "As soon as I find a house, I'm gone," I warned. The house I was renting had been sold, so we would be one big, happy family for the time being.

I hugged my big, strong father and, after he left, watched his black Cadillac cruise away. Roan was so self-assured. I'd heard rumors that he could be mean, but I'd never seen it. His only criminal conviction was for a theft charge. He asked me for the benefit of the doubt, and I gave it to him.

I went to my room, turned up the volume on my metallic red UE Boom speaker, started streaming music, and began unpacking. The speaker has a "+" with a perpendicular "–" right below it for volume. Mom assumed the design was a Christian cross, and I didn't have the heart to tell her differently. This way, she never minds when I have it on.

"Ahhh!" I shrieked when I saw Catania standing in the doorway. I apologized, "I'm sorry if I was making too much noise. I didn't know you were home."

Cat leaned on the door frame and smiled. "This used to be Lorenzo's game room. I hope he's going to be okay with you ending up with the bigger of the two rooms."

"Should I wait before I unpack?"

Cat waved dismissively, "If your dad says you can have it, it's yours. Don't get too comfortable, though; it will ultimately be a playroom for Lorenzo's kids."

"I didn't realize Lorenzo had kids."

"He doesn't yet. That's down the road."

"What does Lorenzo do for a living?"

"He works for me. Enough with the questions. You wearing a wire?"

"No." That was an odd question. "I would never do that—" Before I finished, Cat was gone.

11:00 A.M., FIVE WATT COFFEE
861 EAST HENNEPIN AVENUE, BELTRAMI
NEIGHBORHOOD, MINNEAPOLIS

I DECIDED TO TAKE A break and visit one of my favorite coffee shops. I ordered a "Pollinator," an espresso made with honey lavender syrup and cardamom bitters. I took a sip and considered calling Mom. She must be torqued knowing I've moved in with Dad. But she loved him once, so why can't I?

I watched a young Black man digging in his pocket at the counter. It saddened me for a moment because he had the smooth, boyish facial features of Amir Locke, a twenty-two-year-old who was "accidentally" killed during a no-knock police raid, ironically on 2/2/22. Amir was an aspiring musician with an enchanting gleam in his eyes. I brushed away the thought and focused on the clean-shaven man.

"I can't believe I don't have my billfold," he muttered. With an animated grin, he opened his hands in retreat. "Sorry. Don't mind me."

The barista asked, "No coffee?"

"I'll buy," I stood up and offered. I told the billfold-less man, "You look like you're having a rough day."

Still beaming, he turned to me, "Thank you. I was in a hurry—I will pay you back. I cook, and I work long hours. I make the best pho."

"You can make pho?" I questioned.

"That seems a little racially insensitive."

I wasn't sure if he was serious, but I quickly apologized, "I'm sorry. I just meant—I don't know any white people who make pho. I assumed you wouldn't know any—" I stopped before I dug myself in deeper. "I'm sorry."

"Black people can't make pho?" he snapped. "Or don't you like pho?"

"I love pho."

"Of course you love pho. It's delicious, unlike that lutefisk your Nordic ancestors soak in lye."

"I was trying to be nice. By the way, lutefisk is more of an American Norwegian Christmas thing. Norwegians prefer fresh fish."

He busted out laughing, "I'm just yankin' your chain, woman. I learned to make pho from my grandma."

"Well, see, I'm wrong."

With a grin, he said, "My grandpa Ron brought my grandma Hanh back from Khe Sahn after the Vietnam War. And that's a fact, Jack! It takes about sixteen hours to get the broth perfect."

Now I was laughing. "Ron and Hanh from Khe Sahn? And let me guess, you're Lavon, and your father's Don, or maybe your mother's Dawn?"

"Not even close. I'm Keyshawn."

"And your dad?"

"Fred."

"Mom?"

"Tamika."

"Mmmm, I love the sound of her name." I set a ten-dollar bill on the counter and said, "Get this man whatever he's drinking. But if you throw in any extra espresso shots, you're responsible for him."

"Do you mind if I sit with you?" Keyshawn asked.

"I feel like you really should at this point. Although I should warn you, it's all insanity in my family, and I'm a therapist."

"Just what I need," he teased. "I'm a sous chef. Not a Native Sioux chef, and not a transgendered chef named Sue. Just your run-of-the-mill second-in-command in the kitchen. But someday, I'm going to have my own restaurant." He raised his hands as if he was pointing to a sign. "Friend or Pho. Interracial fusion."

"I love it! Now you have to sit and tell me more."

After hearing the intended menu and design of his future Minneapolis restaurant, Keyshawn stopped himself and said, "Tell me about your insane family."

I nervously moved my cup in a slow circle in front of me. It was safest to start with the oldest. "For the first eight years of my life, I thought my mother, Beth, was my oldest sister. But when I reached age eight, Beth was an adult, and she took me in." I hesitated, uncertain how much more I should share. I could feel my eyes well up for a second, as they always do when I think about that night. Wabasha County Child Protection said I would be in their custody when I was released from the hospital. Beth announced she was my mother, and I was going with her. At first, I thought she was lying. I went with it because I wanted to stay with my sister. But once she got me to my new home, Beth explained to me it was true. Breaking my trance, I told Keyshawn, "Beth is great, but she vigilantly warns me of potential dangers. Mom is like having a guard tower looming over you."

"Why was your mom so overprotective of you?"

Instead of answering, I powered on as if I hadn't heard the question. "I have a sister/aunt, Misty, who is a great dater. She's dated some of the nicest women I've ever met, but she always pulls away after a couple of years. I've stopped thinking her next partner is 'the one' and instead see her as simply 'the next one.' Misty has always been kind to me." I took a sip of my warm beverage. "I'm the only child in the next generation, and I was conceived when my mom was sixteen."

"Next?"

"There's my former brother, Mike, now my uncle, who intentionally married a woman who can't have children. He didn't want to chance even an accident. Mike is only married on weekends."

"How does he pull that off?" Keyshawn laughed.

"Like I said, everyone in my family is certifiable. Mike is a workaholic, so his wife divorced him. A few years alone left him miserable, so he offered to pay her to be his wife on weekends, and she accepted. After a few years of that, they remarried with the understanding Mike works day and night, Monday through Thursday. But when he gets off work on Friday at 5:00 p.m. until Monday at 7:00 a.m., he doesn't work. They're alone for four and a half days a week, other than sleeping in the same bed, but friends and lovers on weekends. And they're happy."

With concern, Keyshawn questioned, "What was the tragedy?"

I'd given away more than intended. On a roll, I decided to put it all out there. "There were two more kids. Ricky shot and killed my brother Blake and my grandparents when I was eight. That's why Beth took over parenting me. I pulled up my sleeve and showed him the scar from a bullet wound on my arm. "He shot me, too, but I survived."

Keyshawn rubbed his eyes. "I'm sorry."

"Me, too. Ricky was recently released from prison."

"Are you worried?"

"No. Not at all. Ricky was an immature kid when it happened, and Grandpa incessantly bullied him. Ricky has turned his life over to Jesus and helps people every waking hour. Like I said, it's all insane. I think I'm only telling you because I'll never see you again."

"Why won't you see me again?"

Now I smiled. "Keyshawn, I'd love to see you again, but after hearing this, I imagine you're running for the hills."

"I'm not. I shared my dream with you, and you never rained on it. Not one drop." He reached over and squeezed my hand. "I intend to pay you back by buying the coffee the next time we meet."

"I'm thirty years old." Following my mother's advice, I've been super careful with relationships. I'm almost twice the age she was when she became pregnant with me, and I'm still hoping to be a mother myself someday.

"I'm not sure what that means. Is that a problem?"

"No, not for me. I wanted you to know in case it was a problem for you."

"I'm twenty-five," Keyshawn smiled. "Are odd numbers a problem for you?"

"I thought maybe you were younger." I liked this guy. "Are you single?"

"Yes."

Keyshawn just made my day. "I am, too."

25

JON FREDERICK

8:30 A.M., MONDAY, NOVEMBER 25, 2019
HENNEPIN COUNTY SHERIFF'S DEPARTMENT
350 SOUTH 5TH STREET, GATEWAY
DISTRICT, MINNEAPOLIS

Zave Williams introduced me to law enforcement staff at the sheriff's department as someone who had worked for the BCA, which was true. I was allowed to sit behind the mirror and watch Zave interview Dick Doden.

Dick had scraggly black hair and a smooth baby face. He was husky, and I could easily picture him gaming online day and night. Dick wore a dark green jail jumpsuit, and he nervously rubbed his nose as he gazed at the floor.

Zave was seated with his back to me.

Next to him sat Hennepin County Attorney Bridget Bare. Her long chestnut hair was turning silver, flowing down her back like a cascading waterfall. In an angry tone, Bridget told Dick, "We know you killed Debra Grant. We have your DNA on the knife and her body. We have your fingerprints on the murder weapon. We have proof beyond a shadow of a doubt that you killed her. I want to know why."

Dick glanced up. "What kind of deal are you offering?"

Bridget laid pictures on the table in front of Dick and stated, "There will be no deal. You brutally beat this poor woman to death. You stabbed her fifty times. Debra Grant was a pillar of the community. A great mother who helped with fundraisers and was a Scout leader. The best you can possibly do is cooperate and hope the judge takes this into consideration at your sentencing."

Dick scratched his neck. "It wasn't supposed to go down like that. I was just supposed to knock her out and drown her. But she came to and fought like a fucking banshee. And then my gun jammed, and everything went to shit. It was a brawl that wouldn't end."

"Why?" Bridget tapped a picture. "Why did you kill her?"

"$10,000. I needed the money," Dick mumbled.

Zave cleared his throat, "Who paid you $10,000?"

"He said to make it look like an accident, but she wasn't havin' that. I don't think the guy who gave me the cash set this up. I think it was Tug," said Dick.

Behind the mirror, I rubbed my forehead.

Bridget softened her tone as she asked, "Did you ever meet with Tug?"

"No."

She continued, "Did you ever talk to Tug on the phone?"

"No."

Bridget tried one more time, "Did you ever have any contact with Tug anywhere? Think hard."

"No."

Zave asked, "Did the man who paid you ever mention Tug?"

"Never," said Dick.

"How did you know where to go? Who to kill?" Zave pressed.

"He gave me her picture and her address."

"Do you still have them?" Zave asked.

"No. I called and told him it was done, but he wasn't gonna like it. He told me to destroy everything, so I did."

Bridget asked, "Do you have the phone?"

"No. It was a burner phone. I threw it off the Mississippi bridge."

Zave repeated, "Why do you think Tug hired you?"

"I was told to go to the Grants' house at 5:00 a.m., and the back door should be open. Wait in the basement until 8:30. The phone will ring at 8:30. She'll answer it in the kitchen. Then, step out of the basement. The back door was open at 5:00. The call came at 8:30. Who else but Tug could control that?"

I couldn't help thinking, *What if Roan took a house key during his visit days before and returned early the next morning and opened the door for Dick?* There was no explanation for Roan's visit. Tug wasn't even aware of it. Roan may know that Tug always calls at 8:30.

Zave asked, "Why would anyone want Debra Grant dead?"

Dick looked directly at Zave. "I asked him, 'What did she do?' The guy seemed to get a little sad about it, and then he said, 'nothin'. She didn't do nothin'.' And I wasn't gonna do it, but I didn't have any money, and $10,000 is a lot of money. He said someone was going to kill her, but he couldn't do it."

Bridget demanded, "Who paid you?"

Dick stopped. "I'll call an attorney tomorrow, and then we'll talk again. You sure you can't make some kinda deal?"

Irritated, Bridget told him, "Positive. Your only hope of ever seeing the light of day again is turning state's evidence. I wouldn't take too long. Somebody's going to realize you're a loose end."

26

WESLEY "DREADS" WASHINGTON

10:45 P.M., MONDAY, NOVEMBER 25, 2019
1249 FREMONT AVENUE, NEAR NORTH, MINNEAPOLIS

I sat on the front steps, waiting for the boys to stop over. The three teens, Jamarcus, Montrel, and Ahmad, pulled up in a gunmetal gray Toyota Rav 4.

Jamarcus stepped out and was immediately ragin', "This is bullshit. Caruso killed Deondre, and he's rubbin' it in our face. By not respondin' we look weak."

Montrel joined in, "I can't sit and watch my sister cry day after day and not do a damn thing. You gotta give us the go-ahead."

I turned to Jamarcus, the most athletic member of the crew. "What do you think?"

He spat, "I'm doin' this with or without your permission."

"How old are you?" I asked.

"Sixteen this year," Jamarcus bragged.

I turned to Montrel, "And you?"

"Nineteen."

I asked the kid with them, "And what are you, seventeen?"

"Almost," Ahmad quickly replied.

"Almost what? Don't lie to me," I threatened.

"Almost fourteen," the boy sheepishly responded.

Stupid kid.

"He can drive," Montrel interjected.

"Montrel, I know you want to shoot, but you should drive if you want to get out alive." Montrel was the most experienced behind the wheel. I continued, "I'd lose the kid. A boy should get laid before he gets buried."

"Awright," Montrel said appeasingly.

I turned to Ahmad. "You look at Montrel and Jamarcus, and you think these cats were doing this at your age. What you don't see is the brothers we buried—just as tough as you. This isn't a zero-sum game. The graveyard and prisons are full of losers."

"Deondre was our brother," Ahmad responded.

I thought about it for a hot minute. "I can't give you permission, but I'm not standin' in your way. Fox told me there won't be any blowback on you from the Disciples. But we never talk about this again, and you never spoke to me. I don't care if the Italians torture you to death. If you ever mention my name with this, I'm comin' after you and your family. We good?"

They nodded in agreement.

"You got his address?" I asked.

"Yeah. I drive by it every night." Montrel said.

"What do you got for firepower?"

"Hella dope," Montrel responded. "Automatics."

I had scouted out revenge for the killing of my friend Deondre, waiting for a go-ahead from our governor, Fox, which never came. "The front of the house is three bedrooms. Roan and Catania entertain in the backyard, so you walk into the dining area and living room from the back. The master bedroom is the window to the far left as you face the house.

He and his wife don't always sleep together. There's a spare bedroom next to it where Catania goes when she can't sleep. Focus on the master bedroom."

They nodded in unison.

I reminded them, "No music. If they hear you comin', you're the ones gettin' buried. I stood up. "There's no order for this. It's on you. Don't call me. Don't text." I sighed. "Abscond, brothers."

I watched as Montrel got in the driver's seat, and the three boys cruised away. I needed to report to Fox, so I got in my car and followed.

11:10 P.M.
PIERCE STREET NORTHEAST, BELTRAMI, MINNEAPOLIS

WHEN THEY TURNED EAST ON Broadway, I knew this was happening. They turned right on Filmore, right on Spring, and pulled over. With lights off, I watched from a distance. They switched drivers. What they don't understand is that shooting is the easy part. Knowing when to bail is how you survive. The Rav-4 continued on its way, and they rolled up on Pierce Street.

They were now sitting directly in front of a one-story Tudor-style rose brick house. The car windows rolled down. The king of his castle was about to be assassinated.

A curtain was pulled back in the middle room.

The boys immediately peppered that window with their automatics. Dammit! I told them to target the master bedroom. Slaughtering innocent people just keeps the war goin'.

The window-peeper was dead for damn sure. Shards of glass showered from the windows. When they rolled to the master bedroom, I could see a flash coming from the middle room. Someone was still alive and was firing back.

Lights were coming on in the neighborhood. People had to be calling the cops. I gunned it and got the hell out of there.

27

ROAN CARUSO

11:18 P.M. MONDAY, NOVEMBER 25, 2019
PIERCE STREET NORTHEAST, BELTRAMI, MINNEAPOLIS

Catania lay beside me in a red silk nightgown, reading *Burning Bridges.* She set her reading glasses on the nightstand and turned to me, "Never trust a whore." Both 'never' and whore' seemed to be absent of 'r's. She added, "That's the lesson here."

I heard a low hum and leaned forward. *Was a car cruisin' up the block?*

Cat placed her hand on my chest. "Don't be so damn paranoid. Let me check."

Before she was out of bed, bullets from an automatic weapon rained into our house. I realized the shots had started with the room next to ours but soon were pelting our bedroom. The glass shards from our window seemed to drop in unison, like a chandelier crashing, onto the maple floor.

I rolled Cat out of bed underneath me and told her, "Stay below the window. Our house is brick. They can't hurt you unless you get above the window ledge."

"Check on Lorenzo," she ordered.

I quickly crawled to the next bedroom. I hoped to hell Halle wasn't hit.

Lorenzo was standing in the dark, firing a gun out of the shattered window. I ran at him and tackled him, yelling, "Stay down!"

Lorenzo turned to me on the floor and said, "She's dead, Dad. She went to the window, right before the shooting started."

The streetlight shining through the window revealed blood on his shirt. "Are you okay?"

"Yeah."

Now I wanted to cry. My girl had survived a mass murder attempt only to be slaughtered in my own home. "Give me that fucking gun." I tore it from his hand. I stood up and fired at the car.

The shooters were focused on the master bedroom, which allowed me to fire unopposed.

I continued to fire at the escaping killers until the magazine was empty. I felt a deep sense of anguish as I watched the car pull away.

When I looked down, I saw that Lorenzo was calling 911.

Catania crawled into the room.

When Lorenzo hung up, he turned to me and said, "I think I hit one of' 'em, Dad. One of the shooters stopped firing."

I saw the bullet-riddled body of a young woman in an oversized T-shirt lying face down on the floor, her long, tanned legs protruding from the shirt. I told Lorenzo, "You're going to tell the police you fired a warning shot in the air to get them to leave, and I took the gun from you and fired at the car." I bent down and turned the girl face up.

Lorenzo stood, and Cat rushed to him and hugged him. "Thank God you're okay."

Still in shock, Lorenzo told her, "They killed Aurora. She was pregnant."

I was relieved it wasn't my daughter. Aurora wasn't my responsibility until she married my son. But this didn't mean Halle was okay. I ran to the next bedroom.

Halle was huddled on the floor, shaking. She was on the phone whispering, "Mom, you have to come and get me."

"You okay?" I placed my hand on her back to comfort her and felt her rapid breathing.

"I haven't been shot," she said.

I felt relieved, only to have Cat come in and confront her, "What are you doing in Lorenzo's bedroom?"

Halle lowered the phone. "Lorenzo wanted the bigger bedroom."

Cat screamed, "Aurora and the baby would still be alive if you wouldn't have been here!"

I went to Cat and hugged her. "Hey, it's not her fault. She's leaving, and I anticipate I'll be spending the night in jail. Make Lorenzo stick to the story."

Cat squeezed me, then stepped back and wiped her eyes. "I love you, Roan. It means everything to me that you're being a stand-up guy here. And I hope you killed one of 'em."

I heard sirens closing in on our house and returned to Lorenzo.

He was kneeling over Aurora's body. He turned to me. "I can't let you take responsibility for what I did."

I went to him, knelt by him, and gave him a hug. "Admitting what you did won't absolve me. They want me. There's no point in surrendering yourself, too. It won't lessen my sentence. Let me do this. You'd do it for your son."

He nodded. "It was self-defense."

"Yeah. I'll get ahold of Tug. He'll help me out.

28

JON FREDERICK

11:40 P.M. MONDAY, NOVEMBER 25, 2019
HENNEPIN COUNTY SHERIFF'S DEPARTMENT
350 SOUTH 5TH STREET, GATEWAY
DISTRICT, MINNEAPOLIS

Zave had called me back to the Hennepin County Jail. He held the door open for me as I entered and said, "We have an opportunity here, and I'm open to your thoughts. My colleagues are all busy as hell, and I feel like I'm too young to be doing this without feedback."

I didn't mind offering some advice. I asked, "What do you have?"

"There was a drive-by at the Caruso home tonight. Roan appears to have been the target, but he survived. His son's fiancée was killed. Roan returned fire and killed nineteen-year-old Montrel Johnson. A fifteen-year-old is in the hospital, and a thirteen-year-old is in custody. I'm making Roan spend the night in jail. I'm going back at Dick Doden, hoping he'll implicate him. I can't tell him I know Roan paid him, but if I could let him know Roan is here in jail, I think Dick would give him up."

"Simply state Caruso is here. Let him give you the rest."

Behind the one-way glass, I watched Zave sit down with Dick Doden.

"What now?" Dick asked angrily.

Zave stood over him. "We're bringing Roan Caruso in on a homicide charge, and there's a good possibility he will be placed in your cellblock. You already lawyered up, so we can't ask you questions, but I thought I'd let you know." Zave stood and turned to leave.

"Wait." Surprised, Dick said, "How did you know? Only Roan and I knew."

"This is simply a news brief," Zave remarked.

"I don't need to talk to my attorney. I'm declining the offer of an attorney."

"Do you have something you want to tell me?"

"You can't put me in the same cell block with Roan. He'll kill me."

"You need to give me a reason for preferential treatment. If you don't, you're on your own."

"Alright, Roan Caruso paid me $10,000 to kill Debra Grant. Roan gave me the gun."

"Did the Albanians have anything to do with it?" Zave asked.

"No. The gun was stolen. Roan liked the Albanian flag on it because he thought it could throw off investigators if they found it. I'm not kidding; Roan will kill me. I need protection. Guys like him think nothin' of killing someone to tie up a loose end."

As the interview was wrapping up, I could hear yelling from the hall. It sounded like Tug.

I stepped out of the observation room to see Roan Caruso cuffed and Tug yelling at the sheriff's deputies, "You need to release my client. You can't break into his home and arrest Roan without a warrant."

"He killed a man," The officer said unemotionally.

"Do you have a witness? He hasn't made an admission." Tug challenged the cop.

The officer furrowed his brows and responded, "Two men were shot right in front of his house."

"This was clearly a case of self-defense," Tug argued.

Zave stepped out of the interview room and said, "Roan Caruso, you're under arrest for the murder of Debra Grant."

Roan showed no outward reaction to the directive, as if being accused of murder was just a normal part of his day.

Tug was furious and immediately got in Zave's face. "Release him!"

Zave continued, "Roan, you will need to find another attorney."

"And why's that?" Tug tried to intimidate Zave.

Undeterred, Zave turned directly to Tug. "Because you're next."

As the police escorted Roan away, I grabbed Tug by the arm and pulled him aside. "You can't defend Roan."

"Why not?" Tug argued.

"Step back for a second. Roan's accused of hiring a hitman to kill your wife. How do you think defending him is going to make you look?"

Tug was taken aback. "You're right." He rubbed his forehead. "Yeah. What the hell am I thinking? I'll call Cat and let her know. What evidence do they have?"

"I'm not sure, but I'd recommend getting your affairs in order." I decided not to tell Tug that Dick Doden was in custody. If Dick was assaulted tonight, it would help clarify that the order didn't come from Tug. I assured Tug, "Zave sounded serious. They're coming for you."

29

LINCOLN GRANT

2:40 P.M. SATURDAY, NOVEMBER 30, 2019
CASA MARINA LANE NORTHWEST, ALEXANDRIA

I had spent Thanksgiving with my maternal grandparents. I didn't think I'd ever say this, but I miss my sisters. This has been a weird month. It's hard to believe Mom was alive three weeks ago. We've always been the quiet kids in school who didn't get invited to much, but we had each other. Mom taught us to be humble and respectful. Dad was the celebrity in the family. Since Mom's death, my sisters and I have been invited everywhere. Our newfound "friends" parents would pump us for inside information, hoping to be the sleuth who broke the case.

Today, Dad and I went to our cabin on Lake Darling, where Mom used to take us when Dad had to work weekends in Brainerd. Dad had to leave and take care of some business, so I called Kailee, a girl I met at Arrowhead Resort last summer, and asked her to meet at Zorbaz on the Lake to share some "Macho Nachoz." This would be my very first date.

Without a ride but determined to make the date, I biked the icy roads to Zorbaz, and man, was it worth it! Kailee was sweet and funny. Strawberry blonde hair with freckles and blue eyes. She thought her front teeth were a little too far apart, but she was a goddess. I went from being so nervous I wanted to puke to enjoying the most meaningful conversation I'd ever had. When I talked about Mom, she put her hand on mine to comfort me. It felt like a warm blanket. Time went so fast. I was excited and had butterflies in my stomach. *Is this what love feels like?*

5:45 P.M.

I WAS EXCITED AND KNEW Dad had to be wondering where I was. I pedaled home as fast as I could. When I came around a corner, my bike hit a patch of ice and slid out from under me. I pressed my arm against the tar to protect my head and felt my stomach burn as I slid. When I came to a stop, I was initially worried, but after realizing I had no broken bones, I laughed. I will always remember my first date. I had road rash on my arms and stomach. When I picked up the bike, I could see the front wheel was bent and no longer rideable. I held up the front end and began the long walk home. It was still worth it!

6:30 P.M.
CASA MARINA LANE NORTHWEST, ALEXANDRIA

DAD STOOD STERN AND STRONG as he waited at the door. He watched me walk my bike up the driveway and grumbled, "Where were you?"

I was in trouble and prayed for understanding. I took a deep breath and said, "I was biking home from Zorbaz, and I slid on some ice." I lifted my shirt and showed him the large blood-red scrape across my stomach.

Dad winced and said, "For God's sake, why were you out biking in the dark?"

"I had a date and I didn't have a ride." His hardened face seemed to soften, so I continued, "It was our first, so I couldn't cancel."

Dad started laughing, "Well, now that makes perfect sense." He put his hand on my shoulder. "Get in the shower and rinse off the gravel. I'll put some Neosporin on it."

"Okay." I appreciated his understanding. It was as close as we'd ever been.

"Do you need something to eat?"

"I ate, but I could eat again."

"Get cleaned up, and I'll throw in a pizza."

9:40 P.M.

DAD AND I WATCHED *AVENGERS: Endgame* tonight. He had to step out to take a few calls, but it was a good night. Dad told me to pay attention to small cues that indicate my girl's likes and dislikes. It will separate me from the other guys who express interest in her. The Neosporin on my road rash burned and itched like crazy, so I couldn't sleep. But Kailee; what a girl! Her parents might be gone tomorrow. If they are, she wants me to stop over. If I have to walk through a blizzard, I'll be there.

Suddenly, my curtains lit up with flashing lights. I heard cars crunching onto the frozen tundra of our driveway. When I peeked out the window, I saw squad cars. They hadn't turned the sirens on, but their presence would soon be known by all the neighbors.

Dad came into my room. He was bothered but, in his cool manner, told me, "Get dressed. You're going to Otto and Greta's. It's a chance for you to spend some time with your sisters. I'll be home in a couple of days."

I could hear the police knocking on the door. "Tilmore Grant. We have a warrant for your arrest."

"Why would they arrest you?" I asked.

He dismissed my concern. "It's just something they do after a spouse is killed. They need to rule me out as a suspect. Ignore the gossip. Don't worry about it. It'll all be okay."

He told the officers, "You don't need to cuff me," and they were fine with walking out with him. Dad wasn't as mad as I was. We were finally making a connection. They can't separate us now. When I looked at Dad, it just seemed to be one more court formality he was dealing with.

An officer agreed to stay with me until Grandpa Otto arrived. The officer led me into the living room and turned ESPN on the TV. Mom used to tell me, "We talk about sports because there are too many things in life that are too hard to talk about. And that's okay." I miss Mom. When I was with Mom, I felt safe. I knew what was going to happen next. Now, everything is so uncertain.

I needed to think about what I was going to tell Kailee. She would hear about what happened here tonight.

11:30 A.M. SUNDAY, DECEMBER 1, 2019
ROME AVENUE, HIGHLAND PARK, ST. PAUL

THE MINNESOTA VIKINGS DIDN'T PLAY today because they were playing the Seahawks on Monday night football. Grandpa Otto and I sat at the table and worked on putting together an old model plane of his.

My sister, Rebecca, approached us with tears in her eyes, and Grandpa hugged her. He told her, "Hon, it will all be okay by the time you get married." Rebecca loved animals, was a bit of a teacher's pet, and was once annoyingly self-assured. It bothered me to see her so beat down.

"What are you talking about?" I wondered.

"I was supposed to go to a birthday party tomorrow, but now they don't want me there," Rebecca said.

"Why not?" I asked.

"Because of Dad," she whined.

"But Dad didn't do anything," I argued.

Grandpa held Rebecca, who was now limp, and told us, "This is just how it's going to be for a bit. I'm sorry."

I wanted the annoying Rebecca back. I wanted my old life with Mom.

Grandma Greta came into the room and, frustrated, told Grandpa, "That's the third call today. These people are ridiculous. None of these girls did anything wrong. They're not responsible for Tug's behavior. How can they be so cruel?"

It was clear Grandma was blaming Dad for her daughter's death. My phone was buzzing in my pocket. Maybe it was Dad with some good news. When I pulled it out, I saw I had a text from Kailee. It read, "My Dad says I can't talk to you anymore. Please delete my number from your phone. I can't respond."

I was outraged. It wasn't fair! People are supposed to be innocent until proven guilty. Even if he was guilty, we hardly even knew our dad. He was never home. When they named Tug Grant the youngest head of the bar association, Mpls. St.Paul Magazine stopped over and took a picture of Dad throwing me a football. It was the only time he ever did.

We had gone from being kids people barely noticed in school to celebrities to kids people purposely avoided. It would have been better to have never been popular. From now on, all we had was each other. I could feel a tear trickling down my cheek.

With his free arm, Grandpa pulled me into his hug with Rebecca. "We've taken some hits, but we're not defeated. One day, they'll regret how they handled this, but we won't. Your grandma and I couldn't love you more, and we're going to respond with kindness and love." He turned and gave Grandma Greta a wink, "And ice cream."

Grandma scoffed, "It's still morning."

Grandpa said, "Time means nothing to ice cream."

Grandma shook her head and went to the freezer.

My grandfather was a great man. He was the first adult who made it clear to me and my sisters that he was going through this with us and would be at our side every step of the way.

30

HALLE DAY

1:30 A.M. MONDAY, DECEMBER 2, 2019
LAKE OF THE ISLES, CALHOUN ISLES, MINNEAPOLIS

That damn drive-by. I was five years nightmare-free before the shooting. It was dark, and I was lying in bed. My body was shaking with cold sweat for the sixth night in a row. Dammit! Please, God, just let me sleep. I slid out of bed and peeked out the window, hiding my body behind the curtain. No one was outside. The crescent moon was waxing, getting a little bigger each night. I'm in the waxing phase myself, mostly because of nervous snacking. On the plus side, the nightmares weren't as bad tonight. I didn't see my dead family lying beside me in the basement.

I was staying with Mom for the time being. She entered the bedroom, shooed me back into bed, and sat beside me. Mom left for a minute, then returned and pressed a warm, wet washcloth against my forehead. *It felt so good.* She used to do this when I was little. Why did my life have to blow up? I had been working for a clinic, renting a house, and had my girlfriends. Well, I still have my friends. They are my rock. The clinic went belly up because the collections department was screwed over by insurance companies who were always trying to find ways to avoid paying for services. The home I was renting had been sold. I was developing a relationship with my father, which almost got me killed, and now I'm back living with Mom, who thinks she needs to protect me like a one-woman army. Dad's in jail, charged with hiring a man to kill his attorney's wife. My brother's fiancé and baby were just murdered. I can't sleep. My mass killer of an uncle might be the most normal person in the family at this point.

Beth said softly, "It's going to be okay. You're safe with me now."

"Thanks." I lay on my side facing her and put my arm around her in a hug in appreciation for her kindness. "I'll talk to Liz tomorrow." One of my old colleagues is a trauma therapist. One of the nice things about being a therapist is knowing the right therapists to talk to.

"That's a good idea." Mom bent down and kissed my forehead. "What are you going to do if Roan gets out of jail?"

I didn't want to decide tonight, and I didn't want to argue with Mom, so I closed my eyes and pretended I was falling asleep.

"Well?" she repeated.

Eyes closed, I rambled, "Buy a beret and an AK-47. Hang with Dad and my homie—Catania. Spend some time at the shooting range firing bullets into the berm."

"That's not funny." Mom shook me.

I thought it was, but I reassured her, "I'm staying with you until I can get a decent night's sleep. I don't know what I'm going to do about Dad."

Beth was comforted and, in a loving mother's tone, whispered, "Okay. I'll stay here until you fall asleep, Honey."

"I'm sorry this is happening again, Mom. I know it's hard on you." I patted the bed behind me.

"You know the drill."

With a smile, Mom laid in bed next to me. I know she needed to be comforted, too. While she scratched my back, I pictured Keyshawn Harris lying in bed in his boxers, processing his pending menu. Maybe one day, we'll be together, sharing our dreams. I told Mom, "I'm going to look for a house, and I'm thinking of starting my own private clinic." I'll be happy again, hopefully with Keyshawn. I just need to get through right now.

31

RICHARD DAY

8:00 P.M. WEDNESDAY, DECEMBER 4, 2019
OAKLAND AVENUE, PHILLIPS, MINNEAPOLIS

I'm renting the basement of a home owned by an elderly woman I met at St. Mary's Basilica. Mrs. Benjamin told me she was terrified of living on her own in Phillips, and I told her I was looking for a place. I wanted her to know my history first. Her response was, "Well, you'd be as likely to kill an intruder as anybody," and she asked me to move in. Her only conditions were that I fed her cats daily and that my rent was on time. Phillips is a poor but diverse area. The American Indian Movement was founded in this neighborhood in 1968.

Today, my sister Beth was paying me a visit for the first time in my adulthood. I bought coffee and splurged on a couple of doughnuts. I maintain a simple, humble existence. I waited for Beth at the basement entry door and welcomed her in.

Beth was now in her forties with beige hair instead of the blonde I remembered. I wondered if this happens when blonde women start to gray, but I for damn sure wasn't asking. It's hard looking at someone I love and sensing her deep hatred for me in her cold blue eyes—all justified. Beth was an older version of Halle, although not as happy. Beth sat with me at the small white table by my fridge.

"I'm sorry, Beth. I want you to know that."

She waved off my apology. "That's not why I'm here. Look, I know it was hard with Dad."

"Nothing justifies what I did." I gently patted her hand. "And to go after Mom, and Blake, and your daughter. It was insane. I am so sorry."

Beth swept a strand of her long hair from her face as she said, "Do you believe in fate or divine intervention?"

"I'm a Christian. I wouldn't call it fate, but I believe there are rewards and consequences for how we live."

"I made the mistake of having a baby with a mobster. Roan is going to be the death of Halle. But then I remembered I have you in my life. Maybe there's a reason you were released. I need a favor from you."

"Anything Beth. I'd do anything for you."

She squeezed my hand and said, deadly serious, "Halle was over at Roan Caruso's home when it was shot up. Roan's daughter-in-law was killed. Roan killed one gang member and injured another."

"Michael told me about it. He said she was okay." My brother Michael is the one person who maintained contact with me, even when I was at my worst. He was hard on me but gave me hope.

Beth continued, "She's alive, but she isn't okay. Imagine holding a child who's shivering in terror night after night—for years. And now the nightmares are back. Roan will ruin her. He's going to get her killed. I want you to keep Roan from ever seeing Halle again."

"How am I going to do that?"

"Any way you can, Ricky." Her eyes welled up. "By any means necessary."

"Beth, I'm not going to do anything violent. I'm not that person anymore."

Disappointed, she grumbled, "Sure, when your rage can finally be put to good use, you won't do it. You're still turning your back on your family, Ricky. Everything is always about you."

"Beth, I can't."

She squeezed my hand harder. "Yes, you can. The question is, will you? Will you help me?" Beth stuck a Post-it with an address on it on the table in front of me.

"Roan was arrested." I reminded her.

"I heard he's out on bail." Beth pulled her hand away and walked to the door. "If you don't change your mind, don't ever call me again. You're dead to me." She slammed the door and left.

Am I a Christian only when it doesn't involve suffering? My freedom was unraveling at the seams. Maybe there can be no freedom for someone like me. I decided to act. My life could be over in an hour, and there wasn't anyone I wanted to call. Michael, Misty, and Halle were all kind to me, but honestly, my death would probably provide them with a sense of relief. They all have friends who have stopped visiting since my release out of fear that I might show up. I fed Mrs. Benjamin's cats for the last time. She would find another caretaker for her cat colony.

8:45 P.M.

PIERCE STREET NORTHEAST, BELTRAMI, MINNEAPOLIS

I CAUTIOUSLY APPROACHED ROAN CARUSO'S rose brick house. The front windows were now boarded up. I took a deep breath. I was afraid of dying. Maybe, if I died violently for the benefit of Halle living, I could be forgiven. I wasn't going to hurt anyone. I'd give it the Gran Torino ending. All I had to do was show up, and Roan would attack me. My GPS would put me at his door so the suspect would be obvious. I'd count on him getting arrested and, therefore, being removed from Halle's life.

As I stepped onto the porch, an icicle fell from the roof and broke into pieces, interrupting my thoughts. Jeremiah 29:11 flashed in my head: "For I know the plans I have for you, declares the Lord, plans to prosper you and not to harm you, plans to give you hope and a future." I contemplated retreating. My veneration should be to Jesus, who is loving, rather than to Beth, who desires retribution.

The door swung open, and a young Italian guy in his mid-twenties angrily asked, "What the hell are you doing here?"

I cleared my throat, "I'm here to speak to Roan."

"You got his son, Lorenzo, instead." He punched me in the face and, when I backed up, said, "I know who you are, you piece of shit. You damn near killed my sister Halle." His next punch knocked me to the ground.

I was dazed and saw stars. He continued his attack with a rageful volley of punches. When I fell to the ground, he began kicking me. I covered my head as best I could to prevent brain damage, but a kick to my head blackened my world.

9:15 P.M.,
15TH AVENUE, SOUTH & 6TH STREET SOUTH
CEDAR-RIVERSIDE (WEST BANK), MINNEAPOLIS

I WOKE UP AS I was being dragged out of a car.

I could hear a woman's voice say, "We're not gonna tell Roan about this. He's got enough on his plate. Dump him, and let's get out of here."

I was dropped hard on a cold sidewalk. My head throbbed, and my body ached. The monster was still standing over me.

The woman's voice screamed, "Get in the damn car! We can't have witnesses seeing you kick him again. We have to get home and erase our security footage before law enforcement stops over and confiscates it."

He hesitated for a moment, spat on me, and entered the car from the passenger side.

32

JON FREDERICK

10:00 P.M. WEDNESDAY, DECEMBER 4, 2019
15TH AVENUE SOUTH & 6TH STREET SOUTH
CEDAR-RIVERSIDE (WEST BANK), MINNEAPOLIS

I was about to leave the metro and head back to Pierz when I received a frantic call. "Jon, this is Beth Day. I asked Richard to confront Roan Caruso, and now I can't find him. Please help me. I called his attorney, Tug. He referred me to you."

The obvious question was, "Why?", but not being one to waste time when someone's life is at stake, I asked, "Can I call you back at this number?"

"Yes."

I hung up and called Richard Day's Intensive Supervised Release agent. Richard was wearing an ankle bracelet that can be tracked by an ISR agent 24/7. After I shared the family's concern and that I had seen Roan stalking Day, the agent agreed to call Midwest Monitoring and Surveillance Incorporated (MMS), the company that does the GPS tracking of offenders.

The agent quickly called me back. "The tracking places Day at the homeless encampment on the West Bank. It doesn't appear that he's moved for the last half hour. The address is 15th Avenue and 6th Street. I'll meet you there."

When I arrived at the encampment, I immediately noticed a body lying on the sidewalk. It was only thirty-two degrees, and a brisk chill hung in the air. I found a battered Richard Day quivering, with a dirty army blanket draped over his body.

Richard gave me a pained smile and said, "He gave me a blanket. Can you believe it? That homeless guy gave me his blanket."

I called for an ambulance and, at Richard's request, made sure the blanket was returned.

The ISR agent arrived and told me, "The GPS tracking placed him at Roan Caruso's address right before he ended up here."

"I thought Roan hadn't been released."

"He was supposed to be released, but his bail was revoked after Dick Doden was found badly beaten in jail." Roan hadn't directly pummeled Doden, but it was believed Roan had orchestrated the assault. The ISR agent concluded, "Caruso wasn't released, but his son was home."

11:00 P.M.
HEALTH FAIRVIEW, UNIVERSITY OF
MINNESOTA MEDICAL CENTER
WEST BANK, 2312 6TH STREET,
CEDAR-RIVERSIDE, MINNEAPOLIS

RICHARD'S SURVIVING FAMILY MEMBERS MET me at the hospital. Beth threw her body across Richard, who was now in a hospital bed. He groaned, and she pulled back. "I'm sorry. I'm so sorry. I never should have asked you to talk to Roan."

Halle, who had been standing back, stepped forward, "You asked Uncle Ricky to confront Roan?"

Beth nodded apologetically. "I can't lose you, Halle. I wanted him to get Roan to stay away."

Staying out of their conversation, I told Richard, "We need you to make a statement."

"I won't," he responded. With a forced smile, he added, "Can you believe that guy gave me his blanket?"

Flabbergasted, Halle turned it up a notch with Beth. "Are you out of your mind? Is this what my parents do—anytime you can't get along, you just put a hit out on people? You're all nuts!" Halle rushed out of the hospital room, and I took off after her. I didn't want her frustration with her mom sending her running back to Roan.

"Halle—Halle, please stop and listen for a second."

She paused and slowly turned to face me.

"I know what your mom did was crazy, but understand she loves you. Imagine what you'd do for your child. Roan is dangerous."

"Roan has made some bad choices, but he's trying to turn it around," Halle said. "He's committed his life to wind energy to make the world better. People can change. Look at Uncle Ricky."

I smiled at her naïveté. "Do you understand that wind energy is big business for the mob?"

Bewildered, Halle asked, "What?"

"It is. Nobody really knows how much the projects should cost. They just know the parts are expensive. There are big government contracts and lots of tax credits for investing in renewable energy. Everything the mafia loves."

"Do you believe Roan's into this for Cosa Nostra?"

"I do. Think about it. Roan isn't an engineer. He isn't a wind turbine technician. So, what do you think he does?"

Embarrassed, Halle responded, "I haven't really thought about it."

"He puts pressure on people to steer contracts in a

certain direction for kickbacks. Catania and Roan are in it together. The restaurant doesn't pay for their lifestyle."

Deep in thought, Halle responded, "Thank you for telling me. Mom still shouldn't have sent Uncle Ricky after him."

"I agree."

1:30 A.M. PIERZ

I FINALLY ARRIVED HOME, AND Serena snuggled against me in bed. After I shared everything that happened, Serena commented, "Richard and Tug's lives keep winding around each other, don't they?"

"Not by Richard's choice." I loved the feel of Serena's body covered only by a well-worn T-shirt.

Resting her head on my chest, she asked, "Do you think it's odd that Deb was killed shortly after Richard's release from prison?"

"I'm not sure what to think about it." I was tired, and my brain was fried. "I'm staying home tomorrow if you want to sleep in."

"I'm sorry I didn't get much out of my conversations with Meg. Tug's sister is nice enough. Meg talked about about Tug being ostracized in school. Tug has hyperesthesia, a hypersensitivity to tactile stimuli. Bullies used to tickle Tug until he passed out and throw him in ditch water to revive him. Do you think it's odd Tug had Deb thrown in water? The term 'trauma bond' comes to mind."

"You're assuming Tug had her killed. I'm not sold on that. When is your next hair appointment?"

"Two weeks." She sighed, and we were both done talking about the case. Serena purred, "I'm still not pregnant."

"Do you want to do something about it?"

"Would it help you sleep?" Serena said with a tired smile.

"It seems to help with everything…"

33

SERENA FREDERICK

10:00 A.M. WEDNESDAY, DECEMBER 18, 2019
VOLUME 10 HARNESS ROAD, LITTLE FALLS

It turned out I was pregnant, but I miscarried. Jon took some days off from the investigation and stayed home, which I appreciated. Still, I don't think a man can ever fully understand what a woman goes through. He was kind and caring, but it was my body that went through it. I was expecting to hear his logical comments about how "during embryogenesis, chromosome errors occur, and the embryo can't survive. It's not your fault. The embryo was never wired to survive." Instead, he held me as I cried and told me he loved me over and over—and now I was ready to move on.

My mom can't keep a secret and unfortunately, Mom shared with Nora that I was pregnant and now lost the baby. Jon agreed to talk to Nora about it. He grabbed a bucket of legos and sat with Nora at the kitchen table. Curious to see how he was going to pull this off, I stood off to the side holding Jackson, observing. I would hand Jackson off and clean up the mess if his explanation didn't take.

Jon and Nora started out by randomly putting Lego pieces together exploring possibilities. Finally, he told her, "Let me show you something." He put together pieces with a wide base and asked, "Is this going to fall over?"

"No," Nora said, but knocked it over anyway.

"Babies grow in a mommy's tummy one piece at a time. And sometimes they grow solid like you and me and Mom and Jackson and they stay standing. But sometimes the pieces come together wrong, and they don't make it." Jon built a tower that was larger on top that quickly toppled over on its own." He told her, "With the baby Mom lost, the pieces didn't come together right."

"Why?" Nora wondered.

Jon smiled, "There's millions of ways the pieces can come together. That's why we're all different. And sometimes it just doesn't work. I honestly don't know why. But if we're going to try to have babies, we need to understand that a lot of time it just doesn't work. That's why when it does, we're so happy. It's a miracle."

"Oh." Nora stacked more Legos.

"It's nobody's fault because the pieces stack themselves," Jon continued. "I can't change it. Mom can't change it. You can't change it."

Nora added with certainty, "And Jackson can't change it."

"Not even Jackson can change it." Jon shared.

Nora turned and smiled at Jackson, laughing at the thought of her little brother fixing anything. Nora got serious and asked Jon, "Do you like your job?"

"I do."

"What do you like about it?" Nora questioned.

"I solve problems for a living, and by solving those problems I keep more people from getting hurt."

Nora wrinkled her nose, "But sometimes it makes you mad."

"It does. Because they are often not easy problems to solve. But when I solve them, it feels good." Jon winked at me, "But I know a guy who doesn't like his job at all."

"Is this a dad joke?" Nora grumbled.

"I promise to catch you if you fall over laughing," Jon teased.

"Not happening," Nora replied. "Okay, what did he do for a job."

"He crushed pop cans."

Jon was so patient with silence, but Nora wasn't about to give in, so I intervened. "Pray tell, why didn't he like crushing cans?"

"It was soda pressing." Jon laughed, much louder than the joke deserved.

Nora shook her head but couldn't help smiling. I carried Jackson to Nora and we hugged. I asked, "Are you okay honey?"

"Yeah." Nora asked, "Are you still trying to have a baby?"

"Yes." I kissed her forehead. "I'm going to take a break for a bit and then try again. But if we don't have a baby, I am lucky to have you and Jackson." I decided to tell her I'm taking a break because I don't want her asking me every day if I'm having a baby yet. And I am ending all the craziness. No more taking my temperature and keeping track of my periods. No more anxious thoughts about 'we should be having sex now.' No more lying on my back after sex for 15 minutes to increase my likelihood of getting pregnant. More manja—playfully goofing around and not worrying about needing to have intercourse.

Meg Grant was due for a trim at Volume 10 today, which meant I was, too. We sat next to each other, both of us wearing comfortable faded jeans and sweatshirts. Meg was a petite blonde with shoulder-length hair.

After asking each other about our kids, Meg went into a tangent about Frozen. "How come no one is shocked in the movie when Elsa brings a snowman to life? Isn't that even bigger than her ice powers?"

"My kids think Olaf should have received the best actor award for that movie. His line, 'some people are worth melting for,' warmed my heart," I said.

Okay, that was good," Meg agreed. "I understand the parents keeping Elsa home, with her freezing everything and all, but why keep Anna locked up? Where were Norwegian Child Services when Anna needed them?"

"Arendal is on the Skagerrak Strait between Norway and Denmark." I remembered Nora's excitement when I showed her that the mythical Arendelle was based on a real city. "It's famous for timber and fabricating. They may have thought the neglect reports were fabricated."

Ignoring my weak attempt at humor, Meg continued, "And then people online think Elsa should be a lesbian. I don't care if she loved a woman or a man, but she's obviously had a suitor. Do you know anyone that moody who isn't in love?"

"Steven Wright said, 'I remember the first time I was in love. Before that I'd never even thought about killing myself.'"

Straight-faced, Meg said, "Everybody thinks my brother killed his wife. Why don't you?"

I honestly believe Tug killed Deb, but I shrugged and told her, "I don't think it's fair for me to judge." That was also true. I didn't express my opinion to anyone but Jon. I've been wrong before.

"Tug loved Deb. He wasn't always the best husband, but he loved her. Deb almost made it too easy."

"What do you mean?"

"It's not really a criticism of Deb. It's more of a criticism of Tug." Our hairdresser was ready for Meg, but Julaine patiently allowed the conversation to continue. "Deb took care of everything for Tug, making it easy for him to do very little at home. But in the end, he was trying."

"It's got to be so hard for you and your family," I said.

"You don't know the half of it." Meg teared up. "Tug told me not to tell anyone, but they're coming after him. And the case is so obvious."

"What do you mean?"

"They arrested the guy who killed Deb. He admitted he was paid by Roan Caruso. Still, Tug is being charged with Deb's murder even though there is nothing connecting him to it."

"Why would Roan want to kill Deb?" I asked.

"When Tug started college, he was a smart, nerdy kid. Roan took him under his wing and told Tug to 'act like the man he wanted to be. Soon, everyone will treat you like that man.' Tug changed the way he dressed, the way he greeted others, everything. Honestly, I miss the old Tug. But people loved the new Tug. Soon, Roan's lover, Deb, left Roan for Tug. Roan ultimately killed her for it. It's that simple. If Deb wouldn't have been so damn tough, Roan might have committed the perfect murder."

"Roan must be a terrible person."

"A narcissist like Roan could never accept that his apprentice became his master." Meg dabbed at her eyes. She briefly squeezed my hand, "I know Roan had it tough, too, but Roan had money from illegal activities already streaming in when he got to college."

She had me considering possibilities.

Meg added, "Do you know why Tug defended Ricky Day?"

"No."

"Roan told him, 'I want you to get Ricky out of prison as soon as possible. When he gets out, I'm going to kill him with my bare hands. Nobody goes after my kid.'"

"Has Tug told anyone this?" I wondered.

"Just me. He won't make a statement against Roan. Tug never had a lot of friends, so he protects Roan to a fault. That's how good he is. I told Tug, 'I'd testify for you. I'd even lie for you to get you out of this charge.' Tug told me, 'Absolutely not. They won't believe you if you speak on my behalf because you're my sister, and if you lie for me, they will damn sure convict me.'" Meg stopped herself. "I'm sorry for going on and on. I've got to get my hair done."

34

HALLE DAY

8:30 A.M. MONDAY, DECEMBER 23, 2019
ADULT CORRECTIONS FACILITY, HENNEPIN COUNTY,
1145 SHENANDOAH LANE, PLYMOUTH

I wasn't allowed to visit Dad face-to-face in jail. Instead, I sat looking at him on a screen with his name, CARUSO, ROAN, on the corner of the screen. This process was started in murder cases across America when the Hillside Strangler, Kenneth Bianchi, passed his semen to his admirer, Veronica Compton, during an in-person visit inside a latex glove. She then attempted to strangle a woman and left the DNA at the scene to make people think there was still a killer free who had Bianchi's matching DNA. Fortunately, the intended victim survived, and the plot unfolded.

Dad, now unshaven and wearing a bright orange jumpsuit, told me on the screen, "I love you, Halle. Thank you for the visit."

I wasn't sure if it was true, but it felt right to say, "I love you too." Dad's trial was over, and we were waiting for the verdict. We wouldn't have it until after Christmas. Tug Grant demanded a speedy trial, so they rushed Roan's prosecution through first, hoping Dad would be willing to make a deal to implicate Tug. Dad not only didn't betray Tug, but he also refused to testify on his own behalf. Dick Doden testified that Dad had paid him to kill Debra Grant, and Dick was believable. There was no question in my mind Dad would be found guilty. Prosecutor Bare referred to Dad as "the Merchant of Death." It just didn't seem like Dad. Maybe I'm naïve, but I don't believe the truth came out. I can't help feeling justice went wide of the mark here.

Dad picked up on my mood immediately. "Hey, what's wrong?"

I wanted to say, "You're going to prison for the rest of your life, Dad. Isn't that enough?" Instead, I said, "Did you hear what happened to my Uncle Ricky?"

"No."

"He was assaulted and dumped on the sidewalk."

This seemed to improve his mood. "I had nothin' to do with that."

"I know. But I want you to request that Ricky be left alone. Dad, I will visit you as long as Ricky's safe."

"I have no idea what you're talking about."

"You know the attacker."

"Honestly, I don't."

In barely a whisper, I repeated, "You know the attacker."

Dad picked up my hint and immediately warned me, "Everything that's said here is recorded."

"Are we good?"

"Yeah. Consider it done."

"Thank you. I want to say this for the record. The night the Disciples rained bullets on us, I was proud of you for firing back. What were you supposed to do—wait for them to execute your entire family? I'm grateful that you defended us, and if they bring any charges forth, I'm willing to testify on your behalf."

Dad smiled.

10:39 A.M.
FIVE WATT COFFEE
861 EAST HENNEPIN AVENUE, BELTRAMI, MINNEAPOLIS

KEYSHAWN HARRIS AND I STOOD at the counter of the coffee shop, looking over the menu. I wore form-fitting jeans that were so light blue they were almost white and a baby blue tunic. I might have to make the first move on this young man. He calls and texts regularly, and we've hinted at being intimate friends, but behaviorally, we haven't stepped out of the friend zone. I picked him up a nice mortar and pestle set for making pho, wrapped it, and put it in the back seat of my car.

Keyshawn was clean-shaven, and his black hair was cut short. His handsome, boyish face and sparkling brown eyes didn't go unnoticed by the teen clerk waiting on us. Keyshawn smiled and told her, "I'll take the Northeast Fog." The menu described the Fog as a combination of tea, milk, vanilla, coriander, and fennel.

"Why do you order a different beverage every time?" I asked.

"To open my palate to new flavors."

"Okay." I decided to take a chance on something other than my usual. "What's in the Chaider?"

"My favorite," the barista responded. "Apple cider, chai, and vanilla. Healthy and heavenly."

I grinned. "Well, in that case, I'll have to try it."

Keyshawn and I sat at a table. His white T-shirt and thin gold chain seemed illuminated by his dark skin. Today, he wore wire-rimmed oval glasses.

"I love your glasses. You've kind of got that Ghandi thing going."

"Wow. So, I dress like a guy who died eighty years ago."

"A comparison to Ghandi is about the best compliment I could give to anyone."

"But you didn't say I had his wisdom," Keyshawn laughed. You said I looked like him. It's kind of like saying, 'You have Einstein-like hair.' It isn't really a compliment."

"Do I have Einstein-like hair? Sigmund Freud believed nothing is said by accident. It's not serendipity that 'Einstein hair' was the first thing that came to mind."

"People who don't believe in coincidence haven't seen all the brothers convicted by being in the wrong place at the wrong time."

"Point taken. But as a matter of semantics, is there ever a right time to be in the wrong place?"

He rolled his eyes, so I followed with, "Okay, compare me to an old famous person, and I will silently accept it."

He studied me and said, "You've got that mysterious blonde Kristen Stewart vibe workin'."

I wanted to say Kristen and I were about the same age, but instead, I took a slow sip of my cider and appreciatively told him, "Thank you."

"I'm working at Shuang Cheng now," Keyshawn said.

"I didn't think they had pho."

"They don't. I know how to make pho. I need to learn how to make everything else."

I reached over and took his hand. "I'm sensing Ghandi-like wisdom."

Keyshawn flashed that million-dollar smile. "I've been thinking about your history. Here you are, living in Minneapolis, where there's a shooting every night. And even in light of the recent incident, you don't seem to be running away from it."

"I'm hoping I can make a difference."

A screeching female voice shattered our serenity. "You have got to be kidding!" Catania Turrisi towered over our table.

Crap. I furrowed my forehead. "Is there a problem?"

Cat stood over me. "They just killed your sister-in-law and her baby, and here you are yuckin' it up with them. Have some respect for your family. This one's on you." Cat grabbed my hot drink and dumped it in my lap, and it burned.

Keyshawn sprang to his feet and stepped between us. "Back off." He stepped into her. "What is wrong with you?"

Catania pointed her big nose in his face. "Look, Harry Potter. All of your sorcery won't save you from the bullets Cleopatra attracts."

I stood up and, with urine-colored cider dripping down my light jeans, shouted, "Leave us alone!"

Cat laughed and said as she walked away, "Don't stop over."

"I don't plan on it," I retorted weakly. Humiliated, I slipped my coat on to cover my lap. "I think I better go."

Keyshawn followed me to my car. As I started it, he got in the passenger seat and asked, "Are you okay?"

"Yeah."

"You know I don't know any of the guys who shot up your house?"

"Yeah, that's just Cat's racist bullshit."

"Why did the Disciples shoot it up?"

"Have you heard of the Turrisi mob family? My stepmother is Catania Turrisi. Cat's a direct descendent of the mob boss, Don Pepé."

Keyshawn was quiet. I wasn't sure how to read him. He finally said, "At least she called you Cleopatra, the Queen of Egypt."

"It wasn't a compliment. Cleopatra was a bastard child like me and was responsible for the deaths of three of her siblings. Catania was implying I was responsible for the deaths of my family."

"You think Cat knows all that?"

"Yeah. She was the one who told me about Cleopatra. I don't plan on ever setting foot in her house again." That gangster bitch resented my existence.

Keyshawn took my hand, "I'm sorry, Halle, but I can't do this. I'm trying to start a business. She could destroy me."

I had to let him go. I felt sick and stopped hearing Keyshawn. He didn't deserve my family. No one does. My damn sick, violent family!

I reached into the back seat, grabbed his gift, and said, "You're right. You are absolutely right." I pushed the gift into his lap. "You need to get out, and I need to go. It's best."

"I'm sorry." Sadness weighed on him as he slowly opened the door.

I softened my tone. "Hey, I'm not upset with you. I understand." It was all I could do to hold back my tears. "Merry Christmas, Keyshawn."

When he hesitated, I said, "Please go," and he left.

35

JON FREDERICK

10:00 A.M., MONDAY, DECEMBER 30, 2019
MINNESOTA CORRECTIONAL FACILITY–
OAK PARK HEIGHTS
5329 NORTH OSGOOD AVENUE, OAK PARK HEIGHTS

Roan Caruso had received the maximum sentence for murder for hire in Minnesota of twenty-five years. He'd been placed in Oak Park Heights, the only maximum-security prison in the state. Much of the prison was underground. Appearing to have his back to the wall finally, he agreed to meet with me.

With his wrists cuffed to the table, the big brute in the orange jumpsuit was unable to sit back. Roan yawned and said, "Come to wish me a happy New Year?"

"I'm not quite that cruel." After watching him rattle his chains, I recited, "The chains would never have bound you, but for the formation of the first link on one memorable day."

Roan curiously responded, "Dickens?"

"Great Expectations."

"I appreciate the reference. Professionals think because I'm big, I'm stupid."

"I know better."

"So, what do you want to talk about?"

"I want to understand your role in Debra Grant's murder."

"What makes you think I had one?"

"You've been convicted. You have nothing to lose now."

"Don't I? Not everything is what it seems. I'm not talking about Deb. I already have an appeal for the conviction in place."

He may have agreed to the interview simply to break up the monotony of his day. I prodded, "You live by the Cosa Nostra code of silence."

"Omerta." He nodded.

"You know as well as I do that almost everyone in the mafia talks to save their ass. I've seen it a hundred times."

"But I don't." Roan studied me for a moment and said, "I've given it a lot of thought, and there's something I need to ask. How did you know?"

"What?" I knew exactly where he was going. Latrice Johnson, Deondre Smith's lover, had told me Roan had asked Deondre to kill Debra Grant. Deondre refused, and Roan killed him, leaving nineteen-year-old Latrice alone to raise their child. There wasn't any circumstance where I would ever give up her name. They'd kill her in a heartbeat.

"Who gave me up?" Roan glared at me.

"It was a lucky guess. You were Tug's right-hand man and Deb's estranged lover, so the investigator pretended he already knew you contracted the hit. Doden fell for the lie and gave you up." I moved on like what I just said was fact. "You took an incredible risk and lost. I can't believe Catania thought it was worth $100,000."

Roan sat in silent irritation. He seemed to understand there wasn't a safe way to respond. His failure to argue that he hadn't hired Doden proved that his conviction was justified.

After a minute, I asked, "Why Dick Doden?"

He continued to quietly study me as he waited for another question.

"You could help Tug Grant," I suggested.

Roan finally broke his trance by reciting, "If you dance with the devil, then you haven't got a clue, for you think you'll change the devil, but the devil changes you."

"A quote from J.M. Smith," I smiled. "Diablos Danzantes." The tradition of dancing devils was started in Venezuela as a tribute to the Catholic Church.

"There's no changin' Tug," Roan said. "At the moment, there isn't a lot of incentive to help him." He shook the chains on his wrists. "I think I have a better chance of winning my appeal if Tug is convicted."

"How so?"

"If Tug is set free, he loses his motivation to have my conviction overturned. If he's convicted, he's fighting right alongside me."

"What's there that could help both you and Tug?" When he didn't respond, I thought out loud, "The man who committed the murder is the only one who's claiming you were involved."

"I'm done talking about Doden."

"You must have really hated Deb." There was a sadness in his eyes that surprised me. Is it possible someone else set up Deb's murder? The thought popped into my head: Tug had a fervid affair with Melanie Pearson, yet she's flown under the radar this entire investigation. Could Melanie have hired Roan? Refocusing on Roan, I pointed out, "You'll never be convicted for killing Deondre. What was said between the two of you that led you to take his life?"

"First of all, I'm not saying I did. But let's say two people need to trust each other, and one says you're not capable of understanding the plight of Black America. That didn't really leave me an option."

Aghast, I asked, "You shot him because he said you don't understand Black America?"

"He didn't say it would be difficult." Roan clarified. "He said I'm not capable. So, there was nothing further to say. If I'm not capable of understanding him, I can't trust him. Deondre died after he convinced me he was right."

I took a deep, angry breath and walked out before I did something I regretted.

As I walked to my car in the prison parking lot, I considered Tug's comment about Roan. "He will mess with your head, and it will be time wasted." I might have just been played. Racism ends the conversation. It's possible that Roan killed Deondre out of racism. It's also possible Roan told me this to keep me from investigating the young man's death further.

36

JON FREDERICK

9:00 A.M. FRIDAY, JANUARY 3, 2020
TARGET CORPORATION, TARGET PLAZA SOUTH,
1000 NICOLLET MALL, MINNEAPOLIS

The Target Corporation is a beautiful three-story building with a glass semicircular corner window. I flashed my badge and was escorted into a conference room in the office area to speak to Melanie Pearson. I wanted to find out why Melanie is on the witness list for the prosecution.

The thin redhead was dressed professionally and nervously squeezed her hands as she entered the room. Melanie studied me hard before she asked, "What are you doing at my work?"

"I'm a private investigator, and I need to speak to you about Debra Grant," I offered.

"I've seen you before." She stood across the table from me and grinned. "You were with that hot brunette at Hoppy Girl."

Getting right down to business, I asked, "Have the police ever interviewed you about Deb's murder?"

"Yes. Security video verified that I was at work. There were no calls made from my cell phone between 8:00 and

10:00, the time around Deb's murder." Melanie cautiously held her skirt against her thighs as she sat. "The prosecutor said I shouldn't talk to anybody before the trial, but I have nothing to hide. The cameras show I never left the building, and my phone records show I didn't make any calls."

The rules of disclosure allowed the defense the same access to those phone records. I'd call Tug when this interview was done and request them.

Melanie disgracefully admitted, "Honestly, I didn't really know Deb."

"Tug has shared details about your affair. At the very least, you knew of Deb. What is your gut feeling about her?"

"If I could talk to Deb, I'd say, 'I'm sorry.' Tug was such a player. I didn't know he was married when we started, and once it took off, Tug was an addiction I couldn't walk away from."

Melanie scratched her wrist, anxiously, I thought. This was a young woman consumed with shame. Instead of finding a path out, she struck me as someone who would keep making one guilt-inducing choice after another for a momentary reprieve from her pain.

"Did you own a burner phone at the time?" Melanie had just admitted to being obsessed with Tug.

"I wouldn't even know where to buy one." She gave me an awkward, coquettish smile.

My initial thought was that Melanie badly desired attention and affection. She reminded me of a histrionic adolescent, and I imagine she was an easy play for Tug. I pointed out, "You didn't answer my question."

"No, I've never owned a burner phone." Melanie studied me nervously. "I know it looks bad that I wasn't at my desk for a half hour. I was under a lot of stress at the time. I was learning a new job and still getting over Tug. I was engaged, but Darius canceled the wedding after our first argument. But we're engaged again, and the wedding is back on."

"What was the argument over?"

"He accused me of still loving Tug after he found a picture I kept of Tug and me together."

"Do you still love Tug?"

Melanie hesitated and then unconvincingly muttered, "Nooo."

"Where were you for the thirty minutes you weren't at your desk?"

"The camera showed I went to the bathroom. Honestly, I don't recall what was going on with me that day. I did a lot of crying back then. I imagine I was trying to pull myself together. I wonder sometimes if people sense when something bad is about to happen to someone they know."

I tried a new line of questioning. "Tug was scheduled to be the keynote speaker at the Minnesota Bar Conference not long after Deb's murder. How far in advance does Tug have his presentations ready?"

"Months." Melanie smiled. "Tug likes to run a lot of risks up to the last minute, but speaking is not one of them."

I'd have to return to that thought later. "Do you think Tug killed Deb?"

"No," Melanie adamantly replied.

"Are you and Tug getting back together?"

"No! I'm engaged to Darius. I'm testifying for the prosecution."

"What are you going to say?"

"Bridget said if anybody working with Tug tries to talk to me, I should mention you're tampering with a witness."

"Let me clarify that," I smiled. "I'm only tampering with a witness if I threaten you. I simply want the truth."

"Am I obligated to talk to you?" Melanie asked with a snarky grin.

"No." It was clear Prosecutor Bare had told Melanie to avoid me.

"Then I'm going back to work." Melanie stood up.

I handed her my card. "Please call if you have something to share."

37

JON FREDERICK

9:00 A.M. MONDAY, JANUARY 6, 2020
HENNEPIN COUNTY COURTHOUSE
300 SOUTH 6TH STREET, CENTRAL MINNEAPOLIS

The courtroom was packed with reporters on the first day of Tilmore "Tug" Grant's murder trial. Tug demanded a speedy trial, which is a good move if you don't feel they have enough evidence to convict you. With an arrogant grin, he sat flanked by two over-priced gray-haired attorneys.

Bridget Bare stood before the jury in a black blazer with a pristine white button-down shirt beneath, her silver hair pulled back in a tight ponytail. She explained in her opening statement, "We will demonstrate that Tilmore Grant, the man they call 'Tug,' murdered his wife, Debra Grant, in a callous and premeditated fashion. Tug paid a man $10,000 to make it look like an accident. Tug didn't anticipate the fight his wife would put forth to survive another day with her children, and it ended up being a brutal murder. A murder for money that would eventually leave her four wonderful children parentless. Tug took out ten million dollars' worth of life insurance on Deb, most of it during the last year of her life.

"We will have insurance agents who will share with you that Tug told them not to explain to Debra that the forms she signed were all for insurance. Dick Doden, the hired killer, will testify that Tug left the door open for him. He was instructed to enter the home in the early morning, lock the door behind him, and hide in the basement until 8:30 a.m. At that time, Tug would call home. Tug removed the extra phones from the home, requiring Debra to answer the call in the kitchen. This ensured Dick could come up from the basement unnoticed, and he would know her exact location. The killer was told to make it look like she fell in the bathtub. Tug filled the bathtub with water before he left for work that day. Tug called the home at 8:30 a.m. Tug was having an affair with his secretary and had told her in eleven months, he would be single and financially stable. Eleven months have now passed. Breaking the hearts of his children, Tug even got rid of the family dog just days before Debra's murder. His own children acknowledged their dog would bark at strangers."

It was clear Zave had helped the prosecutor develop a strong case. Zave hadn't returned my calls recently, and I didn't blame him. I wouldn't have offered information to a private investigator when I worked for the state unless I absolutely knew that I could use him.

Melanie Pearson had texted me, stating that she was instructed not to talk to me. Tug had finally given me Melanie's phone records, so while sitting in the courtroom, I paged through them, looking for anything that seemed odd. There were no calls in the hour before or after Deb's murder. Melanie's phone history suggested this was not unusual, as she'd go hours without making calls during the workday. There was no indication Melanie ever called Roan Caruso. There was a Brainerd phone number that piqued my curiosity. Melanie had called it once a month until seven months before Deb's death and then called one more time fifty-four days before the murder.

6:00 P.M.
ANGRY INCH BREWING, 20841 HOLYOKE
AVENUE, LAKEVILLE

I MET WITH TUG AFTER the first day of court. The prosecution had a good case, but it had holes. While Dick Doden believes Tug ultimately hired him, Dick never met with Tug. Dick never received payment from Tug. Instead, he was recruited and paid by Roan Caruso. Dick got the gun from Roan Caruso. And Roan Caruso wasn't talking.

Tug and I sat at a table away from the other customers, and Sne, the bar matron, delivered our beers. Appreciating her friendly and efficient service, I left her a generous tip. Sne thanked us and headed back to the bar.

Disgruntled, Tug sipped his glass of the Ale to the Queen. "We'll tear their witnesses apart one by one."

I took a large swallow of the Creamalicious Cream Ale and asked, "Why did you get rid of the dog?"

Tug dramatically turned his hand as if he was offering me something, "It was pissing on the carpet."

"Didn't you have the dog for seven years?"

"Okay, I don't know why it started doing that. I didn't kill the dog. My sister kindly agreed to take it so the kids could still visit Milo. And those damn insurance agents saying I told them not to tell Deb what she was signing—that's ridiculous. They just don't want to pay the money they owe me. They are suggesting *they* had Deb sign life insurance policies without knowing what she was signing. Wouldn't that be pretty unethical of them?"

"Yes—I agree." I scratched my chin. "Melanie Pearson is testifying for the prosecution. She didn't leave work that day, but it looks like she was in the restroom from about 8:15 until 8:45 a.m. on the morning Deb was killed. I'm not sure if her going off the grid at the time of the murder is significant or coincidental."

Deep in thought, Tug said, "We can't go after Melanie as the killer. If the jury thinks Melanie killed her, they're going to blame me."

"You met monthly with Melanie at Grand View Lodge in 2018. Melanie called Grand View one more time on September 13, 2019. Any idea what that was about?"

"Non-issue. Let it go. Melanie is a red herring. And when this is all over, my bet is she comes back to work for me."

"Melanie's obsession with you makes her even more suspicious. What if Melanie had Roan arrange the hit on Deb?"

"There was no love between Melanie and Roan. She didn't like him or trust him. Mel's just a spurned lover. I'll tear her apart as a witness. I have no worries about her." Tug smiled, "If you can find solid proof Melanie contacted Roan, we'll go with it. But if we implicate her without solid proof, it will backfire on me. Trust me, I know how these cases play out in court."

"You made a couple of payments to Roan Caruso right before Deb's murder."

Surprised, Tug commented, "That's good work." He sipped his ale.

"Anticipate this is going to come up."

"We were always lending Roan money. Roan was Deb's old lover. I stole her from him. He's a dangerous guy, so I had to let him down easy. You know what they say: Keep your friends close and your enemies closer."

You gave Roan $100,000, and he never paid you back. Why would he need to borrow money? With his marriage to Catania Turrisi, he's sitting on a bigger pile than you are."

"But the Turrisis' money isn't his money. Roan will pay me back. He always does."

"Roan's in maximum security."

"For now."

I couldn't help noticing that was the same thing Roan said. Tug and Roan aren't enemies—at least from Tug's perspective. I said, "I've spoken to Dreads and Roan, and there's something I can't make right in my brain. At Roan Caruso's court hearing on Deondre Smith's murder, you said that Roan was driving by the site when Deondre was shot. I've spoken to a Disciples gang member who claims Deondre had agreed to return the items that were previously stolen from Roan's car that night. The valuable item was believed to be a leather folder with an old piece of paper sealed in plastic with a signature on it."

Tug shrugged his shoulders. "I didn't even ask him about it. It was an illegal search and seizure. That's all that mattered."

"I saw the signature. I did some research, and a document with this signature on it was stolen from a home in Texas three months before Deondre was killed. If it's authentic, it's worth $722,000. Caruso would need someone above his grade to sell it."

Tug shut down. "Okay, I don't know anything about that." Agitated, he remarked, "Jon, I need you to focus on my trial and stop worrying about Roan. I could go to prison for something I didn't do."

"If Caruso doesn't implicate you, all they have is the word of a killer. Dick Doden claims he isn't getting a deal to testify. If your attorneys find the prosecutor made an agreement with Dick in exchange for his testimony, it will prove that he's lying."

"That's what I'm talking about!" Tug smiled. "I'll see what they can do. Keep looking."

I purposely never revealed that the signature belonged to Button Gwinnett. I thought it was interesting that Tug never asked.

38

JON FREDERICK

1:45 P.M. TUESDAY, JANUARY 7, 2020
HENNEPIN COUNTY COURTHOUSE
300 SOUTH 6TH STREET, CENTRAL MINNEAPOLIS

It was day two of Tug's murder trial, and I sat back on the wooden bench in the gallery, watching the proceeding. Twenty-one-year-old Dick Doden was on the stand today. Dick had oily dark hair that looked like it had been styled with a garden rake. He wore his prison-orange jumpsuit. His left eye was purple, his cheek was swollen, and the rest of his face had the greenish tint of bruising that was slowly healing. After much debate this morning, it had been clarified that Dick was assaulted in jail by an acquaintance of Roan Caruso.

Prosecutor Bridget Bare had walked Dick through the murder of Debra Grant and showed the jury how his testimony was consistent with the evidence. The biggest surprise for me was Dick's level of functioning. He seemed only a few lucky guesses above intellectually disabled. Tug would have never hired him to kill his wife. It surprised me that Roan had. Dick returned to the stand in the afternoon for redirect by Tug's attorneys.

A gray-haired lawyer with traditional side-parted hair approached Dick. I could picture that attorney drinking cognac at the Spearmint Rhino's Club with the "good old boys" at the end of the day. It rubbed me the wrong way when Bridget Bare told me Tug's attorney friends headed to the strip bar at the end of the block to discuss cases. It was a place she never felt welcome, and I understood. Welcome or not, I wouldn't go there. The slick gray solicitor asked Dick Doden, "Did you ever meet with Tug Grant?"

Dick looked straight into the solicitor's eyes. "No."

"Did the man who paid you ever mention Tug Grant's name?" the attorney asked.

"He told me to go to Tug Grant's house; the target was Tug's wife."

"Did he tell you what Debra Grant had done which made her worthy of murder? Was she cheating on him, or had she threatened him?"

"Roan told me she didn't do anything. It was an insurance thing."

The attorney paused. "And still, it was okay in your brain to murder a loving mother of four who hadn't done anything wrong?"

Dick put his head down for a second and then looked up and said, "Man, I wish to God I wouldn't have done it. It didn't seem real. And then it was…" his voice trailed off.

"And we're supposed to believe a man who could rationalize beating to death an innocent woman—a woman who was a pillar of society. In other words, you're a heartless killer, but you wouldn't lie to us."

Dick appeared tearful as he responded, "I'm not lying."

Tug's attorney ended the redirect, and I couldn't help thinking the prosecutor won this exchange. For as criminal as Dick Doden was, I believed him. I imagined the jury did, too.

39

TUG GRANT

9:00 A.M. WEDNESDAY, JANUARY 8, 2020
HENNEPIN COUNTY COURTHOUSE
300 SOUTH 6TH STREET, CENTRAL MINNEAPOLIS

I honestly thought Melanie would back out of testifying against me. It started as a slow burn but was now raging inside me. I had done so much for her, and she appreciated it so little. I'm the reason she wasn't homeless a year ago. I fired my attorneys and decided to defend myself. Melanie would never keep it together during a direct confrontation with me. Taytum suggested I hire her to sit next to me and give me feedback to keep my emotions in check. She wore a classic gray suit, but I wasn't wild about the blunt bob her blonde hair was now styled into. To me, it said, "bitchy white professional."

Horseface, the prosecutor, asked Melanie, "Did you have an affair with Tilmore 'Tug' Grant?"

Melanie wore a light blue scarf around her neck, and she tugged on it as she responded, "Yes. I didn't know he was married when I first slept with him."

"Objection!" I stood up. "Her ignorance wasn't part of the question." I wanted Melanie to know I wasn't going to take her betrayal lying down.

The judge seemed slightly annoyed by my quick intervention but said, "Sustained." He turned to Melanie. "Just answer the question."

When I sat back down, Taytum whispered, "Be careful. You don't want to turn the judge against you."

Bridget flashed an arrogant grin at me before continuing. "Melanie, could you tell us about your affair with the defendant? Was he married? How long did it go on?"

"As I was saying, I didn't know he was married when we were first together. Tug didn't wear a wedding ring and never mentioned he had a wife and children. I fell for him, and the affair went on for nine months."

"How did it end?" the prosecutor asked.

"I caught him having sex with his assistant in the office." Melanie gave Taytum and me an angry glare.

It was all I could do to keep from laughing. I reached under the table and briefly gripped Taytum's leg.

Taytum stared stoically ahead, white-knuckled as she tightly gripped her hands together on the table.

The prosecutor asked, "Did Tug ever tell you he was going to leave his wife?"

"Yes."

That wasn't true. I may have implied it, but I never said it. Instead of objecting, I'd confront Melanie in my cross-examination.

"What exactly did he say?"

Using her right hand, Melanie brushed her copper hair back. "He said, 'If you stay with me, I'll have enough money for both of us to live well in eleven months.'"

I'd forgotten about that. That was stupid. How could I counter this?

The prosecutor continued, "And it was in that eleven-month period of time that his wife died, correct?"

"Yes." Melanie was ignoring my glare.

Prosecutor Bridget Bare directed her arrogant smile at me as she said, "No more questions."

Picking up on my irritation, Taytum whispered, "It might be best to let her go. Minimize the time she's on the stand. She could toast you if this spins the wrong way."

Determined to win this, I stood by the table and, tamping down my fury, asked politely, "Do you mind if I call you Melanie?"

"That's fine." She finally looked at me.

"Do you remember what you did on June 7, 2018?" I asked.

"No." She shrugged nervously.

"It's the day we met for the first time. I had scheduled a job interview with you, and you invited me to a waterfront home and engaged in sex with me. Do you remember that?"

"Yes, but—"

I cut her off. "Do you remember when we last had sex?"

"I don't remember every time we've had sex," Melanie said softly.

I don't imagine you do. It was a lot, wasn't it?" I laughed out loud. "I just want you to remember the last time."

"I thought we weren't going to talk about that."

"I changed my mind." I turned to the jury. "I want everyone to know the truth. It is why you're testifying, isn't it?" I slowly turned back to the witness.

Melanie pulled on her scarf. "I'm testifying because it's the right thing to do."

I stepped toward her. "Well, I imagine you do remember our last date. Did I call you and set up that date—or did you call me?"

Melanie blew out a long breath. "I called you." She stared at her fiancé, who was seated in the gallery, attempting to apologize with her eyes.

"You set up the date. And you rented the room in your name, correct? I can show you a copy of the receipt if needed."

Melanie reluctantly replied, "Yes."

"Do you remember what you did when you entered the room?"

"I imagine I unpacked my bags."

"No. You did something even before that. Let's see if I can refresh your memory. You dropped down on your knees, undid my belt, and performed oral sex on me. Do you remember now, or do you need me to show you a picture of my slacks?"

"I remember," Melanie quietly responded.

I wandered back behind the table while I let the jury think about the credibility of this witness.

Taytum tugged at my sleeve and whispered, "Enough."

But I powered forward, "I'm sorry, I didn't hear you."

Humiliated, Melanie answered, "I did."

Ignoring the judge, I remarked, "I believe it was what they call a facial."

"Language," the judge interrupted.

Why wasn't the prosecutor objecting? I glanced over at Bridget and watched her rifling through her notes. I could destroy Melanie while the old gray mare was distracted.

Taytum told me, "Don't go there."

Proud of humiliating Melanie in front of her fiancé, I stepped away from Taytum and approached Melanie again. The degradation she was facing was a long way from over. "Do you remember me bending you forward against the wall and taking you from behind—doggy style?"

"Language," the judge repeated with increasing agitation.

Melanie was staring straight down when she answered, "Yes."

"How many times do you think we had sex that weekend?"

"I don't know."

"More than a couple of times?"

"I don't remember—"

Before she could finish, I interjected, "I believe they call that a cream pie."

Now visibly angry, the judge demanded, "DO YOU HAVE A POINT?"

"Yes. I will get to it, Your Honor. There will be no more questions about Melanie's promiscuity." I turned to Melanie. "How long ago did this happen?"

"It was the beginning of October—a little over a month before Deb's death." Before I could cut her off, she blurted, "You offered to put $100,000 in a bank account for me to live off of until we could be together permanently."

"Stop. Please just answer the questions you are asked." That damn slut was irritating. I turned to the judge for support, but he ignored me. I needed to counter her last comment. "Did I ever put $100,000 in a bank account for you? I don't recall doing that."

"No. I declined your offer."

"Ms. Pearson, do you understand there are laws against perjury? You could serve five years in prison and pay a $10,000 fine."

"I'm not lying."

I spoke over her response, hoping the jury didn't hear it. "The question was, do you understand there are laws against perjury?"

Melanie took a deep breath before responding, "Yes."

Bridget had coached her well. I pointed out, "There is no evidence that I offered you $100,000, is there? No lover's note. No texts. Not even a single call to your phone after that weekend. Is that correct?"

Melanie thought for a moment and said, "Yeah."

"You didn't even initially remember what you did when you entered the room, but suddenly, you remember a ridiculous offer of money?"

"Yes—"

"Did I ever call you again after that weekend?"

"No."

"Doesn't it seem odd that I would offer you $100,000 but never talk to you again? Wouldn't it make more sense that I saw the weekend fling for exactly what it was?" When Melanie didn't respond, I added, "You were engaged at the time, right?"

"Yes."

"So, I knew you were going to marry someone else. You didn't hide that, did you?"

"No," she responded defensively. "I told you."

"You're clearly not trustworthy. An engagement is a commitment, isn't it?"

Melanie exclaimed, "You were married!"

I could feel her desperation as she watched her fiancé exit the courtroom, and it was deeply gratifying. *Who the hell is she to turn on me?* I responded, "And even that couldn't stop you from chasing me like a dog in heat." Before the judge admonished me, I quickly asked, "Are you aware that my wife and I had reconciled after that and went on vacation to celebrate renewing our vows?"

"No."

Taytum nodded in approval of my change in questioning. I wanted to make one more point. "And your booty call to me was one-weekend tryst, months after we were over—for good, right?"

"Yes," Melanie admitted.

"Why would I kill my wife for you? I could have you anytime, any way I wanted. What did you have to offer me? I had nothing to gain from being with you."

Taytum was shaking her head at me, attempting to get me to back off. Taytum was usually right.

I questioned, "Did I ever ask you to end your engagement?"

"No."

"No more questions."

Melanie glared at me all the way back to the defendant's table. Before I sat down, I noticed the judge had glanced down to read a document. I raised my thumb and pinky finger to my ear, signaling to Melanie, *Call me.*

Melanie shouted, "Go to hell!"

The judge looked up, hit the gavel, and stated, "Let's call it a day."

After the judge exited, I smiled at Taytum and said, "I can't believe the prosecutor never objected."

"Why would she?" Taytum looked at me dumbfounded. "You got the entire jury to hate you. Everyone in this courtroom knows you ruined Melanie's engagement. The entire jury watched her stare at her fiancé as he walked out while you went into the disgusting details of your sexual escapades. You might not be guilty, but you're going to get yourself convicted if you grandstand like that again."

"I'm the one facing prison here. I needed her to admit I never asked for a future with her."

Taytum packed up, "You could have done that without saying anything about your sexual behavior. It was humiliating for me to be sitting at this table."

"I'm doing what I have to do."

"No, you're not. You're doing what you want to do, which is to humiliate women because your mother left you as a child. I won't stand for it. If you want to win, your ego can't be more important than proving your innocence. And don't touch me again in court. You're acting like a perv. I came very close to punching you."

Remember your place, Taytum. You're my understudy.

She grabbed her briefcase, and I watched the strong Scandinavian woman walk away.

I didn't need her anyway. Ultimately, I'm alone. Debra was nice and did a hell of a lot for our family, but no one could ever truly appreciate me. John Steinbeck was right when he said, "All great and precious things are lonely." Greatness separates me from the masses and, in the end, isolates me.

I approached Jon Frederick, who was standing in the aisle, and told him, "You need to find out who did this, okay?"

"You lied to me," Jon remarked.

"A beautiful woman called and promised to rock my world. I did what any man would do, and I never promised Melanie anything would come out of it."

"You do understand the prosecutor was just giving you rope to hang yourself by pretending to be busy, right?" Jon said.

He's giving Bridget more credit than she deserves. I destroyed Melanie.

Jon asked, "How long have you been romantically involved with Taytum?"

"Who said I was with Taytum?"

When Jon didn't respond, I acquiesced. "Off and on when we're both desperate. Taytum gets it. She never gives me an ultimatum. She understands it's just scratching an itch, and then we go on with life."

Jon looked toward the judge's chambers, "Would you like me to check into the possibility that Taytum may have hired someone to kill your wife?"

Both Taytum and Jon had serious concerns about today's hearing. For the first time, I considered that I could actually be convicted. I didn't want to throw Taytum under the bus. She's been my one friend through all of this. I suggested, "Find a way to connect Richard Day to this. I still think he's my best shot of coming out of this clean."

"It's not Richard Day. It's a mistake to go after Day if you're innocent. If you go after him, you'll look desperate."

"How do you know it's not Day? Every person I talk to says, 'Do you think Day might have killed her?' I just need reasonable doubt. He thought nothing of killing his entire family. Why would it bother him to kill mine?"

"I've checked into him, as you asked. It's not Day. Did you ever play football?"

"Elmore Academy Wildcats. The hometown of Walter Mondale."

Jon continued, "Going after Day is a last-ditch effort like throwing a Hail Mary pass in the hope of escaping a loss."

"Maybe I want to throw one to guarantee a win."

"Do you know why teams don't throw a Hail Mary pass when they're ahead?" Jon countered.

"No." I'd never really thought about it.

"Because you're more likely to lose than win. If you're winning, you don't risk it."

"Just be ready to take the stand tomorrow," I told Jon. "I need a witness who can stand up to Bridget's scrutiny, and I have a lot of faith in you. Remember who's paying you."

40

JON FREDERICK

7:00 P.M. WEDNESDAY, JANUARY 8, 2020
BLUELINE SPORTS BAR & GRILL, 1101
2ND STREET SOUTH, SARTELL

Taytum had business in St. Cloud after court. I went home for a few hours, and she called and agreed to meet me at the Blueline Sports Bar in Sartell. With a friendly smile, Penny delivered a cold glass of Fat Tire amber for me and a Starry Eyed Cream Ale for Taytum. She wore a rose gold pendant featuring a ram's head around her neck, which stood out against her dressy but unadorned black blouse.

Quietly reflecting, she took a slow sip of her ale and then asked, "Did Tug send you? He couldn't handle my walking away."

"No, he didn't." I smiled. "How long have the two of you been romantically involved?"

"Since we first met four years ago. What did Tug say?"

"He was very vague."

"Of course." Taytum grinned. "I'll go back and help him. I get frustrated that all it takes is for Prosecutor Bare to take a few jabs at him, and he loses it and acts like a thirteen-year-old."

Serena has described narcissists as "the empty actor." They attack out of fear that others will discover that, deep down, they are a weeping fraud.

"I have nothing to hide, Jon," Taytum revealed confidently. "I'm just taking care of my life. I'm a happy single woman with no desire to be a mother. I've never hidden the fact that I plan on being a judge. Tug knows my relationships take a distant second to my career." She laughed. "I expect nothing from Tug. I'm just happy to learn from him. The man is a genius."

"You're the only partner of Tug's I've encountered who has a relaxed attitude about him."

"I'm the only person who understands him. People see the fancy suits, the cars, and the workout routine, and they're intimidated. I see a man who's desperate for acceptance. I let him know he's adequate but imply there's competition. She held the elegant pendant between her thumb and forefinger. Any idea of the cost?"

"None," I shrugged. I was terrible at appraising jewelry. It could be $25 or $25,000.

"It's a Van Cleef Arietes. $22,000. From Dad. But when Tug asks, I tell him, 'A gift from a man,' and he desperately tries harder to win my affection. Tug can't accept losing."

"Would you mind sharing your thoughts about Debra Grant?" I studied her expression.

"While Tug can act like a brattish teen, his larger choices are brilliant. Like me, Tug is all about being a successful attorney. The difference is that Tug wanted children, so he found himself a supermom."

"Tug didn't spend much time with the kids."

"He didn't want to parent. He wanted a legacy." Taytum held her cold ale in front of her with two hands. "Think about how drug runners hire mules to get drugs into the country. They don't really care about the carrier; they simply want the drugs delivered. If the mule gets there, okay, that's better because you can use her again. Deb was Tug's baby mule."

It wasn't a very complimentary view of Deb, but I wasn't going to interrupt Taytum.

"Tug needed a woman who would take full responsibility for raising the children. Deb fit the bill perfectly. I had no desire to replace her. I admired Deb."

"Still, you were sleeping with her husband. There had to be some hard feelings." I sat back and waited for her response.

"I don't brag about it," she said as she sipped her ale. "Tug and I were both passionate about law, and that enthusiasm carried over." she shrugged and let the sentence trail off.

I sat silently, waiting for her to continue.

Instead, Taytum smiled at a fond memory.

"Did Deb ever confront you about sleeping with her husband?" I asked.

"She did. I told Deb that's a conversation she should have with her husband." Her pleasant smile was now gone. "I know Deb hated me, and I felt bad about that." She glanced down briefly, and I sensed shame when her eyes met mine again. "But I didn't hate Deb. I don't see Tug killing Deb, either. Why would he? His life was exactly what he wanted."

"Ten million dollars," I suggested.

With a surreptitious smile, she said, "He does love money. But the childcare would then fall on him, which would be too much of an annoyance. Tug and I will always be together. What we have, neither of us could have with anyone else."

"Were you jealous of Melanie?"

"Tug destroys women like Melanie." She chuckled, "Melanie's the car he drove to work every day. I'm the Corvette he takes out on special occasions."

Taytum's hollow laughter seemed insincere. As nonchalant as she presented on the surface, Taytum's relationship with Tug wasn't painless. If she were as tormented as I believed, she would keep trying to explain herself.

She continued, "I warned Melanie, but she insisted on trying to please him. There is no pleasing him. Tug's an empty vat for affection. There are only moments. You have to squeeze everything you can out of those moments."

And there it was. Taytum wanted more of Tug. Still, she knew Tug better than anyone I'd encountered. Knowing Tug would always be this way, would Taytum kill him? I doubt it. I suggested, "Moments of elation are typically followed with equal moments of despair."

"I don't know." She dismissed the thought. "I didn't stick around for them…"

9:00 P.M.
SEMINOLE AVENUE, WEST ST. PAUL

I FELT LIKE THE INVESTIGATORS had dropped the ball on Carlos Garcia, so I drove to Garcia's home to talk to him myself. When I pulled up to the house, I could see Carlos and Luciana sitting on the couch watching television together.

I stood in the cold January air and knocked on the door.

Carlos was frustrated when he answered, "Do you know what time it is?"

"I do. I'm working as late as needed to get answers before this trial is over."

Luciana came to the door and, after seeing that it was me, walked away. I could see the guilt in her eyes for giving me inculpatory evidence against her husband.

Carlos hesitated but finally invited me in. "What do you need?"

"You lied to me about your past charge. The naked picture was still on your phone when the police confiscated it."

"I didn't want to be in more trouble."

"And I understand there was a naked picture of Deb. I'd like to know where it was painted and how that all came about."

Carlos glanced at where Luciana, who was sitting with her back to us. "It was painted here. It was before Luciana and I were together. Luciana found the picture and burned it."

"Was Debra Grant here a lot?"

"No. Debra was never here. And the truth is, I've never seen Deb naked. Back then, I had this thing about wanting pictures of women. If I couldn't get a naked picture from them, I'd paint one. I painted one picture of the photo I had of Deb, standing fully clothed in her house. And then I painted the same picture of her standing there naked. At the time, I told myself it was more artistic—hiding nothing."

"Were there other naked pictures of women?"

Carlos glanced back at Luciana. "Yes. But they're all destroyed now."

"Did you tell the investigators this?"

"They never asked. Look—they know I had nothing to do with Deb's death. I was stupid back then. I don't look at any woman other than Luciana like that anymore. I don't want any trouble."

"Have I seen all of your pictures?"

He glanced back at Luciana and said, "Yes."

I sensed he wasn't being honest with me, but there was nothing more I could do tonight.

"If you're done, I've got to get to bed," Carlos said. "I have snow removal tomorrow." He closed the door firmly behind me.

6:00 A.M.
THURSDAY, JANUARY 9, 2020, PUBLIC
STORAGE, 246 EATON STREET, ST. PAUL

I SAT OUTSIDE CARLOS'S HOME, waiting for him to leave for work. He didn't have room in his garage for all his landscaping and snow removal equipment, so he needed a storage shed. At 6:30, I slunk down in my Ford Taurus and watched Carlos get into his truck. I followed his truck to a strip mall of orange garage doors encased in concrete called Public Storage. Carlos parked in front of a garage door, lifted it open, and headed inside. I followed. From the open garage door, I observed Carlos digging out tools.

He finally turned and noticed me. "You scared the hell out of me. What do you want?"

"Are there more paintings here?"

"No. I told you I got rid of them all."

"Do you mind if I have a look?"

"No. Have at it. Close the sliding door when you're done. It will lock itself. I've got nothing to hide. I don't want to be deported. I did nothing wrong." Carlos watched me for a minute and then left.

I moved items and meticulously returned them to their location but found no additional paintings. I wasn't sure what I was looking for, but I carefully looked through the drawers of an old metal desk. There was a house key with a handwritten address on the keychain: 1979 Misty Lane, Dancing Waters. I took out my phone and quickly took a picture of it.

7:00 A.M.

1979 MISTY LANE, DANCING WATERS, WOODBURY

AT THIS POINT, I HAD nothing implicating Carlos, but I decided to check out the address anyway. Dancing Waters is a neighborhood east of St. Paul, near the Wisconsin border, in Woodbury, Minnesota. My GPS brought me to a small, white, two-story house with an unplowed driveway surrounded by woods. I parked on the road. There were no lights, and the smooth drifts of snow suggested the driveway hadn't been entered for weeks. I had a decision to make. *How far do I go to look for evidence that Tug is innocent?* I was driven by the desire to know the truth.

I popped the trunk, put on gloves, and grabbed my RF detector and a set of blunt keys. RF detectors can detect the presence of surveillance devices. It looks like a walkie-talkie, but it can detect radio frequency signals from wireless transmitting devices such as cameras or microphones. Blunt keys easily open most household locks. When I walked up the steps, I was blatantly aware I could earn a burglary charge for this. But curiosity was killing me. Carlos had a key to a house in the middle of nowhere. *What was inside?* Having worked a variety of homicide cases, my imagination ran wild. *What if there was a painting of Debra Grant under the water in a bathtub?*

I unlocked the door and stepped inside, and the red light in my RF detector went on. I was on camera somewhere. The downstairs had an open floor plan. I was standing by a small kitchen table and could see into the kitchen. Paint brushes rested on a towel on the counter. There was a couch in the living room but no television.

The paintings had to be upstairs. Instead of walking away, I headed right up the steps. The second floor was also completely open. There was an easel, and paintings all around the room, all with the backs facing outward. In front of the easel was a double bed. It was a fantasy chamber. I quickly started turning pictures to get a glimpse of what Carlos was fantasizing about. The first picture was a naked painting of Luciana. So was the second and the third. Above the last canvas was a note painted on the wall written in a woman's cursive handwriting, *"I love you, Carlos!"*

I walked over to the window and looked out at a beautiful view of the sun glistening off the ice of Dancing Waters Lake. It made me think of the room differently. It was a love nest for Luciana and Carlos. He had transferred his fantasies to Luciana. Carlos wasn't involved in Deb's death. He had moved on.

My phone buzzed.

"What are you doing in our house, Jon Frederick?" Luciana asked.

"I'm sorry. I discovered you had a second residence you hadn't told me about, and I had to see if there was anything here related to Debra Grant. I owe you an apology. You're right. I shouldn't be here." She obviously had a wireless residential camera and was watching me on her cell phone. I walked down the steps and told her, "I'll lock the door."

"Are you finally convinced Carlos is innocent?" she questioned.

"Yes."

"You didn't believe the polygraph?"

"I wasn't aware Carlos had been given one." The prosecution had failed to release some pertinent information.

Luciana reassured me, "Carlos passed a lie detector test indicating he had nothing to do with Debra's death." She sighed. "I cleaned up her blood."

"What?"

"I clean at one of the homes on the Grants' block. When the investigators were done, they told me to clean up Debra's trail of blood from her home to the four homes she tried to enter. Guys like Tug complain about the immigrants until they have a job they can't get anyone else to do. Then they call us and ask for our help."

"I'm sorry you had to do that." I locked the door and stepped outside. "Can you forgive me for violating your space?"

"Yes, but please contact us ahead of time if you need anything from us again."

"I certainly will. I appreciate your forgiveness." I ended the call and rushed to court.

9:00 A.M.
HENNEPIN COUNTY COURTHOUSE
300 SOUTH 6TH STREET, CENTRAL MINNEAPOLIS

WHEN I ARRIVED AT THE courthouse, I discovered the prosecutor had rested, and Tug called his thirteen-year-old son, Lincoln, as a witness. Taytum Hanson was back at Tug's side. The two wore fashionable navy blue suits that fit them perfectly. Tug's bright red tie made him look like a presidential candidate.

Lincoln looked like a young Tug dressed in his private school uniform—light blue shirt, dark blue slacks, and dark blue tie.

Once sworn in, Tug brought him a piece of paper and asked, "Do you recognize this report as a copy of your current grades at school?"

"Yes sir, I do," Lincoln responded.

Tug turned to the judge, "Let me identify this as Exhibit 34."

The judge nodded.

Tug turned back to his son, "All A's. Very impressive."

"Thank you, sir."

Tug asked, "Did your mom, Debra Grant, ask you to do her a favor on the morning she passed?"

"Yes. She asked me to turn the light off in the basement."

"What did you say?"

"I said, 'Okay.'"

Lincoln had repeatedly said that the only thing he said to his mother on her last day was, "I hate you." I wasn't sure what to think about Lincoln's response.

Tug scratched his chin. "Who turned the light on?"

"I don't know." Lincoln shrugged. "It gets left on all the time."

"Did you go into the basement?"

"Yes. There's a light on the top of the steps, but it seems like it's the one downstairs that always gets left on."

"Did you see anybody in the basement?"

"No."

"If someone was in the basement, would you be able to see him?"

"Yes. It's all one room."

When Tug was finished, Prosecutor Bridget Bare questioned, "And you know with certainty when you go into the basement if anyone else is present—all the time?"

Lincoln said, "Yes."

"Why didn't you tell the police?

"I forgot about it. I didn't think it was significant until Aunt Meg told me."

Tug had them. If no one was in the basement, the prosecutor's story wasn't accurate.

Once Lincoln was released as a witness, his Aunt Meg met him in the aisle and escorted him out of the courtroom.

I was the next witness for the defense. After I stated and spelled my full name, as directed by the judge, Tug asked, "Would you mind stating your profession and how you are uniquely qualified to perform this work?"

"I am a private investigator who previously performed investigative work for the Bureau of Criminal Apprehension for seven years."

Tug continued, "And you have been involved in solving cold cases and, more recently, in cases where you've had to examine the behavior of your colleagues in law enforcement, correct?"

"Yes."

"And you had no issue investigating people you once worked with?"

"I can't say it didn't bother me, but it didn't keep me from doing my job. The law should be applied equally to everyone."

"So, if you thought I was guilty of, say, killing my wife, you'd have no difficulty prosecuting me?"

"I would not."

"And I hired you to find my wife's killer shortly after her murder two months ago?"

"Yes."

"And with your reputation as a sojourner of justice, you're still not working for the prosecutor?"

"That is correct."

"It's fair to say you believe I could be innocent." Tug continued, "At the very least, there is certainly reasonable doubt regarding my guilt."

"Objection." Bridget stood and shouted in an exhausted tone. "First of all, Tug is testifying. Second, this is conjecture. We don't bring in random people to share opinions. We have a jury. Does he have any solid proof? We're not interested in theories."

The judge asked me directly, "Do you have solid proof?"

"I do not," I admitted.

The judge responded, "Objection sustained." He turned to Tug. "If you have evidence that somebody else did this, present it. We can hear the opinion of professionals about the evidence after."

"I'm trying to figure out who killed my wife." Tug appeared surprised. When no one responded, he capitulated. "Okay, then, I guess I have no more questions."

Bridget now had her opportunity for cross-examination. She stood up and said, "I believe Officer Williams showed you the DVD *Dial M for Murder* after it was found in Tug's garbage."

"He did."

Bridget said, "Please tell us how the murder was committed in that movie."

Tug catapulted to his feet and shouted, "Objection!"

"Based on what, Tug?" Bridget grinned.

Tug regained his composure and said, "Relevance. Is the theme of a movie relevant? What's next, the Scooby Doo movie?"

Scooby's catchphrase, "Ruh Roh," came to mind. Scoobert "Scooby" Doo was an investigator, a talking Great Dane who always managed to solve crimes by pulling the mask off the perpetrator at the end, a level of sleuthing that I have yet to achieve. I knew the discarded movie was a problem for Tug the first time I saw Zave holding it.

"*Dial M for Murder* was in your garbage on the day of the murder," Prosecutor Bare stated. "This makes it relevant."

"The objection is overruled," the judge responded.

Bridget repeated, "Please tell me about how the murder was orchestrated in *Dial M for Murder*."

"It's an old Alfred Hitchcock mystery. In the movie, a husband sets up his wife's murder by letting a man in the house. He then leaves and surrounds himself with witnesses. The husband calls home on a landline at a predetermined time, which allows the killer to know her exact location in the house."

Bridget clarified, "The husband hired a hitman to kill his wife. He let the hitman in the house and called home to make it easy for the killer, correct?"

"Yes." Even though I was Tug's witness, Bridget won again. My testimony may have just gotten Tug convicted of murder. Tug's explanation was that the DVD was in the garbage because Deb didn't like the movie and threw it away. There were no fingerprints on the DVD, but there were no fingerprints on most of the Grants' DVDs. They loaded them carefully by the edge so as not to damage them. The DVD case had rubbed against other items in the garbage, so any fingerprints on the outside had been smudged and were unreadable. I was about to say, "I have *Dial M for Murder* at home, too," when news reporter Jada Anderson entered the courtroom. Everything stopped for a moment. Jada and I had dated before I met Serena. She now had a child with my boss, so we still ran into each other socially on occasion.

Jada went to the prosecutor's table and, in a voice loud enough for me to overhear, told Bridget's assistant, "Tell Jon to call home immediately once he is done testifying." Jada dabbed a tear from her eye, gave me a sad nod, and left.

The impending doom of her message skyrocketed my anxiety. In half a decade of testifying, I have never had someone leave a dire message for me to call home. I wondered if something happened to Serena. I should have stayed home instead of taking this job in Minneapolis. I absolutely can't lose her. I've told Nora a million times to stop jumping down multiple steps. If she broke her neck…Jackson was running a temp last week. Had it come back with a vengeance? Is it my parents? They were sixty, and I hadn't heard anything, but Dad would never tell me if there was an issue.

Aware that my testimony would not further benefit the prosecution, Bridget Bare declared, "I have no more questions for this witness at the present time. Jon appears to have a family emergency to address. Out of respect, I would like to let him address it."

When the judge dismissed me, I rushed out of the courthouse to my car and immediately called home.

I felt relieved when Serena answered. She said, "Your mother had a terrible stroke. She's incoherent and dying. The doctor said it's a matter of hours to days. Certainly, less than a week."

"Where is she?"

"St. Gabriel's Hospital. I'm with her now. She's unresponsive."

"I'll be there as fast as I can."

"Drive carefully, Jon."

I started my car and headed north.

1:30 P.M.
ST. OTTO'S CARE CENTER (ATTACHED TO ST. GABRIEL'S HOSPITAL)
920 4TH STREET SOUTHEAST, LITTLE FALLS

MOM HAD BEEN MOVED FROM St. Gabriel's Hospital to St. Otto's Home for hospice care. Dad had headed over to Charlie's Pizza with my siblings, Theresa and Vic, to get something to eat. I sat hand in hand with Serena next to my mother's bed. Camille was breathing, but other than that, she was as motionless as she'd lie at her wake. Serena continued to talk to her as if she was still awake.

Serena massaged Mom's hand and told her, "Camille, Jon is here now." Mom's eyes opened and moved slowly down to her wrist. Serena told her, "Nora made you a bracelet."

I smiled at the beaded bracelet on Mom's wrist. In some ways, Mom was closer to Nora than she was to her own daughter. Nora was young enough to listen to and appreciate Mom rather than argue like Theresa did through her growing pains. I don't blame Theresa. I don't know how I would have handled Mom's conservative sermons, always ending with implications of the dangers of not being a "good girl." And honestly, I was complicit in my silence. But in my defense, I was only eight years old, and Theresa was fourteen when the war between them had reached its summit.

Serena was gently telling Mom, "Bill will be right back. Jon and I want you to know we love you. We're all praying for you."

For a second, Mom opened her eyes, looked at us, and looked down at the bracelet. In a barely audible voice, she said, "Cursive," and closed her eyes once again.

I smiled and said, "Nora is learning to write in cursive, just as you taught her. You're my hero, Mom, like I've always told you. I love that you did your best every day and loved us without ever expecting anything in return." Mom wasn't perfect, but she was better than anyone I knew. I felt my heart breaking and an emptiness only a mother could fill. Losing Mom was like having the heat turned off. The significance of her impact became more evident as I faced losing her. Serena is the most important person in my life, but Serena and I are equals. Parents and children aren't equal. Initially, the power is with the parent, and later, it's with the child. The parents are left on the sideline, cheering or jeering. Mom was always cheering.

1:52 P.M.

MOM OPENED HER EYES AGAIN. I stood over her and said, "I love you."

She stared calmly past me, fixated on something only she could see.

A nurse entered the room and addressed the family. "How is everyone doing?"

"She isn't looking at us anymore. It looks like she's staring at something in the corner of the room."

The nurse studied Mom for a moment and said, "Sometimes, as people approach the end of life, they appear to see things we don't see. Many people believe they're seeing others who are waiting for them to cross over. But if it ever seems like she's anxious about what she's seeing or is otherwise uncomfortable, please let me know. We have medications available to help keep her comfortable."

"How close to the end?" I asked, not wanting to hear the answer.

"Once a person has stopped eating, drinking, and making urine, it's usually no more than a few days."

"Will the doctor see her again?" I asked.

The nurse said, "The doctor only sees patients on admission, and the hospice care team takes over after admission to our wing. After that, it's a matter of keeping her comfortable. That's what I'm here for. Call for me anytime you think your mom needs something, and I'll come to see her. I've known Camille for a long time, and I'm honored to be a nurse for her and for your family."

"The staff at St. Otto's have been amazing," Serena said.

I hate our medical system. Mom goes from normal to dying, and a doctor doesn't need to see her? I took some deep breaths but said nothing. I knew it wasn't the nurse's fault.

Serena squeezed my hand. I was expecting her to say *there's nothing anyone can do*, but she simply said, "I love you, Jon."

Not long after, Mom's breathing got quicker and sounded shallow. I called for the nurse, and she came in with a medication syringe. "This will help her. Respiratory distress can be painful. This morphine will ease her respirations so she's not so uncomfortable." She slid the syringe under Mom's tongue and squeezed a few drops of morphine out. "This will help her rest."

Camille was soon in medicated peace.

I said softly, "Mom, you told me when I was struggling after high school, 'If you ever lose your faith, you will still have mine.' That was a powerfully gracious vote of support, and I've never forgotten it. Thank you."

6:45 P.M.

SERENA HAD LEFT FOR HOME to spend time with our kids before she put them to bed. My dad, Theresa, and Vic sat in chairs around Mom's bed. We would never see her coherent again.

Vic was unusually quiet. He struggled with schizophrenia and made a variety of odd decisions, which included dyeing his long hair blond while leaving his mustache dark. Today, he was wearing a red bandana.

"I heard you're helping clean a construction site," I said to Vic. "How's the new job going?"

"Dad always said a good worker is hard to find, so I spend a lot of the day hiding," Vic replied.

I laughed.

Dad told Vic, "You better be kidding."

Theresa had the same lanky build Vic and I shared. Like Vic, she had dyed blonde shoulder-length hair. Her dark roots were starting to grow out. Theresa was both rugged and pretty. We were raised as hard-working farm kids and maintained our strength into adulthood.

Theresa smiled at me and said, "Remember when you shamed Mom into saying 'I love you?'"

Dad gave me a weary look, "How?"

"Yeah, how *did* you do that, Jon?" Theresa laughed.

She always enjoyed getting me in trouble. I gave her an evil eye and told Dad, "We all knew Mom loved us."

Theresa interrupted, "We were sitting around the table, and I asked, 'Mom, why don't you ever say you love us?'"

"Then I told Theresa, 'Mom doesn't say "I love you" to you? She says it to me all the time.'" I laughed.

"Then Mom said, 'I do not.'" A sad giggle managed to sneak out from Theresa as she added, "But she told me she loved me every day after that. She didn't want me to think she was saying it to Jon but not to me."

Dad turned to me. "That was mean."

Theresa asked Dad, "So when are you going to start saying, 'I love you'?"

"We don't talk like that," he responded. "If you don't know, after everything we've done for you, there's no point in telling you."

I laughed. Dad firmly believed that being emotional was a concession of weakness he wasn't willing to make.

11:30 P.M.

MY FRIEND, BRUCE, PICKED UP Vic at the hospital and gave him a ride home. Dad fell asleep in the chair next to Mom and refused to leave.

I told Theresa, "I'm headed home, but I'll be back as soon as I wake up in the morning."

Theresa walked me outside, and I stood with her while she smoked. Theresa said, "You and Vic are the only two people who don't smoke who will step outside to talk to me while I smoke. When Vic was out here with me, I asked him, 'What do you think will happen to Mom when she dies?' He said, 'Well, for damn sure she won't smoke.'"

"Unless we cremate her," I remarked.

Theresa laughed and then punched me in the shoulder. She held her arms open and, still holding the burning cigarette, hugged me. After I released her, she puffed and said, "You know I'm not going to be funny anymore." Theresa opened pictures on her phone showing her standing by our very conservative mother. In picture after picture, Theresa was posing outrageously, holding two tassels from New Year's Eve's whistles, two cantaloupes, and a variety of other pairs of objects in front of her breasts for photos while Mom unassumingly stood next to her with no clue what her daughter was doing.

"Mom was your perfect straight person," I commented.

"She was a fucking saint," Theresa declared.

"Mom's faith was unshakeable. The older I get, the more I respect her. Everybody has temptation, but Camille always made the right choice."

A tear trickled down Theresa's cheek. "I think that's why I gave her so much grief. How could morality always be so easy for her?"

"I don't believe it was easy. Dad drank too much and was out of control for half of our childhood. They lost the farm.

Vic was psychotic. You were boy-crazy, and I was accused of murder. As much as she suffered, she focused on doing what was right, regardless of what people said. Do you ever remember Mom going on a rant complaining about someone?"

Theresa smiled, "Never." She put out the remains of her cigarette and said, "I worry sometimes that you're too much like Mom."

"How so?"

"Serena brags how you rub her feet every night and give her back rubs on demand. Camille was a martyr for Dad before he got his act together, and I just can't respect that. It wasn't good for her, and it wasn't good for him. I don't want you to be the same. I have no issue with Serena getting what she wants, but for God's sake, there needs to be a little give, too."

"There is give." I smiled. "What I do for Serena, like rubbing her feet, she can tell you about. What Serena does for me, a respectful man doesn't talk about."

Theresa stepped in front of me and looked directly into my eyes. "Shit. You're telling the truth! My stock in Serena has just skyrocketed." She punched my shoulder. "Damn, Jon. No wonder you smile so much. I don't know that I'll ever look at Serena without grinning again."

Theresa assumed my comment was completely sexual, and while it was, partially, there's a peace she brings to me I can't describe—so, as a respectful man, I don't talk about it.

4:35 P.M., THURSDAY, JANUARY 9, 2020

DAD, THERESA, VIC, SERENA, AND I sat in Mom's room. Theresa and I played guitar while we sang "Will the Circle be Unbroken." We were singing the second verse:

I said to that undertaker
Please drive slow

For this lady you are carrying
Lord, I hate to see her go
Will the circle be unbroken
By and by, Lord, by and by
There's a better home a-waiting
In the sky, Lord, in the sky...

Theresa looked at the bed and said, "Mom's stopped breathing."

I stopped breathing for a moment, too. It was over. I would never hear Mom's voice on this earth again. She finally ended the conversation. I never questioned Camille's love for me. Her faith never wavered. She showed up every day and offered compassionate help, and not just with words. She'd ask, "What can I do?" and we'd get to work. Mom was a great Christian, and I told her again and again that she was my hero. I'll never regret that.

Vic had said little during the entire hospital stay. He now said, "I wonder what heaven is like. I imagine hell's a lot like junior high. When I die, I want one of those all-star wrestling refs to stand over me and do a mandatory eight count and announce, "'He's not getting up.'"

We smiled but didn't respond. Vic added, "I wish I could still talk to her."

Dad patted him on the back and said, "I plan on it. Truth be told, I think our marriage was one long conversation that never ended."

We all had to smile at that. The "Camille Goodbye" was famous for its never-ending nature. Mom wanted us to know she would keep listening if anyone needed to talk. *I love you, Mom, and I'm so grateful. I am a better person for having known you, and I will continue to show up every day and try to be the best person I can be. I don't have the patience to maintain conversations after they've run their course, though.*

Sorry—it's just not me. But thank you, Mom, for everything. I couldn't have done better.

8:30 P.M.
PIERZ

ON THE DRIVE HOME, I tried to make peace with Camille's death. I don't believe a child can ever fully understand the heartache a loving parent experiences, but I try. I thought about Lincoln losing his mother at thirteen. If Camille had died when I was thirteen, I'd be a mess. My family didn't reach a comfortable peace until I was an adult. Theresa settled down, Vic's meds started working, and I became an investigator. Peace came to me when I found Serena. I was blessed to have Mom in my life until after I'd reached homeostasis.

Jackson toddled to me when I entered the door. I picked him up, and he quietly studied my face. It's interesting that even a little guy, almost two years old, realizes that something isn't right. Serena was busy cleaning up toys, and Nora was standing in front of the television, watching a show about animals.

"Why don't we shut the TV off and read?" Serena suggested.

"I'll read before bed," Nora responded.

Serena gave her a tired smile."You'll want to work on a puzzle then."

Nora likes to do puzzles before bed when I'm home because she knows I'll sit and talk to her while she's working on it.

Nora told Serena, "Working on a puzzle is like reading. You take a shape and make a picture, like you take letters and make words."

I grinned at Serena, and she gave me a wink as she said, "The girl's got her dad's logic."

I sat on the couch, and Nora joined me. I asked, "What are you thinking?"

"How did Grandma learn to write so good?"

Camille wrote in perfect cursive. "She practiced."

"Mom says Grandma's in heaven."

Jackson silently observed our conversation.

I hugged them both. "Grandma Camille is in heaven. She was incredibly kind to everyone."

Serena interrupted us. "Either you do a puzzle, or Dad makes up a bedtime story."

"Story," Nora said.

"Story," Jackson repeated.

"Okay, what kind of story?"

"Animals," Jackson said.

I asked Nora, "Are you okay with that?"

"Yes," she said.

"Did you know Santa had a brother? According to the Pennsylvania Dutch, his name was Bells. And according to me, Bells had a dog named Paws Claus. Well, Bells lived in an igloo. Do you know what an igloo is?"

"Yes," Nora eagerly responded. "An igloo is a house made of ice." She turned to her younger brother. "It looks like a baseball hat."

My storytelling continued, "One day, when Bells was ice fishing, Paws thought he'd start a big fire to get the igloo nice and warm for Bells. What do you think happened when he heated up the ice?"

"It melted," Nora guessed.

I retrieved an ice cube from the fridge and returned to their sides. I held the ice in my hand and showed it to my dynamic duo. Jackson carefully observed the water form in my hand and added, "Melted."

"You can have a fire in an igloo," I told them. "But it has to be small, and you need to have a hole in the top of the igloo so the smoke can escape." I didn't bother to explain that igloos only need a small fire since they are well-insulated.

"What happened?" Nora asked.

"That's exactly what Bells said when he came home. The igloo melted completely to the ground."

"Was he mad?" Nora asked.

"He might have been for a second, but he knew that anger is energy. Why waste it tantrumming when he could use his energy to build a new igloo? Bells and Paws worked together. Bells told Paws, 'I know you were trying to be kind, and that's a good thing. We're lucky to live in a place where there is so much snow and ice.' What do you think they did the following week?"

"What?" Nora and Jackson said simultaneously as they eagerly waited for my response.

"They needed new pictures for their igloo."

"Target," Jackson said.

"That's where Paws went because he wasn't a great artist. Who do you think he bought pictures of?"

"Bluey and Bingo," Jackson suggested.

"You are exactly right. And what do you think Bells drew pictures of?"

"Santa, Peppa Pig, Spiderman," Nora suggested.

"All of them, sitting down for Christmas dinner together. I didn't know they hung out together until I saw the picture." We were all laughing. I hugged them both and said, "Good night."

"You know how you say if we promise to do something, we should do it?" Nora said.

"Yes."

"Jackson asked you to tell us a story about animals. You told us a story about an animal and a human. You still owe us a story about animals."

I smiled at her, feeling both indulgent and grateful—it was time to come up with a story about animals.

41

JON FREDERICK

2:35 P.M., THURSDAY, JANUARY 16, 2020
HENNEPIN COUNTY COURTHOUSE
300 SOUTH 6TH STREET, CENTRAL MINNEAPOLIS

I was back at work, and, as Serena knows too well, everything else in my life disappears when I'm focused on an investigation. I had accepted that Tug's case wasn't mine to win or lose. My task was to find out if anyone else could have killed his wife. I explored other suspects and possible motives but continually came up empty. Tug's cross-examination of Melanie convinced me she hadn't killed Deb. If Melanie planned on replacing Deb, she would have accepted Tug's offer of $100,000, and she for damn sure wouldn't have mentioned it in court. Richard Day had nothing to do with Deb's death. Carlos had nothing to do with Deb's death. When I spoke to Roan, he appeared troubled to have brokered the deal that led to Deb's murder. There was no anger or resentment in his eyes when I spoke of Deb. Realistically, Roan had no reason to kill Deb outside of the money Tug gave him. Roan wasn't leaving Catania. They sparred but were content with it. Roan and Cat reminded me of Dad's comment about couples who fought but stayed together: "Manure stinks, but it's warm." Cat would never leave Roan for Tug, as Deb had done, and that quality was important to him.

Today in court, Tug looked restless and troubled. Apparently considering that this case could go either way, he said to the judge, "I would like to take the stand on my own behalf. My assistant will question me."

Clearly, Taytum did not agree with his decision. Tug went to the table and slid his notepad in front of Taytum. He had written out the questions she should ask.

Taytum followed the script. "Where were you when Debra Grant was murdered?"

"I was at work. That is indisputable. I have a witness who is the daughter of a decorated sheriff's deputy. I have electronics, including my phone and a business camera, that verify this."

Tug's reference to Lily Walker made me nervous for him. Lily wasn't a terrible person, but she struggled with substance abuse after her father's death. While Tug likely saw Lily as someone who was vulnerable to his manipulation, using an association with her in court was potentially harmful.

Taytum asked, "Are you familiar with Dick Doden? The man who confessed to killing your wife."

"I had never met him prior to this court hearing. I had never heard his name until he was arrested."

Taytum held the notepad as she reluctantly said, "Mass murderer Richard Day was released right before Debra's murder, correct?"

"Yes."

"You defended Richard, and he was found guilty of first-degree murder, correct?"

Tug paused to make sure everyone on the jury heard. "Yes. And he wasn't happy about it. Richard brutally murdered three family members. I should have hired a bodyguard for Deb, but I thought she'd be safe during the day." Tug dramatically hung his head while Taytum returned to the table.

I thought back to Richard Day's release hearing. Tony Shileto had criticized Ricky heavily, and when his defense attorney, Tug, was given the opportunity to counter with something kind about Ricky, he passed.

Taytum gazed down at the tablet and read, "Debra had hired a man named Carlos Garcia to provide lawn care, correct?"

"Yes. It turns out Carlos had committed a sex offense. Deb liked to give people a second chance."

Taytum continued, "And Debra was only wearing a robe when her body was discovered, correct?" This was going as smoothly as anticipated. The cross-examination that Taytum dreaded was still coming.

The gray-haired prosecutor targeted Tug with wolf-like eyes, practically licking her chops as the cross began. "Let's clear something up. Richard Day had nothing to do with Debra Grant's murder. You defended Day upon his release from prison. You were in high school when Day went to prison, correct?"

"Yes." Tug quickly responded.

"And Richard Day has been wearing an ankle bracelet since his release, correct?" Bridget didn't wait for a response. She informed the jury, "Day's bracelet and witnesses place him at work at General Mills."

"Electronics and witnesses place me at work, too," Tug remarked.

"Let's also clarify that Carlos Garcia didn't kill Debra Grant. We have Carlos on camera at work."

Tug interjected, "It's my understanding that he left work at the time Deb was attacked to make a phone call."

Prosecutor Bare responded, "He made that call in front of

the house he was working at from his truck. The neighbor's security camera indicated that he never left the property."

Taytum stood up, "Objection! This is a Brady violation. We have never been privy to that security camera footage."

The judge glared at the prosecutor, and Bridget explained, "It's clear Carlos didn't kill Debra Grant. Dick Doden admitted killing her, and the physical evidence proves he did."

Taytum interjected, "But the fact that Carlos left work to make a call at about the time of the murder is significant to our defense."

Bridget argued, "Carlos didn't call Dick Doden."

"How do you know?" Taytum asked.

"We have the woman's number. It was just a private citizen who was considering a major landscaping project." Bridget pointed out, "Your entire reasoning process is preposterous. You're arguing that Carlos may have killed Deb because he's a sex offender, but he called someone else to do it? Have you ever heard of a sex offender hiring someone else to commit the offense? And the kicker is, Deb wasn't sexually assaulted."

Taytum restated, "Brady violation."

The judge was upset. He pounded his gavel. "I'll take this into consideration. Let's continue with the questioning for now."

The interaction raised concerns for me about Bridget. She purposely kept information from me that Carlos was innocent to keep me occupied investigating him. Bridget could be as manipulative as Tug.

Bridget turned back to Tug, "How much money are you set to receive from insurance with Debra's death?"

He answered quickly, "Ten million dollars."

"And most of that insurance was taken out during the last year of her life, correct?"

"Yes."

"That's a lot of money."

Taytum stood, "Objection. The prosecutor's testifying."

"Sustained." The judge responded.

Bridget said, "I'll withdraw the statement. Did you ever cheat on your wife, Debra Grant?"

Tug snidely remarked, "You mean like playing cards?"

"No. I mean like having sex with other people during your marriage to Debra."

Purposely defiant, Tug said, "Yes and no."

"Please explain. For most people, it's simple. Either you had sex with someone other than your wife, or you didn't."

Bridget and Tug were going at it like a pair of histrionic teenagers, which was to Bridget's advantage because it might cause Tug to say something he never intended to say.

Tug sat back with cocky arrogance. "I had never planned on leaving Deb, okay? She was my soulmate."

"Was Melanie Pearson your soulmate?" Bridget asked.

"Melanie Pearson made it pretty clear what she was when she took the stand."

"And what is that?"

I watched as Taytum shook her head at him, anticipating his answer.

Tug turned to the jury with a smirk. "Melanie is a whore."

Bridget was sporting a mischievous grin at Tug's lack of discretion. She tasted blood and went after it. "Are you a whore?"

Tug responded softly, "Horseface."

Incredulous, Bridget leaned back, "What did you just say?"

Tug cleared his throat and said, "I said, whore—no way—okay. I'm a man who makes women happy."

Pretending to be confused, Bridget remarked, "Melanie didn't seem happy." Before Taytum could object, Bridget interjected, "Let's talk a little about the daughter of the deputy who is providing your alibi. You're talking about Lily Walker, right?"

"Yes."

"Isn't Lily Walker an addict?"

"She's clean now."

"It has to be less than a year," Bridget scoffed. "Are you aware she has an assault charge?"

"She was never convicted of assault," Tug argued.

"True. But only because she agreed to treatment. Are you having sex with her?"

Lily was in the courtroom. She immediately looked away when I glanced at her.

"No—okay? What difference would that make anyway?"

"So, when I put Lily on the stand, she's going to say you never had sex?"

"We've had sex. But it wasn't until after Deb died. Who cares?"

I began to consider that Tug may have recruited Lily because she was struggling and was subsequently vulnerable. Is it a coincidence that Tug's last two secretaries struggled emotionally and only had one living parent? Lily was another person who had flown under the radar during this entire investigation. I didn't realize she had a prior assault and was now intimately involved with Tug. I needed to talk to her once the day's testimony was over. One of my frustrations with this case was the lack of effort investigators put forth to rule out other suspects. The evidence should lead to the suspect rather than starting with a suspect and trying to use the evidence to convict him.

"Is Lily a whore?" Prosecutor Bare asked.

Tug gave Lily a smarmy grin.

Taytum stood, "Objection!"

The judge pounded his gavel. "Sustained. Where are you going with this?"

"I think his attitude about women is significant," the prosecutor said. "How do the women he's been with earn the label of 'whore,' when he doesn't place himself in the same category?"

Tug interjected, "By definition, a whore is someone who has sex for money. I have never received any money from Melanie, but she got plenty from me."

The judge turned to Tug with distaste. "Shut up. At the moment, you're a witness. You're not allowed to respond unless you're questioned."

The prosecutor backed away with a hint of a smile. "No more questions."

The judge asked Tug, "Do you have any more witnesses?"

Tug confidently replied, "The defense rests."

The judge announced, "We will have closing arguments tomorrow morning. I will then instruct the jury, and they will be sent to deliberation."

After the judge and jury departed, Tug and Taytum sat at the table arguing.

I went straight to Lily Walker.

She looked guilty as sin when she asked, "Can I help you?"

"You can. I need to have a few words with Tug and Taytum, and then I need to speak to you, so stick around."

Lily nodded penitently as she asked, "Can I meet you at Agnes's home in about an hour? I told Tug I'd be at Agnes's if he needed me."

"That will work." Agnes was an irascible woman in her eighties I had befriended during my *Lying Close* investigation. Lily knew Agnes was also originally from northern Minnesota, so she occasionally stopped and took Agnes out to eat.

Agnes respects the need for private conversations, even in her own home, though she's always a little belligerent when she exits the room.

As Lily left the courtroom, I approached Taytum and Tug and asked, "Tug, how would you characterize your relationship with Prosecutor Bare?"

"Hate," Tug sneered.

"At least you read that accurately," Taytum remarked. She turned to me. "Why do you ask?"

"You may not get a Brady violation on the Garcia evidence, but maybe you should consider that Bridget might have withheld other evidence."

Tug said, "You're not having any luck, so I've asked a friend of mine, Brent Parker, to look for a prisoner named Liam Davis."

"Who is Brent Parker?" I asked.

"Former client, now retired millionaire, who wants to help me out." Tug added, "Brent knows I'm innocent."

"And who is Liam Davis?"

"Okay, when I was in jail, I was told there's a guy named Liam Davis who knows why Dick Doden set me up. He said this cover-up is occurring at a federal level, and they're moving Davis around from prison to prison."

"Why?" I wondered. "Why are the Feds interested in you?"

Tug stood, puffed up his chest, and walked around the table. "They know I'm a great attorney, and they're tired of me getting people out of charges. I messed up a federal case by getting Roan out of the conviction. They wanted Roan to turn state's evidence against the Minneapolis Combination."

"Why didn't you tell me about this?"

"I'm not certain I can trust you. You haven't given me anything." Tug pointed his finger at me. "Your testimony might bury me. If I lose this case, it's on you."

"If the truth buries you, I think that's on you. Is Brent here?"

Tug directed me to a man standing in the back of the courtroom, wearing a black turtleneck, gray slacks, and glossy black Ferragamo dress shoes.

I approached Brent. "I'm Jon Frederick." Brent did not offer to shake my hand.

In his low baritone voice, Brent scolded me, "Tug invested a significant amount of money in you based on your reputation, and what have you given him? I'm going to find Liam. Tug told me there was going to be backlash for getting Roan out of that charge long before Deb was murdered. And now Tug's fighting for his life."

I asked Brent, "You and Tug met and talked about this prior to Deb's death?"

"Once. We were going to talk about the potential blowback again on the day she died, but obviously that needed to be rescheduled."

I considered this. "So, when did Tug cancel your meeting?"

"A couple of days before Deb's murder. Tug said something came up, so we would have to reschedule. He wouldn't be at his daughter's concert, so I should just head off to Lake Geneva as planned. And then, of course, dealing with Deb's death superseded everything."

I was stuck on a detail. Tug told me he had promised he'd be at Rebecca's concert on the day of Debra's death. According to her planner, it was the last thing he told Deb. How did he know he wouldn't be able to attend two days ahead of time? When I looked back to the defendant's table, Tug and Taytum were no longer in the courtroom.

CAPELLA TOWER PARKING
225 SOUTH 6TH STREET, CENTRAL MINNEAPOLIS

ONE OF THE PROBLEMS WITH grief is that you don't realize the extent to which it clouds your memory until you're out of it. Watching Tug lie on the stand turned the cards right side up for me, and I saw the hand I was playing. Tug lied to me when he told me his affair with Melanie ended nine months before Deb's death. He lied when he initially told the prosecutor he didn't have sex with Lily. Tug either had Deb killed, or he was protecting someone very dear to his heart.

I called his son Lincoln and said, "Hey Lincoln, this is Jon Frederick. Where are you at? I'd like to stop and ask you a couple of questions."

"If you're looking for Dad, he's not home. He said he was headed to someplace called Alloy. He left a number but said he wouldn't be home until later."

"Are you by yourself?" Lincoln was thirteen, but it seemed odd to leave a child home alone after his mother was murdered.

"No. I've sort of been kidnapped."

I sat up. "By whom?"

"I'm okay." He added, "My grandparents Otto and Greta got some sort of injunction that says I can't stay at Dad's house until court's over. They showed up with cops to keep Dad from intervening."

"Give me the address. I'll be right there."

4:45 P.M., THURSDAY, JANUARY 16, 2020
ROME AVENUE, HIGHLAND PARK,
ST. PAUL

DEBRA GRANT'S MOTHER, GRETA SCARPETTA, met me at the door. Lincoln waited patiently behind her. Greta looked like Deb but was in her sixties, with gray-streaked brown hair. She studied me skeptically. "I don't want you brainwashing this boy. He's been through enough."

"I have no intention of putting any false ideas in his head. I know you don't know me, but I promise you I have no desire to traumatize this poor boy. I thought Debra was amazing, and I'm interested in finding justice for her. I have a feeling Lincoln knows a little more than he's let on, and, for his sake, I'd like him to have the opportunity to get it off his chest."

"Like what?" Greta questioned.

"For example, Lincoln has stated the only thing he said to Debra on the day she died was, 'I hate you.' We both know he didn't mean it, and she understood. Still, he testified in court that he had a conversation with his mother."

Lincoln nervously looked away.

"I'd like to know if that testimony was coerced," I added.

Greta considered this and agreed, "All right, you have fifteen minutes, and then he needs to get to his homework."

We stepped into a study room, and Greta closed the glass double doors behind us.

Lincoln looked back at his grandma, who was watching through the glass, and said, "If Dad gets convicted, Grandma and Grandpa will have full custody of us. Dad was furious when he left here tonight—well, sort of furious. He yelled at Grandma, but I watched him out the window. After he got in the car, he called someone and then was laughing. Probably another woman to have sex with."

I felt sorry for Lincoln when I considered the rumors he was subject to, both in school and online, regarding Tug's affairs. It was a ridiculous amount of drama and trauma for a thirteen-year-old. "Are you okay with living here?"

"Yeah." Lincoln seemed unsure but, with feigned confidence, added, "I'm fine. It'll be okay."

Taytum had commented to me that Tug wouldn't have killed Deb because the responsibility of childcare would be too annoying for him. What if he knew from the very beginning Deb's family would take this task over for him? Tug could rationalize that he did everything he could to keep his kids, and parenting was taken away from him. It was all beginning to make perfect sense.

Lincoln asked, "You work for my dad, right?"

"Yes, I do."

"I just wish I hadn't told Mom I hated her," Lincoln muttered. "That's the only thing I said to her on that last day."

"I think Deb knew you loved her. Parents understand that kids say that sometimes, even when they don't mean it."

I paused, "In court, you said Deb told you to go down in the basement, and you responded to her."

"I know. But I don't think I went in the basement on the day Mom died."

"Why did you testify that you did?"

"Aunt Meg. She said if there was any chance I'd gone into the basement that day, I'd save my dad from prison. I mean, I could have. There was times Mom asked me to go shut the basement light off. Meg kept saying, 'You have to testify. You're the only one who could save him.' But I honestly don't think I did that day. If anybody puts me on the stand again, I'm not saying anything."

"It sounds like you're having doubts about your dad's innocence."

"When I lived with Dad, I was convinced he was innocent. He had so many reasons why he couldn't have done it. But here, they're convinced Dad's guilty."

Innocent people have one reason they didn't commit the crime. Guilty people have ten.

"Do you think the jury will find him guilty?" Lincoln asked.

"I don't know." I felt bad that Lincoln had been put in the position of lying to try to save his dad. "What are you hanging onto, Lincoln? Now's the time to let it all out."

"It bugs me that Mom had to answer the phone downstairs. Remember when Dad told that investigator he had no idea where the other phones were? The other phones were in Dad's car. I saw them when he brought me to school that morning."

By forcing Deb to answer the phone downstairs, Tug gave the killer her exact location.

Lincoln was on a roll. "And our dog never peed on the floor."

"What are you talking about?"

"Dad got rid of Milo one week before Mom died. Dad told the investigator that we got rid of Milo because Milo peed on the floor. Milo never peed on the floor. Grandpa got Milo back for us, and he still doesn't pee on the floor. But he did bark anytime a stranger was around."

Greta opened the door. "Time's up."

"Is there anything else?"

"No. Not that I know."

"Are you going to be all right tonight?"

"Yeah. I better go. Honestly, I feel a little better now that I've talked about it."

"You're a good man, Lincoln. Don't hesitate to call me if you need to talk." I handed him my card.

5:30 P.M.
51ST STREET & WASHBURN AVENUE
SOUTH, FULTON, MINNEAPOLIS

NOW I KNEW WHAT LINCOLN hadn't told me. It was time to find out what Lily hadn't told me. Serena took Agnes Schraut to the Mall of America, which was only eight miles away, so Lily and I could talk privately. I had asked her to bring a T-shirt for the lie detector test. She entered the bedroom wearing a blazer and blouse and returned in an oversized gray tee. Her straight black hair hung loosely down her back.

Lily joined me at the kitchen table. I had a leather bag at my feet and began removing the polygraph machine and setting its contents on the table. Lily carefully watched me set up the laptop and attach the Axitron, the pneumonic breathing tubes, the galvanic skin response measures, and the blood pressure cuff.

"Is this necessary?" Lily asked.

"I think so. Put your feet flat on the floor and look straight ahead." I wrapped the pneumo tubes around her chest. I don't do polygraph examinations. There are experts far better than myself I rely on. However, I do know how the machine works.

"Just ask me," she suggested.

"Were you involved with Tug before Deb's death?" I attached the galvanic skin sensors to her fingers.

"No, but we were the next day. He was so miserable, and I felt so bad for him. Tug can be incredibly charming. He made it feel like that moment with me was all that mattered in the world."

"Tug was going to do a major presentation for the Minnesota State Bar Association only two weeks following Deb's death. Did you ever work on that presentation?"

"No. It never came up."

I carefully placed the blood pressure cuff on her bicep.

"You're not hooking me up to ask me that. What do you want to know?"

"Did you have any involvement in Debra Grant's murder?" The machine wasn't running yet, but I curiously waited for her response.

"Yes." Lily teared up.

I stopped what I was doing and said, "Explain."

"I was the one who called Carlos Garcia at 8:40 on the morning of Debra Grant's murder. Tug asked me to use his client's phone and her name to call Carlos two days in a row at the exact same time to request that he complete a landscaping job. This client struggles with memory issues, so I thought I was doing her a favor. Carlos took a break from work at that time to speak to me. The woman thought she'd lost her phone. Tug returned it after Deb was murdered. I later heard Tug convincing the woman she was the one who made the calls."

"When did you realize Tug may have been setting Carlos up?"

"Today in court. I swear, I had no idea until I heard today's testimony. You can run an exam and ask me if I intentionally had anything to do with Debra's murder. I will say 'No' and pass."

I believed her, and I'm not a great polygraph examiner, so I began unhooking the skin conductivity and respiration measures.

Serena returned home with Agnes. She removed her jacket and revealed the little black dress she had purchased. Serena was gorgeous with her naturally curly brunette hair, sensuous green eyes, full lips, and smooth bare shoulders. The dress melded perfectly to the curves of her body.

Catching my reaction, Agnes commented, "Booty call."

"I had to show it off." Serena laughed and hugged Agnes. "Thank you for shopping with me. You are so entertaining!"

Agnes appreciated the hug but outwardly said, "Deary, I know you're not here to see me. People who tolerate me, they're the real heroes. You've done your time, and I've got reading to get to." Agnes asked Lily, "Are you done letting that self-important little fellow strut around here?"

"You're the one person who was never fooled by Tug." Lily laughed. "I think he's afraid of you. After meeting you once, Tug insisted on waiting at the door for me."

"That man is small in every meaning of the word." As she retreated to her bedroom Agnes added, "Lily, you'd know better than me."

Serena joined Lily and me at the kitchen table. After Lily filled Serena in on her new information, Serena said, "From the onset, I've believed Tug killed Deb. Did you notice in court Tug worked 'okay' into the sentence every time he lied?"

Lily commented, "I never noticed it."

"It started with, 'I never planned on leaving Deb—okay?' When the prosecutor confronted him about calling her horse-face, he said, 'No way—okay.'" Serena softened her tone as she looked at Lily, "When Tug was asked if the two of you had sex, he said, 'No—okay.' I think it's a Freudian slip. His sister told me that after every time Tug was bullied, Tug would lie and say, 'I'm okay.'"

I thought back to my first conversations with Tug. When I asked if he was having an affair, he initially diverted the question by commenting, 'Okay—right down to brass tacks.' He later responded to my question about when his affair ended with, 'Nine months ago—okay?' It had been one month. I wanted to revisit every conversation I'd had with Tug and pay special attention to every time he said "okay." Unfortunately, it wasn't possible. My memory was good, but not that good. I smiled at Serena. "That's good work. Do you know where 'OK' came from?"

Lily interjected, "Didn't have something to do with politics?"

"It did. Martin Van Buren referred to coming from 'Old Kinderhook,' which made him acceptable and then became 'OK.' The community of Kinderhook was formed when a Jewish rancher married his white Irish Catholic housekeeper."

Disappointed, Serena said, "I was hoping it had something to do with water. That would connect the saying to his trauma from being tossed in the river."

"Old Kinderhook is now a resort on Lake of the Ozarks," I offered.

Her smile returned, "Okay—you're saying I'm right."

It was a stretch, but who was I to argue about it?

"Let me talk to Tug," Serena suggested. "I've got our extra room baby-ready. The house is basically good to go. I'm going stir-crazy thinking maybe I can't get pregnant again."

"Procreation is not the meaning of life—Viktor Frankl. Does someone with ten children have a more meaningful life than someone with two? Or none? Something that is meaningless cannot be rendered meaningful by its perpetuation."

"I get a lot of happiness from time with Nora and Jackson."

"Because your relationship with them is meaningful. And the byproduct of doing meaningful tasks is happiness. Time with you is my most precious gift. Time with Nora and Jackson is as meaningful, too."

"Please, let me into this investigation—existential freak," Serena teased. With a sly grin, she added, "Tug's probably stopped somewhere for a drink. Doesn't a cold beer sound good? I'll drive if you both want to step out for a drink. I'm not drinking tonight, just in case. You can't tell if you're pregnant the first couple weeks."

We heard pounding on the front door. Tug was yelling, "Lily!"

Agnes came out of her room in her nightgown and said, "I'll handle him. I know how to talk to Tug."

Lily and Serena slipped into the spare bedroom so they would not be seen.

Agnes opened the door and said, "Fuck off, Tug! She's not home," and slammed the door. With no additional emotion, she returned to her room.

Tug yelled through the closed door, "Tell her I'll be at Alloy Brewing."

I entered the bedroom and said to Serena, "Tug will be at Alloy Brewing."

"Should I leave the black dress on?" she grinned.

"It would be one way to guarantee he talks to you."

Lily said, "This will be the perfect time for me to go to the office and pack my stuff. Once I'm out of there, I'm never going back."

7:00 P.M.
2700 COON RAPIDS BOULEVARD
NORTHWEST, COON RAPIDS

ALLOY BREWING HAD A LONG tar parking lot adjacent to the boulevard. After I dropped Serena off at the taproom door, I parked at the far end of the lot. I needed to occupy my mind with thoughts other than that slimeball hitting on my amazing wife.

The case didn't make sense. Roan Caruso first looks for a Black male to commit the murder in a predominantly white neighborhood. After he's turned down, he hires Dick Doden, a man with a history of criminal incompetence. Was there a reason for this, or was Roan desperate to get the job done, and Doden happened to be available? Roan had no reason to be desperate to get it done—unless he was hired by someone and a timeline was set.

It all comes back to Tug. I've proved everyone else I've investigated to be innocent. If Tug was guilty, the offense was impeccably planned. If I consider that Tug has quite convincingly lied to everyone, the case is clear: Tug is guilty. I thought about the number of times Tug lied to me, and I wrote it off as *he was under a lot of stress.* Tug had lied to me when he said he planned to attend Rebecca's concert. Tug had lied to me when he suggested Deb hired Carlos. His most convincing lie to me was that he had backed off from killing Deb at the last minute. Tug had to know I'd find evidence, and this explained it all away.

Tug's sophisticated plotting made me nervous for Serena. I texted Serena, "Okay?"

"Yes," she quickly texted back.

Nervous over how this night would play out, I called Lily Walker and asked, "Are you out of the office?"

"Yeah. I packed my items, and I'm in my car now. I've left that den of sin for good, and I'll be pulling away as soon as this call ends."

"Did you ever tell Tug I was married to Serena?" I worried about Serena's safety.

"No," she responded indignantly. "Remember how you set up Dad's killer by pretending Serena was your mistress in the Lying Close case? I didn't want to prevent the two of you from using her undercover again."

"Be careful, Lily."

"If Serena's undercover, you might want to check on her. Tug's a wolf."

It was a better metaphor than she knew. Recent studies have discovered that dogs have a gene, absent in wolves, that makes them desire friendship. Wolves are predators who'd kill their family if the moment called for it. More wolves are killed by other wolves than by humans.

"Holy shit," Lily uttered.

"What?"

"Guess who's about to enter Tug's office?"

"I have no idea."

"Melanie Pearson. She's never been at the office when I've been there. Don't you think that's odd—after he skewered her in court?" Lily paused and offered, "Unless the court piece was just an act."

"If so, it was a hell of an act," I responded. Melanie genuinely suffered during her testimony.

"It just seems weird, but as they say, 'Not my circus. Not my monkeys.' I'm outta here. Take care, Jon." I could hear her car start.

"You too, Lily."

I watched Tug exit the taproom and rush to his car. He tore out of the parking lot and was gone.

I was about to enter and check on Serena when she walked out. She looked bothered, so I stepped out of the car and asked, "Are you okay?"

"Yeah," she said dejectedly. "Do you want to throw this in the trunk?" Serena handed me a Crowler of Erik's Red Runner ale.

"Thanks." Alloy has a great red Irish ale.

She got into the passenger side and said, "I'm losing it, Jon. He didn't even look at me. When I approached him, he said, 'I need to get going' and walked away. Tug hit on every one of Deb's friends, but I didn't even warrant a glance."

"He's blind." I took her hand and kissed it. "But I'm not." I found Tug's nonchalance puzzling until the answer came to me. "Tug knows you're my wife. When he saw you, he must have realized I was having second thoughts about his guilt and asked you to check him out. He decided it was best to avoid you."

"You don't need to flatter me," Serena said.

I put the car in gear. I'd witnessed Tug's lecherous glances toward Serena in court.

42

MELANIE PEARSON

9:30 P.M. THURSDAY JANUARY 16, 2020
EAST FRANKLIN AVENUE, VENTURA VILLAGE, MINNEAPOLIS

I still had an extra key to Tug's office. After seeing that the office was dark, I quietly entered and went directly to his desk. Melanie/Mel-on-knees is a top-trending hashtag featuring the raunchiest clips of my testimony, remixed as if I was stuttering. If I had known my testimony would be recorded, I wouldn't have put Dad and my fiancé—now *ex*-fiancé—through it. Tug is going to pay for humiliating me.

I know Tug, and he's a risk-taker. He loved to have sex with me if he knew Deb was coming to the office to speak to him—always making sure we were finished in the nick of time. He has something he's brought back to the office that could get him in trouble. Why did he wait until the day before Deb's murder to get rid of *Dial M for Murder*? Because Tug likes the thrill of having things come down to the wire. There must be something here that he doesn't want investigators to see. Something he could take out and touch periodically for the rush. It had to be handy to conceal. I looked around the office, but nothing stood out.

My memory mystifies me. Since testifying, I've recalled something Tug said to me during our last night together. I was in his arms, dead tired from all the lovemaking. He told me, "I don't mind if you get married. Hell, I was married. Never deny me, and never betray me." I had certainly betrayed him in court. If I don't find a way to send Tug to prison, he'll kill me.

I didn't know what I was looking for, which was frustrating. I sat in his office chair and opened the drawers of his desk. The one on the bottom right didn't open. *This must be it.* I dug through the desk and found a key in the top drawer. I smiled as it opened the locked drawer. Inside was a $200 bottle of Johnny Walker Blue and two whiskey glasses. There were clear cellophane bags, an open box of condoms, a couple of pairs of handcuffs, and a gun—loaded. It was an interesting drawer, but it was just Tug's playthings. *This wasn't it.*

I knelt on the floor and looked under his desk. A metal tray was attached beneath the center drawer, just deep enough to hide a laptop. I slid the computer out and opened it up on the desk. I sat on his chair and stared at the screen as it asked for his password. Tug's code to everything was Cottontop#1. The computer opened.

I reminded myself to breathe deeply as I tried to calm my nerves. When I clicked into the history, I found a search for "A perfect murder." The Gwyneth Paltrow and Michael Douglas movie by that name popped up. I was about to click out of it when I noticed a line in the movie description. *Andrew Davis' 1998 thriller,* A Perfect Murder, *is an updated remake of Alfred Hitchcock's* Dial M For Murder. I remembered *Dial M for Murder* listed as evidence in the discovery. *Bingo! The prosecutor would love to see this.*

I gasped when my glance drifted above the screen. Tug Grant, eyes fierce with anger, stood facing me across the desk. I hadn't heard him come in. I quickly exited out of the laptop's history and stood, "I'm trying to find any way I can to help you."

"You are so dead. How did you get into my office?" Tug said.

"I realized I still had the extra key." My mouth was dry, and I could feel acid coming up from my stomach.

He came to my side and looked at the screen, which was back on the homepage. "You got into my computer."

"I tried your usual password." I was shaking. "But I haven't found anything yet. I just opened it up."

Tug grabbed my bicep and tightened his grip. I could feel his rage. "Serena Frederick tried talking to me tonight, and now I find you at my office. You bitch."

"Tug, I don't know what you're talking about."

"We'll see." Sensing my weak, submissive state, Tug slyly said, "I've never hurt a woman,"—He inched closer to me— "But I know people who have. The Vatos Locos owe me a favor."

Vatos Locos is a Hispanic gang in Minneapolis that was recently involved in a shooting over a territory dispute. They would torture me in every way imaginable—and some unimaginable.

"The boys would be more than happy to provide some discipline to a snitch." He ran his finger through my ginger hair. "We're going to have fun with you, Mel."

"What are you talking about, Tug?" I gulped. "I love you, Tug. After it all, I still love you. I'm trying to help you." Tears trickled down my cheek.

"What have you turned over on me?"

Shaking, I said, "Nothing."

"I'm not stupid. Don't insult me, Mel."

Feeling desperate, I chose the one route I knew would distract him. I placed my hand on his buttocks. "I think this bad girl could use a good spanking."

Tug grabbed my hands and pinned me against the wall. He walked his body into mine until I was unable to move. For a few seconds, I flickered into a dream state. Thank God, I quickly came back. Out of self-preservation, I took it up a notch. "Have you ever had a ménage à trois? I know a sultry brunette who would blow your gaskets."

"Tonight. Right here." His breathing was getting heavy, and his grip loosened. "Get on the phone and get her over here right now."

I squeezed out from between him and the wall and grabbed my phone.

I didn't honestly know anyone who was interested in a threesome. I was hoping just to call someone and let them know I'm here with Tug. Who can I call?

Tug's body pressed against my back and began to grind on me.

I used it as an excuse. "Tug, I can't think when you're doing that."

"You wouldn't be lying to me, would you? I'm sick of being lied to." Tug yanked on the neck of my shirt, and it ripped.

I blacked out again for a second. *I have to keep it together. Stay in the moment.* I forced out, "Let me make the call."

Tug stepped away, and I called Dad. No answer.

"You're the submissive," Tug whispered in my ear. "You do whatever I demand, both to me and to her. Reach down and grab your ankle."

"The call didn't go through." I pled, "Let me try again."

"We'll start without her."

Suddenly, my mind went blank again.

When I came to, I was on my knees. A handcuff clicked around my left ankle, followed by a click around my left wrist.

I was still dressed. I must have been out only seconds. I was dissociating. I had to keep it together. *C'mon, focus.* Tug knew to cuff like a perv, cuffing wrist to ankle instead of wrists or feet together, making it possible to spread my legs when he wanted to. Now unable to stand, I knelt on the floor. Pretending to cooperate, I asked, "How do I get my clothes off?"

"We'll bunch your shirt and bra around your wrist and your jeans around your ankle." Tug gave me a lecherous grin. "One set of cuffs will do."

He was right. I couldn't run. I was in trouble. I was going to die, and nobody would care. Dad would say I deserved it. I felt more alone than ever.

A plastic bag slid over my head, and Tug squeezed the opening tight around my neck. His muffled voice said, "How about a little erotic asphyxiation?"

I closed my eyes and waited to die. The bag inflated and collapsed again with my breaths. I wasn't going to fight it.

"Not yet." Disappointed with my reaction, Tug removed the bag and tossed it to the side.

"I'd rather hear you tell me how much you desire me."

Like a sadistic cat with a mouse, he was playing with me. *Was I weak enough to kill yet, or was he going to torment me further?* I softly said, "Just kill me."

"You're going to be okay." He wanted me to hope. This would make my demise more satisfying for him.

I was on the verge of blacking out again when the office door sprang open.

"What the hell?" Tug turned. "I locked it."

Jon Frederick stood in the doorway. "Melanie, you need to come with me. We received a call that you broke into this office." He stepped closer and told Tug, "Take the cuffs off."

"I'm not pressing charges," Tug told Jon. "It's all good." Still, he bent down and uncuffed me. "Melanie and I have some issues to work out. She's thinking of returning to work here."

Ignoring him, I quickly spun out of his clutches and went to Jon. He held the door open, and I escaped into the hallway with him.

Serena was waiting, gun in hand, just outside the door. She quipped, "Someday, I'm going to have to learn to shoot this thing." She handed the gun to Jon and hooked my arm. "Melanie, I'm going to help you get set up with some counseling."

"Can we wait until after tomorrow? After everything Tug put me through, I have to see this through."

"Okay," she acquiesced.

I turned to Jon. "How did you get in?"

He held up a set of blunt keys, the kind robbers use.

I squeezed Serena's arm as we walked. "Thank you! That could have ended bad."

"Do you want to press charges?" Jon asked.

"No. You've heard the way I was blasted in court. Both Tug and the prosecutor referred to me as a whore in court, and it wasn't questioned. People think I deserve a lot worse than being groped. It's not worth the hassle. I need to see how this ends. Let Tug have his day in court tomorrow." I paused. "How did you know I was in trouble?"

Jon said, "Lily Walker called and told me she saw you enter the office. Serena and Tug were at Alloy Brewing. When I saw Tug tear out of the parking lot, I considered that perhaps he thought Serena was sent as a distraction and someone was back here searching through his office."

43

SERENA FREDERICK

9:30 A.M. FRIDAY JANUARY 17, 2020
HENNEPIN COUNTY COURTHOUSE
300 SOUTH 6TH STREET, CENTRAL MINNEAPOLIS

Jon, Lily, and I sat together in the courtroom, waiting to listen to closing arguments. We now knew Tug was guilty, but no more evidence could be presented.

Lily asked Jon, "Why don't you go to the prosecutor and tell her everything you uncovered last night?"

"I can't. Private investigators are hired to answer questions their clients want answered. Tug paid me to prove that someone else orchestrated Deb's death. I couldn't. P.I.s are restricted by law not to reveal information uncovered during an investigation. Even if I could tell Bridget, the prosecutor can't introduce any new evidence after closing arguments."

The judge entered, and we prepared for the beginning of the end.

9:40 A.M.

BRIDGET BARE STOOD BEFORE THE jury in black-framed glasses that matched her black suit. The shirt beneath her blazer was blood red. Bridget held a notepad in her hand and pushed her glasses up as she reviewed her notes. She set the notebook on the railing in front of the jury as if she were just going to wing it.

She began, "Tilmore, 'Tug,' Grant had his wife brutally murdered for ten million dollars. In premeditated fashion, he watched the movie *Dial M for Murder* and planned the murder accordingly. He let the killer in the house, went to work, and called home to give the killer Deb's location. Tug then tossed the video in the garbage. If the garbage had been hauled away as scheduled, we never would have known this. But the driver was arrested two blocks before he reached Tug's house, and the video remained in the container in front of the house for two days for investigators to find. Tug followed the movie's modus operandi and then discarded the evidence."

Bridget picked up the notepad, carelessly tossed it on the prosecutor's table, and muttered, "Unnecessary. This is just plain obvious." She then stepped back to the jury. "The defense is going to pretend that there isn't enough evidence. But you've seen the evidence—ten million dollars. Who insures their partner for ten million? Somebody who wants her dead. Money is everything to Tug. Remember what he said about Melanie Pearson? "I had nothing to gain from being with you." Tug referred to Melanie as a whore because, in his exact words, 'I have never received any money from Melanie, but she got plenty from me.' Keep in mind Tug never paid Melanie for sex. He was referring to her work salary. Melanie was a whore who owed him sex because Tug paid her salary. Dead, Debra Grant was worth ten million dollars to Tug."

She paused, "Was it really a coincidence that he got rid of the family dog just days before the murder?"

The jury was fixated on Bridget's every word. "You've seen how Tug treats women. He promised his lover he'd be rid of his wife and be financially set in eleven months, and he is. Tug told us what was about to happen. Is it a coincidence that right after Tug got Roan Caruso out of a murder charge, Roan murdered Tug's wife? Tug gave Roan one hundred thousand dollars. He claims it was a loan, but there has been no repayment. Tug is smart. He waited until Richard Day was released so he could blame him. But we proved Richard Day had nothing to do with this. Tug tried to blame his landscaper, but we proved Carlos Garcia had nothing to do with this. It's Tug Grant. It's that simple."

Bridget walked over to the table as if she was about to sit down and turned back one last time. There was no doubt in my mind this was all rehearsed. "Dick Doden was told to make the murder look like an accident. But thank God for Debra Grant's resilience. A picture of Deb kneeling in the garden watching her youngest daughter eat a strawberry came on the screen in the courtroom. Four-year-old Audrey had strawberry juice smeared all around her lips. Bridget's gaze led the jury to the picture as she told them, "Dick punched her, pistol-whipped her, kicked her in the head, and then stabbed her fifty times. But Deb,"—she pointed to the picture— "this loving mother fought and bit and scratched. And she almost survived. Debra wasn't going to give up her life with her children. But Tug took it away from her. And it was brutal. Deb was battered and covered with blood when she was found." Bridget inconspicuously undid the button of her blazer, giving the jury a full view of her blood-red shirt. "Give Debra the justice she deserves." Satisfied, Bridget sat down.

Taytum wore a light gray blazer with a white button-down dress shirt underneath and a gray mid-length skirt.

Her short blonde hair was stretched into a tight ponytail. Taytum walked straight to the jury in a no-nonsense manner. Clearly, she wasn't going to try to get them to love her. She stated directly. "Let's get down to the raw facts. Tug Grant never killed his wife, Deb. Tug never hired the man who killed Deb. Tug has never actually even met the man who killed Deb. The only person Dick Doden implicated in the murder was Roan Caruso—Deb's former lover. Roan has never said Tug was involved. All of this is undisputed. What you've heard is a story created by the prosecution. The killer was supposedly in the basement, yet Tug's son Lincoln testified there was no one in the basement. Shouldn't they have to produce some evidence to convict a man of murder? There is no case for murder against Tug Grant because there is no evidence. This goes far beyond reasonable doubt." Taytum once again enunciated, "There is no evidence!" She sauntered back to the table and sat elegantly.

As convincing as Bridget was, Taytum was right.

Tug sat there, gloating in his silver Havana suit and bright turquoise tie. He put his arm around Taytum, kissed her cheek, and shared his smug grin with the gallery. Taytum quickly pulled away and acted as if it never happened.

The kiss creeped me out. It had an *I'm so proud of my little girl* feel to it.

It would come down to whether the jury believed Dick Doden when he implicated Tug or whether they believed Tug's son, Lincoln, who claimed the prosecutor's story couldn't be accurate. I was surprised Dick had stuck with his story even after he was brutally assaulted in jail.

10:30 A.M.

ONCE THE JURY WAS RELEASED to deliberate, I asked Jon to step into the side room off the courtroom to talk briefly. Before either of us had time to say a word, Taytum opened the door to the small room and said, "Tug wants a moment with Serena in a side room, but he doesn't want the conversation recorded. Do you have your phone on you?"

"No," I responded. "I didn't want to surrender it during the search, so I left it in the car."

"Do you want to talk to Tug?" Jon asked me.

"It will have to be right now," Taytum demanded. "Jon, you can be right outside. There's a glass insert in the door so you can see inside." When he didn't immediately respond, she questioned, "What do you think he's going to do?"

"I don't trust Tug," Jon said.

"I'd like to hear what he has to say," I responded.

"Wait a minute," Taytum said. She took out a walkie-talkie-like object and walked into the room. I had seen RF detectors before. It was used to identify the presence of recording devices. Jon has one. Taytum waved it over my body. When the red light didn't go on, she was satisfied and said, "I'm going to lunch." She turned to Tug. "Can I trust you?"

"Have I ever hurt a woman?" he quipped with a haughty smirk.

"Okay. I'll call you when the jury comes in." Taytum told him, "Keep a low profile until then."

I stepped inside the room, sat across from Tug, and asked, "Why did you want to see me?"

"I won," Tug said, beaming with optimism. The jury's not going to be out long. They never are in cases where the defendant is found innocent. You do understand what this was about, don't you?"

"Determining your guilt or innocence, I presume."

"This is about creating the perfect murder and challenging the best investigator to solve it." Tug grinned. "I can never be retried. Not even the great Jon Frederick could solve this one."

"Jon was trying to help you. It was what he was hired to do," I added in Jon's defense. "Why aren't you telling him this?"

"He's turned on me. That's why he sent you to talk to me last night, right? I won't underestimate the way you use those curves of yours if you don't underestimate my intelligence." His lecherous gaze felt like a snake slithering across my body. "You can tell Jon he's fired, and I'm not speaking to him again. But I will talk to you."

Tug's narcissism left him with the need to brag to someone. The information he shared with me couldn't be used against him anymore. The testimony was all over.

"Why did I take Deb on vacation?" With a sly grin, he said, "Because investigators would think if I wanted to kill her, there would have to be some evidence there, right? Instead, I treated her like a queen. It was nerve-wracking because I couldn't afford to let her get hurt. And Deb was appreciative in every way you can imagine." He laughed. "But not ten million worth of appreciative. Roan almost blew it by hiring that idiot."

"I can't believe you hired Deb's ex-lover to kill her."

"That's the beauty of it." Tug's smile broadened. "If he got caught, Roan was a legitimate suspect himself. I still had an out. Roan hated that Deb dumped him. I guarantee you that Roan would have made it look like an accident. But when it came down to it, Roan couldn't bring himself to kill her. Roan told Doden he couldn't rape her. We respected Deb. It was just about the Benjamins—100,000 of them. If I would have needed to implicate Roan, I would have. It turned out to be unnecessary since he never rolled on me. And for reasonable doubt, I had Richard Day, just coming out of prison, and Carlos Garcia, a gardener with a past sex offense. Garcia wouldn't have raped her. He would have just taken a picture, so the fact that she wasn't raped meant nothing."

Jon was right. It was a scandal of vandals—three different men who rationalized destroying a kind-hearted, respected woman for money. I wondered out loud, "Did you really plan it like *Dial M for Murder*?"

"The fact that the garbage didn't get hauled away was a glitch."

"And the comments to Melanie about being financially set and offering her money to basically be your concubine. What was that about?"

"Who remembers what was said in the heat of passion?" He shrugged it off.

"Apparently, Melanie does," I remarked.

"And Melanie is now the laughingstock of the metro. Who's hated more than a guy who got away with murder? The slut on her knees in front of him."

My maternal instincts made me incredibly sad for Deb and her children. I softly asked, "Don't you worry about Lincoln and your daughters?"

"Deb did well with the kids.." He sighed, "She taught the girls to love me. They will always love me. Lincoln may struggle for a bit, but ultimately, he'll be just like me. Wait and see."

Tug was pure evil, and I loathed him. I was ready to leave. "Anything else?"

He was enjoying the effect his revelations were having on me. "I knew Deb had a planner that she wrote in. I didn't touch it because that's what a guilty man would do. I was so confident in my ability to manipulate her that I didn't have to. I knew there would be nothing to implicate me, and I was right." He sat back, appraising me. "I've considered you an option ever since I saw you at Hoppy Girl. Perhaps you'd prefer a cheesy pickup line. How about this one: You must be from Nashville because right now you're the only ten-I-see. Good one, right?" He laughed.

I stood up to leave.

"I will never admit guilt under any circumstance ever again. I just wanted you to know that the great Jon Frederick was no match for me. Think about Deb, Taytum, and Melanie—all attractive, intelligent women—all obsessed with me. There will be a day when you'll wonder what their fascination was about. When that day comes, I'll be up for a weekend at Cragun's Resort. Wear that black dress, and you'll learn what a real man feels like."

"I know what a *great* man feels like. You're the one on your way to prison and about to learn what a real man feels like." I wouldn't sleep with Tug if he were the last man on earth.

"Not happening, babe! I'll be enjoying a Caramel High Rise at the Ridgedale Lunds tomorrow at noon. Don't deny yourself. Be there." I could hear him laughing as I left.

1:00 P.M.

I SHARED THE CONVERSATION WITH Jon at lunch. I pointed out that Tug hadn't said "okay" once during the conversation. Before we could discuss it, Jon was buzzed back to the courtroom. The jury had reached a conclusion.

Tug looked back at us in the courtroom and smiled. I could feel Jon's muscles tense briefly, but he showed no outward reaction. Instead, he stretched his neck like he was bored.

My anxiety and anger skyrocketed, and I squeezed Jon's leg hard. "If I knew Tug was going to speak to me, I would've brought that tube of tingling lube and said, 'Here's a housewarming present for your new home in prison.'"

Jon laughed. "You do remember we're searched before we enter the courthouse."

"Yeah, that would have been a little difficult to explain."

Seeing that Tug was getting to me, Jon tried to cheer me up. "If the jury is hung, Tug could be retried. That means you could turn everything Tug told you over to the prosecutor for the next trial."

"Would a hung jury come back this quickly?"

"No. A short deliberation generally means a verdict of not guilty," Jon said. "As much as I'd love to hear a guilty verdict, I'm not anticipating it."

Sorrow crept over me as I thought about Debra Grant. She was a kind, hard-working woman who showed up every day for her children. Deb should have been able to see the fruits of her labor—watching her children grow up, marry, and someday become parents themselves.

My melancholy was interrupted when Halle and Richard Day approached us. Halle sat beside me while Richard stood hesitantly at the end of our row. Halle was dressed professionally in sky-blue slacks with a matching blouse. Richard's dress shirt and slacks looked like they came from Goodwill.

"Is it okay if we sit here?" Richard asked.

"Of course." I said to Halle, "I heard about the shooting at the Caruso house. Are you okay?"

"Yes. Thanks for asking." She smiled.

"Halle is opening her own shrink's office," Richard told us proudly.

"Congratulations," I said. "So, do you have a name for the business?"

Before she had a chance to respond, Jon tried to lighten my mood by suggesting, "One Fine Day. Daytime. Opus Day."

"Day Toner—you know, like Daytona," Richard added. "Or Day Care?"

Halle interrupted their banter, "I am thinking of calling it Hope."

"I like that," I told her.

The judge entered the courtroom, and everyone stood. The mood quickly became somber. The judge turned to the jury foreperson and asked, "Have you reached a verdict?"

A woman in her early fifties stood and said, "Yes."

"Would you please read the verdict?"

For a moment, I still had hope.

"With regard to the charge of Murder in the Third Degree, Murder for Hire," she read, "we find the defendant, Tilmore 'Tug' Grant, guilty."

There was a collective sigh of relief in the courtroom. The judge set the date for sentencing, and Tug was immediately remanded into custody. Court was dismissed.

Jon sat as silently as he had when I told him what Tug had told me. He remained seated when I stood, so I asked, "What are you thinking?"

With sad eyes, he said, "Vincent Van Gogh said, 'Great things are done by a series of small things brought together.'"

"Are you talking about Tug's conviction?"

"Perhaps. I was mostly thinking about our family.

"Let's go home." I took his hand.

I love that man. Even though a psychopath had shoved it in his face that he fooled him, all that mattered to Jon was that our family had dealt with loss in the last couple of months, and we have emerged more affectionate and secure. *Tug, I don't care what you tell yourself. You didn't fool us. For Jon and I are one, and I was always certain of your guilt.*

44

RICHARD DAY

1:30 P.M. FRIDAY, JANUARY 17, 2020
HENNEPIN COUNTY COURTHOUSE
300 SOUTH 6TH STREET, CENTRAL MINNEAPOLIS

There is no such thing as a good outcome from the court. Debra Grant is still dead, and now we know her husband killed her. It made me sad. *Why do we destroy our families?* I said somberly to Halle, "Thank you for sitting with me."

"Any time, Ricky." She offered me a pleasant smile.

Pushing my luck, I asked, "Do you want to grab a bite to eat?"

"No, but thanks for the offer. I'm going to the prison to visit Dad for a bit."

As I strolled out of the courthouse, I saw that a group of tabloid reporters had Melanie Pearson trapped against a wall. A man with a mic was asking, "Do you think your steamy affair with Tug contributed to Debra Grant's death?"

Melanie was panicking and protectively covering her face. The media had her surrounded, blocking her escape.

I barged into the center of the fray and ordered the crew, "Leave this poor woman alone. Regardless of her story, she is loved by God. Every one of us was created with dignity and worth, not one worth more than another. This isn't religious happy talk — it's truth. She is suffering. Comfort her or leave her be."

Melanie leaned into me, and I walked her through the gauntlet and out of the courthouse.

"I thought I'd be happy once Tug was sent away. But now Debra's death is my fault."

"It's not. Tug had her death planned before you came into the picture. If my understanding of the timeline is right, he was taking out insurance on her before the two of you met. You were just one more of his victims along the way. You left him."

"I swear I'm going to go crazy, just like my mom," she muttered. "Pills and paranoia until she couldn't take it anymore and then took her life." Tears streamed down Melanie's face as she said, "I'm a terrible person."

"If it's any comfort, look who you're talking to."

She looked sadly into my eyes and then laughed. "Richard Day, right?"

"Yeah. There's nothing you will ever do that will equal my mistakes. It almost seems like a lifetime ago, like it's not real. But unfortunately, it is." I pulled my arm off her shoulder now that she was safely away from the reporters. I continued to walk alongside her. "I'll walk you to your car to make sure you're safe. If you want me to drop back, I will. I understand if you don't want to be seen with me."

Melanie reached for my hand and squeezed it. "I love what you said. Walk with me. I owe you for the rescue. Can I buy you lunch?"

"I'd love to have lunch with you, but you don't have to buy."

Melanie gave me a once-over and said, "You're not much older than I am."

"I went to prison at sixteen, for sixteen years."

She dabbed away tears and, with a chuckle, said, "This question is inappropriate, so if you choose not to answer, it's fine, but it just occurred to me: Have you ever had an intimate girlfriend?

"Nope." I laughed. "They made a movie about me, *The 40-Year-Old Virgin.* I'm not quite forty, but I'll be there soon enough."

Melanie's mood was improving. "There are worse things a person can be."

"Preaching to the choir."

45

ROAN CARUSO

4:30 P.M., FRIDAY, JANUARY 17, 2020
MINNESOTA CORRECTIONAL FACILITY–
OAK PARK HEIGHTS
5329 NORTH OSGOOD AVENUE, OAK PARK HEIGHTS

After listening to Tug Grant testify in court, my daughter, Halle Day, is convinced of my guilt. Taytum Hanson had told the Warden that Halle was temporarily serving as my attorney. Halle wasn't privy to the lie since she wouldn't have consented. This meeting allowed me one last private, unrecorded visit with my daughter. Her entrance to the cement interview room warmed my heart. She was dressed like a professional, and I felt so proud of her for breaking out of my family's legacy of violence.

Halle immediately confronted me. "There is no doubt in my mind that Tug arranged his wife's death. And after digesting it all, I now believe you orchestrated it," she began in a hardened tone. "But you asked me to hear you out, so here I am. You have one chance to explain yourself, and we will never speak again."

"In our last correspondence, you commented that I am antisocial personality-disordered. Do you really think I'm like Tug?'

"Tug's a psychopath," Halle smirked. "You're more like 'psychopath lite.'"

If she wasn't my daughter— I bit my lip and said, "It's hard to understand people like Catania and me."

"Try me," my girl challenged. Before I could utter a word, she said, "Let me guess. You spent most of your high school years in juvie and think that if you could have just stayed in school, you would have been the cock of the walk. So, you play best friends with Tug Grant, who thinks he is God's gift to women. And your borderline personality-disordered wife was a good girl through school who now wishes she would have spent those years in the backseat of a muscle car being banged by some jock."

My girl's pretty damn good. "Okay, I spent the last couple years of high school in Northwestern Minnesota Juvenile Center in Bemidji and the Itaskin Treatment Center in Grand Rapids. Cat had a 4.0 GPA at Hill Murray in Maplewood. The Turrisis may have been mafia, but they were smart. So, what does that say about us now?"

"You're both trying to make up for what you think you missed out on—driving around in fancy cars, bullying, acting like you're both sixteen. The reality is most teens don't live a glam life."

"I'm going to tell you something I've never told anyone."

"Not the first time I've heard that," Halle said.

"But not from your dad. I need you to know the truth because I love you. You can do with it what you wish."

"I struggle with you killing Deondre." Halle rubbed her forehead.

"I didn't kill him because he was Black. Deondre's dead because he stole my car. You enter the game when you take something that means a lot to another person. And people who play the game risk losing their lives. Thousands of cars are stolen in Minneapolis a year. That's millions of dollars' worth of crime. A couple of well-publicized killings of car thieves could slow that trend in a hurry."

"For God's sake, Dad, it was just a car. I can't help thinking Deondre was a young man with his whole life ahead of him."

"The only thing ahead for that boy was prison. He was a thief."

"So were you!" Halle was adamant.

"You're right. I'm not going to argue with you. He entered the game when he stole my car. That's the cost of playing." She wasn't particularly happy, but I surged forward. "I didn't want Debra Grant murdered."

"Dad, you brokered the hit."

"First, I tried to get a Black guy to do it because, in that neighborhood, the presence of a Black guy would lead to a police call."

"You are such a racist prick," Halle uttered with disgust.

"I'm not wrong. Someone would have called the police, and that might have saved her life."

"But you would have ruined that man's life for no reason."

"Don't you think that a guy who agrees to kill a decent woman for money should have his life ruined?"

"You had Dick Doden beaten to the brink of death."

"I have no sympathy for Dick Doden. This wasn't his first murder. Doden's suspected of raping a widow on Mackinac Island. When he was done, he strangled her with her panties. Doden came to Minnesota to escape DNA testing."

"You weren't concerned about him killing Deb?"

"Deb wasn't an older grieving widow like his last victim. She was supposed to kill him." I sighed, "I messed up. There—are you happy?" I silently reminded myself that my self-loathing wasn't Halle's fault. I took a deep breath and softened my tone. "Please stop interrupting me. You said I have one chance to say my piece. Let me say it."

"Fair enough."

"Tug told me he was going to have Debra killed. He wanted me to do it. If I didn't, he'd find someone else. I told him I'd do it. I got this guy who was kind of a fuck-up to do the job. Dick Doden could never seem to do anything right, so I thought he was perfect. I told him it had to look like an accident, to make it difficult. I handed him a gun that didn't fire to give him a false sense of security and made him promise he wouldn't take another weapon into the house. I went to Deb's home the day before and threatened her to put her on edge. Doden chickened out the first day. So, I gave him two options. He could either give me the money back or go to Deb and tell her Tug hired him to kill her. Instead, he killed her. I should have known. You give a fuck-up a task, what's he going to do? Fuck it up."

"He could have killed her the first day," Halle suggested.

"No, he couldn't. I was outside the house to make sure he didn't follow through. I would have killed Doden before I would have let him hurt Deb. I had a job I had to do the second day, so killing her wasn't one of the options I gave him. And Deb had a gun. I gave it to her. I taught her how to fire it. The investigators think she ran back to the bedroom out of modesty because she came out wearing a robe. I think she went to the bedroom to get that gun. I hadn't considered that Tug would make sure it was out of the house. She was supposed to kill Doden. I think when Deb saw that gun was gone, she realized Tug arranged the hit, and part of her gave up."

"How come investigators didn't know the gun was missing?"

"It wasn't registered. Halle, I couldn't turn the job down. The only way to keep Tug from killing Deb was to create a failed attempt on her life. It would be too much of a coincidence then if she was murdered later. But son of a bitch—" I decided not to finish that sentence. Angry swearing wasn't going to win over my daughter. "I didn't want Deb dead. And it's not because I was obsessed with her. It just wasn't right. I love Cat. Deb and I—that ship sailed years ago, and I was long over it. But she didn't deserve to die. You might not understand why I love Cat, but I do love her."

"I know why you love Cat," Halle smirked. "I imagine the sex is great."

"Girl, have you no boundaries? I'm your dad. How the hell would you know that?"

"Cat is off the rails with every other emotion. Why would passion be different?"

"I hope you never hear me say this again, but I messed up. I've had the Midas touch since I turned eighteen, and Dick had a history of falling flat on his face. The one time, more than any other, I needed to succeed, and Dick needed to fail, the winds changed, and it all went to hell." I could feel my eyes well up, but I closed them for a second and managed to pull the tears back. "Anyway, I wanted you to know the truth. I wanted you to know that I'm proud that you're my daughter. I love my son, but his greatest weakness is he's too much like me. You're amazing—because I didn't raise you." I stood up. "I love you, Halle."

Halle mulled the conversation over. Finally, she stood and opened her arms to me.

I hugged her and squeezed tight. I was optimistic. She had forgiven Ricky for shooting her, so maybe there was hope for me, too.

The guard outside the door must have witnessed the hug through the plexiglass window and immediately marched into the room, commanding, "No contact."

When Halle stepped back, a paper fell from her pocket onto the floor. I picked up the note and saw it was written on the back of a menu.

Halle blushed. "If you must know, a friend of mine is opening that restaurant, Friend or Pho. He sent me a personal invitation to join him one-on-one the week before the opening to taste his food."

I read the note out loud:

Halle,
I tell my friends about you. I once had a confidant who sacrificed our friendship to keep me safe. Your agonizing pain was tangible. I was afraid, so you told me to walk away. You desperately needed a friend, but you chose to be alone rather than put my dreams at risk. I should have stayed, but I didn't. You're a diamond in the rough, and if I could get a redo, I'd be forever indebted. When I think about what you did, I find myself wanting you more than the restaurant. I'm hoping you believe in second chances.
Keyshawn

I glanced up at Halle. "Sounds pretty intimate."

"I hope so." Halle beamed. "Keyshawn asked me if I was still single before the invite came. I'm excited about it."

"You should be. If anyone deserves special recognition, it's you." I had to give Keyshawn credit for expressing his appreciation of Halle. Nothing felt better than to see my daughter happy.

46

JON FREDERICK

10:30 A.M. SATURDAY, JANUARY 18, 2020
ST. JOSEPH'S CATHOLIC CEMETERY, PIERZ

I stood alone on the frozen tundra in the cemetery by Mom's grave. This was the first time it had been above freezing in a week. The warm sun on my face felt like a blessing from Mom. I got up early, scrolled through my old emails from Mom, and reminisced about our conversations. She was strong on morality but struggled with technology, and I had to laugh at the calls that started with, "I need my computer fixed." Serena was at Mom's home at least once a week, helping her work through her difficulties, and Mom was always so appreciative.

Mom made grammatical corrections on my casual notes to her and returned them to me with messages like, "Alright isn't acceptable English. All right is two words." I never felt insulted. She was worried that being raised on the farm put me at a disadvantage among my professional colleagues, and she didn't want to be embarrassed. It was her way of saying, "I love you."

I feel blessed with my family. I should have visited more. I got busy with life, work, and kids and took my parents for granted. For me, Camille is still leaving, and yet Camille is gone. Letting go doesn't happen overnight, and, in some ways, it's unnecessary. I put my angst over my regrets into loving my family—something she would appreciate. Still, Camille remains part of my existence. She taught me most of the words I use. She was with me during my fevers and my failures, in the field, on the court, and by the river. Camille is the embodiment of my morality. The blocks of the church are no more concrete than her influence on me. Our separation is only visible on the outside. I knelt, put my hand in the snow, and said, "I love you, Mom." Your prayers for me were always more needed than my prayers for you. I know you're fine. I'm letting go, knowing you will always be with me.

I stood up and considered the case. It wasn't my best investigative work. Tug hired me to find an innocent person to blame. Mom's death made it difficult to focus on the investigation. Mom's life made it easy to handle it in a moral manner. In the end, that's all that matters.

47

SERENA FREDERICK

9:45 P.M., SATURDAY JUNE 3, 2020
BON TON TAVERN, 212 MAIN STREET
SOUTH, LUCK, WISCONSIN

I had talked Jon into playing the "chance meeting" game tonight at Bon Ton Tavern. Feeling it was good luck, I wore the same copper wedding dress to Luck that I wore when we played the game at Hoppy Girl in Wabasha.

I entered the tavern through the old wooden porch entry.

Jon was at the bar with a glass of Totally Naked Lager, brewed by New Glarus Brewing, in front of him. He stepped forward and gave me a once-over. Jon wore blue jeans and a cream-colored button-down shirt. His boyish grin always made my heart melt. He was a good man, and I never got enough time alone with him. Two men and two women were sitting at the bar to his left, so I approached from his right. I wore my hair down and had my makeup done. My copper dress had thin shoulder straps over my shoulders, a slit up the side, and molded closely to my body.

Jon was telling the crew, "I'm the guy who puts up the orange 'End Road Work' sign at the end of road construction sites. I volunteered because I thought it was a protest."

When Jon didn't feel like talking to strangers, he'd make up some absurd job to shorten the conversation.

The fortyish woman behind the bar was wearing a Spotted Cow baseball jersey. I approached and said, "I'll have the house cab."

One of the guys bumped Jon and said, "What do you think about her?"

"She's hot enough to scald a loon," Jon responded.

I enjoyed the way he drank me in.

"You from around here?" Jon asked.

"Funkley. The smallest city in Minnesota. The only business is the Funkley Bar, but it's a good bar." I flashed my cell phone. "We are still able to communicate with people from the world outside of Funkley, even all the way to Wisconsin."

"We live in a world where losing a phone is more significant to some people than losing their virginity," Jon remarked.

"I wouldn't know. I've never lost mine." I winked. "What do you do for fun around here?"

"The Luck Fireman's Corn Feed has been described as 'fun for the whole family,' so unless you hate fun or families, you wouldn't want to miss that. And in winter, the Annual Iceman 500 is an SXS race on the ice of Balsam Lake. No need to bring a cooler."

"SXS?" I wondered.

"Side by side," Jon explained. "All-terrain vehicles where people can sit next to each other." Jon said, "So, tell us what puts the funk in Funkley?"

"Curling. My mom bought me my first broom at four, and I've been sweeping the floor since."

Jon's left hand rested on the bar, and the man next to him tapped the wedding band on Jon's ring finger.

"Are you into swinging?" Jon asked. It was loud enough to capture the attention of everyone at the bar.

"The broom?" Honestly, I blushed a little. We hadn't rehearsed tonight's scenario, so I wasn't sure where he was going with this. "What do you have in mind?"

"Have you ever been with a man in a Donald Duck costume?"

It was all I could do to keep from laughing, so I bit my lip and pretended to ponder the question before responding, "Let's see, a wolf in sheep's clothing—yes—but no duck."

"We could sneak onto the Luck Municipal Golf Course. The 7th hole has a dogleg with a narrow green guarded by a stone-lined pond." He softly nudged me. "See where I'm going with this? You can say you had a birdie." When I hesitated, Jon continued, "Which is impressive for using a wood driver."

I giggled at the puns. "So, you're part of the furry fandom looking for a yiff?"

"I'm not a furry." Jon dismissed this. "Donald Duck was one of the first reality stars. It was a show about an anthropomorphic drake dealing with the stressors of everyday life."

"It was back when you could get by with wearing a hat, a shirt, and no pants on TV," I said. "It was Donald's red bowtie that enamored me."

In his best Donald Duck voice, Jon uttered, "Aw, phooey!"

I tried to remember what I could about the cartoon. "Didn't Donald Duck have some weird family stuff going on? He was an uncle to Huey, Dewey, and Louie and was dating Daisy, who was their aunt."

"All legal." Jon smiled. "The three nephews were from his twin sister Della. Daisy was Della's husband's sister, which makes her the boys' aunt, but no relation to Donald."

"I feel much better having that clarified." We had the full attention of our audience. I inwardly laughed at the research Jon had done on both Donald Duck and Luck.

"Can you blow bubbles?" Jon asked.

"Who's Bubbles?"

Jon didn't expect that and blew out a long breath to keep from laughing. Finally composed, he said, "Forget about the bubbles. We'll get a bubble machine to set the mood."

"Is this a scramble or a round robin?" I asked.

One of the guys interjected, "I'm in!"

"It's just you and me, Funkley lady, but I'd take a mulligan if needed," Jon said.

I stepped close to him and rubbed his ring finger in clear sight of everyone at the bar. "Is your partner a voyeur?"

"Yes. When we met, I thought she meant *voyageur*. I bought her a kayak, but she never took it out. And then we married, and there was no going back."

"As wonderful as getting railed by Donald Duck on a dogleg amidst bubbles sounds, I think I'm going to pass."

"If it helps, I honestly don't have a partner, other than potentially you, of course," Jon interjected. "I only wore a ring to keep these guys from hitting on me." He nodded to the four people to his left.

"That does help, but still, no thanks." I left a tip on the bar and took a large swallow of wine as if I were about to leave.

"I want to thank you for the conversation," Jon said. "A conversation with a good-hearted person is more valuable to me than internet access. I wish you well."

I moved closer to Jon and raised an eyebrow seductively. "A man who handles rejection with class is *the* biggest turn-on."

"I should add, there's no 'fowl' play. I don't have a duck costume, either," Jon said. "That was just an icebreaker."

"It keeps getting better." I winked at him. I grabbed my phone off the bar and glanced at it with frustration. "Awww, sorry, I just received notice that my flight's been moved up, so I need to get to bed early. Won't be able to do it."

A chorus of "boos" came from the crew next to him.

"I understand. Best wishes on your next adventure, Funkley lady."

"Perfect response. I was just testing you. Now you're mine tonight." I leaned into him and kissed him. I took his hand and began escorting him out of the bar, saying to the crew, "I'm going to have some fun with this guy."

1:30 A.M., SUNDAY, JUNE 4, 2020
LUCK COUNTRY INN 10 ROBERTSON ROAD, LUCK

THE BLUE NIGHTLIGHT IN OUR hotel room reflected off my dress on the floor. My nakedness was comforted by the warm sheets and lover by my side. I kissed Jon and covered him with the blanket. I had received a text from Mom hours earlier that both Nora and Jackson were sound asleep. The people I loved most were at peace, and so was I. Placing my hands low on my stomach, I wondered what the future would be like for my family. Maybe I won't have another baby, and that's okay. I felt tranquil. I got out of bed, pulled a T-shirt out of Jon's suitcase, and slipped it on. I crossed my arms and enjoyed the comfort of it. I walked to the window, gazed out at the full moon, and thought about my little moon-finders at home. Somehow, the world was being set right again. I could feel it.

7:30 P.M., SUNDAY, JANUARY 19, 2020

NORA AND JACKSON HAD ENJOYED a full day of our undivided attention. After a day of indoor fun with the kids, our house became a bit of a mess, so Jon and I were now cleaning up. Our dynamic duo was captivated, watching the Lady and the Tramp slurp spaghetti noodles while gazing lovingly into each other's eyes.

They're falling in love," Nora said gleefully.

"Falling in love?" Jackson asked his older sister.

Nora placed her hand over her heart and gently moved it to Jackson's little heart. "Mom's love fell, into Dad's heart."

"Oh," he responded as if it made perfect sense.

I beamed. Nora was right. I was lucky to have my family. Everything we have can be lost so quickly. I said a quick prayer for Jon's father, Bill. Camille was in good hands now. It's the rest of us who need guidance.

This was a scandal of vandals. Three men, Tug, Roan, and Dick, were involved in the hit on Deb. And there was Ricky—who killed his family and Melanie and Taytum—who both had long-term affairs with Deb's husband. I like to have something tangible so I can announce, *Here is the evidence that solved the case!* But we didn't have that. Jon had warned me. Sometimes, cases just end. But Nora and Jackson are healthy. Jon and I are deeply in love and solid in our commitment and faith, so we are blessed. Sometimes, the best gift we have is today—an uneventful, nothing planned day. And I'm going to enjoy the heaven out of it.

If you enjoyed this book,

the story finishes with the sequel,

titled *The Sun.*

About the Author

FRANK WEBER is a forensic psychologist who has completed assessments for homicide, sexual assault, and domestic abuse cases. He has received the President's Award from the Minnesota Correctional Association for his forensic work. In 2024, he was given the outstanding achievement award from the Minnesota Psychological Association for his work in reducing sexual abuse. Frank has been interviewed in forensic shows and has presented at state and national conventions. He teaches college courses in social problems and developmental psychology. Raised in the small rural community of Pierz, Minnesota, Frank is one of ten children (yes, Catholic), named in alphabetical order. Despite the hand-me-downs, hard work, and excessive consumption of potatoes (because they were cheap), there was always music and humor. Frank has been blessed to share his life with his wife, Brenda, since they were teenagers.